TOKYO
DREAMING

ALSO BY EMIKO JEAN
Tokyo Ever After

TOKYO
DREAMING

EMIKO JEAN

FLATIRON
BOOKS
NEW YORK

TOKYO DREAMING. Copyright © 2022 by Emiko Jean. All rights reserved. Printed in the United States of America. For information, address Flatiron Books, 120 Broadway, New York, NY 10271.

www.flatironbooks.com

Library of Congress Cataloging-in-Publication Data

Names: Jean, Emiko, author.
Title: Tokyo dreaming / Emiko Jean.
Description: First U.S. edition. | New York : Flatiron Books, 2022. |
    Series: Tokyo ever after ; book 2 |
Identifiers: LCCN 2021059412 | ISBN 9781250766632 (hardcover) |
    ISBN 9781250862198 (international; sold outside the U.S., subject
    to rights availability) | ISBN 9781250771360 (ebook)
Subjects: CYAC: Princesses—Fiction. | Dating (Social customs)—
    Fiction. | Japanese Americans—Fiction. | Tokyo (Japan)—Fiction. |
    Japan—Fiction. | LCGFT: Novels.
Classification: LCC PZ7.1.J43 Tm 2022 | DDC [Fic]—dc23
LC record available at https://lccn.loc.gov/2021059412

Our books may be purchased in bulk for promotional, educational, or
business use. Please contact your local bookseller or the Macmillan
Corporate and Premium Sales Department at 1-800-221-7945,
extension 5442, or by email at
MacmillanSpecialMarkets@macmillan.com.

First U.S. Edition: 2022
First International Edition: 2022

10 9 8 7 6 5 4 3 2 1

For all the girls out there. Life is a poem.
I hope you write it.

THE IMPERIAL FAMILY*

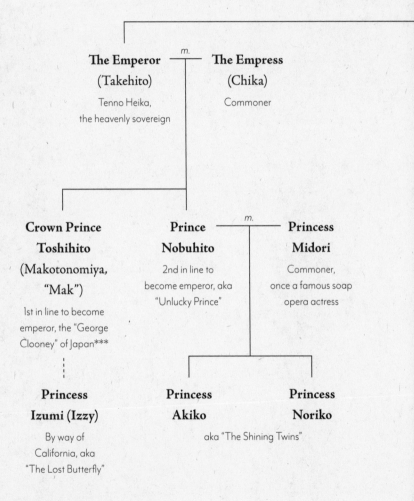

Emperor Chōwa**

The Emperor
(Takehito)
Tenno Heika,
the heavenly sovereign

m.

The Empress
(Chika)
Commoner

**Crown Prince
Toshihito**
(Makotonomiya,
"Mak")
1st in line to become
emperor, the "George
Clooney" of Japan***

**Prince
Nobuhito**
2nd in line to
become emperor, aka
"Unlucky Prince"

m.

**Princess
Midori**
Commoner,
once a famous soap
opera actress

**Princess
Izumi (Izzy)**
By way of
California, aka
"The Lost Butterfly"

**Princess
Akiko**

**Princess
Noriko**

aka "The Shining Twins"

* an annotated, unofficial genealogy
** deceased
*** pre–Amal and twins

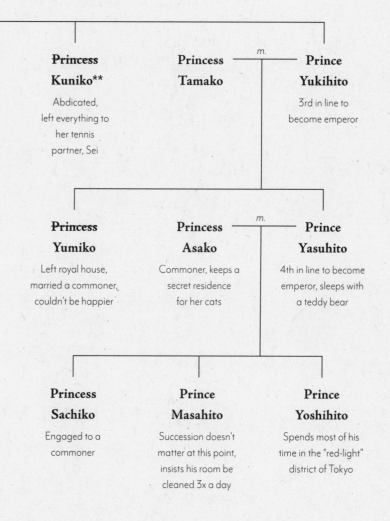

m.

Empress Aimi**

~~Princess~~ **Kuniko****

Abdicated, left everything to her tennis partner, Sei

Princess Tamako

m.

Prince Yukihito

3rd in line to become emperor

~~Princess~~ **Yumiko**

Left royal house, married a commoner, couldn't be happier

Princess Asako

Commoner, keeps a secret residence for her cats

m.

Prince Yasuhito

4th in line to become emperor, sleeps with a teddy bear

Princess Sachiko

Engaged to a commoner

Prince Masahito

Succession doesn't matter at this point, insists his room be cleaned 3x a day

Prince Yoshihito

Spends most of his time in the "red-light" district of Tokyo

TOKYO
DREAMING

TOKYO TATTLER
SPECIAL SUMMER EDITION

Love is in the air!

August 21, 2022

It was a blink-and-you-might-have-missed-it kind of moment. Late last evening, the usual crowd spilled into the streets after a Bunraku performance at the National Theatre. A couple darted through the crush and into a black sedan idling at the curb. It was His Imperial Highness, the Crown Prince Toshihito, and his latest love interest, American Hanako Tanaka, mother to his illegitimate child, HIH Princess Izumi. The couple sat in general admission seats for the play. Those near them had no idea the Crown Prince was in their midst.

Thirty days ago, Ms. Tanaka arrived in Japan quietly via commercial airliner toting a fraying LeSportsac duffel and Tamagotchi, HIH Princess Izumi's pet dog, a mutt with unknown breeding (a far cry from the purebred Shiba Inus the empress favors).

"Both mom and dog are tearing up the palace," a member of the imperial staff says. "Ms. Tanaka refuses to let any of the staff wait on her. The dog is a menace and smells foul."

The Crown Prince has taken his lady love's lead. He's eschewed the heavier police escorts to venues, opting for unmarked vehicles and surprise visits instead. Gone are the imperial flags announcing the Crown Prince's arrival, and the Imperial Household Agency's rigidly prescheduled tours are a thing of the past. And in a *stunning* breach of imperial protocol, the couple has been openly affectionate—holding hands and whispering in each other's ear while out in public.

It is no great secret the Imperial Household Agency wishes for the prince to marry and produce a male heir to uphold the line of succession. But bridal candidates never included one such as Hanako Tanaka, an American with no ties to the former aristocratic families of Japan and who, at age *forty*, is well past her prime childbearing years.

Very little is known about Ms. Tanaka other than she met the Crown Prince at Harvard. He was there on a one-year exchange to study and practice his English, and she on biology scholarship. Despite the Ivy League degree, Ms. Tanaka teaches at a community college with open enrollment.

"I don't see the appeal," imperial blogger Junko Inogashira says. "The Crown Prince could have anyone. *Anyone.*"

Still, the Crown Prince has let his preferences be known. "His Imperial Highness is temperamental in regard to Ms. Tanaka. It is his way or no way," a member of the imperial staff tells us. "The Crown Prince is enthralled." So enthralled, he has broken tradition and allowed Ms. Tanaka to stay on imperial grounds—*in his house.* The Imperial Household Agency says it's all aboveboard. "Ms. Tanaka is residing in the palace but in separate guest quarters."

HIH Princess Izumi has ripped a page from her father's notebook, opting for only one imperial guard and a small unmarked imperial vehicle when going on dates with her former bodyguard turned beau, Akio Kobayashi. *And* inspired by her mother, she's been donning pants in lieu of the pastel dresses usually favored by imperial women.

It's impossible to ignore that all three—the Crown Prince, Ms. Tanaka, and HIH Princess Izumi—are turning up their noses at imperial traditions.

"The Imperial Household Agency hopes *both* romances fizzle out. They are marking their calendars for the day Ms. Tanaka returns to America and when Mr. Kobayashi departs for Air Self-Defense Force Officer Candidate School. They firmly believe the distance will cool the hearts of both the Crown Prince and HIH Princess Izumi."

1

Once a year, in late August, the Asian Girl Gang conducts its annual meeting. Attendance is mandatory. The agenda is preset. It is a closed-door event; only those sworn to uphold the five covenants of the AGG are permitted to attend:

1. ABS—always be snacking.
2. Secrets make the bond healthier. (One of us writes Jonas Brothers fan fiction. One of us shaves our toes. And another clogged the school bathroom toilet so terribly with a pad that an outside plumbing company had to be called, after which the principal was prompted to hold a female-students-only assembly on the proper disposal of feminine products—it was me; that girl was me.)
3. Motivate and encourage one another.
4. My clothes are your clothes.
5. And, I'll do it if you do it.

I stare at my three friends—Noora, Glory, and Hansani—on the computer screen. It is the first time we've conducted the meeting in separate locations, scattered all over the world in different time zones.

It's eight p.m. here. I'm all the way in Tokyo, by far the farthest away from home. In Tōgū Palace, in my new room, which is all soft whites and earthy wood tones that could easily be featured in Japan's *Architectural Digest*. It's early morning in New York, where Noora is. She arrived a few days ago to move into the dorms at Columbia University. And even earlier for Glory and Hansani, four a.m. (they drew the short straw on time). Both are on the West Coast. Glory is visiting her dad in Portland before heading to the University of Oregon tomorrow. And Hansani is still in Mount Shasta but at a twenty-four-hour diner because she lives in the boonies and her father refuses to pay for the company to wire for the internet at home. She'll leave in a couple days and be off to UC Berkeley. Among the three of them, my best friends are always the smartest people in the room. There is nothing these ladies can't do. Hand to God, Glory can even field dress a deer. Their futures are set.

And mine?

Well, I'm trying to figure things out. My world teetered and turned upside down when I learned spring of my senior year that my father was the Crown Prince of Japan. Overnight I became a princess. It's hard to believe and I'm still adjusting. I've been pretty much living in Tokyo (with one brief jaunt home, to Mount Shasta, after my relationship with my bodyguard was splashed all over the media). And my only goal has been to continue to get to know my father. That's it.

Only . . .

Mr. Fuchigami, palace chamberlain and ruthless overlord, has been leaving catalogs to Japan's elite schools all over the rooms I frequent in the palace. He's even wrangled me into touring University of Tokyo tomorrow. Just my father's and my grandfather, the emperor's, undergraduate alma mater. No pressure. Only some pressure. I am standing in the past royals' shadows. It's far from a done deal. And I've made it clear I'm considering my options. So the question is: Gap year or school? The answer: I don't know. Each option represents a different path. School in Japan leads me further down the princess conveyor belt. A gap year, further away from it—I'd be the first imperial princess in one hundred years *not* to go to school right away.

I pull Tamagotchi from his stinky nest at the foot of my bed and sink my nose into his wiry hair. He squirms from my embrace, planting himself farther down on the bed. *Dumb dog.* All I want to do is love him and be loved in return. Granted, he's been a little out of sorts after arriving in Japan and being quarantined for fourteen days.

A server approaches Hansani and pours her a fresh cup of coffee. The mug steams, and she wraps her hands around it. "Thanks," Hansani says to the server, smiling unsurely. "I'm sorry, I've been here so long. I promise I'll tip you a lot." The server says to take all the time she needs.

Hansani is like that. She projects an I'll-mow-your-lawn-for-free vibe. Parents love her. She waits a beat for the server to leave, then stares directly into the camera and stage-whispers, "I barely have enough cash to cover this coffee. We need to end this now."

"We're almost done," Noora pipes in. Behind her, there is a calendar with neon stickies. Already she's enshrined in schedules and notes—it's her happy place.

So far, we've covered: One, how we'll keep in touch while out of state/country and in different time zones—it's open season on texting; whoever is available will reply. Two, we all agree we must support each other emotionally during this transitional time. Three, when we will reunite—sadly, not until next summer at the earliest. But Noora will be visiting me in Japan during her winter break. I'll be playing hostess, showing her the Tokyo sights.

"We have one last item to discuss," Noora imparts.

"This is silly," Glory grouches. "We don't need to talk about number four on the list." She sits back in her chair and crosses her arms.

Noora gives Glory the stink eye. "Last item on the agenda—"

"We are not going to spend our final meeting minutes going through which movie with a couple should be recast with two men or two women as leads," Glory cuts in. She turns her cheek and says under her breath, "*Titanic.*"

"Honestly, I've spent a lot of time thinking about this. Mine would be *Dirty Dancing*," Hansani says. "The scene in the river? C'mon."

Movement in the hall catches my eye. "Ladies," I say. "I hate to cut this groundbreaking conversation short, but I have to go."

"What?" Noora whines. "I haven't even put forth my nomination. I had a whole five-page essay on my choice, *The Notebook*, prepared." She holds up a stack of papers.

"I love you all." I blow them a kiss. "But you're all wrong. The correct answer is *Pride and Prejudice*." I slam my laptop shut and scoot from the lavish bed and into the hall, Tamagotchi at my heels.

Mom whips around, startled. "Izumi. Hi. I thought you were with Akio."

"He'll be here soon." I eye her carefully. Tamagotchi sits and twists his body to suck on his toes. "What are you doing?" The only room past mine is Dad's.

She splays a hand against her chest as if surprised and offended. "Me? What am I doing?" she asks, clearly buying time. "Nothing. I was going to your father's room. He wanted to show me something . . . a, uh, a plant?"

I purse my lips and cross my arms. "Are you asking me or telling me?"

She places a hand on her hip and huffs. "I don't have to explain myself to you. If I want to have—"

I hold out a hand. "For my mental health, I'm going to need you to stop." I try to think of non-sexy things. Baseball. Cultivating wheat. Socks with sandals.

Mom bites back a sigh. "I'm a grown woman."

This is Mom's second trip to Tokyo. The first had been in June and we'd been in semi–crisis mode (that whole bodyguard-scandal thing). Despite the chaos, it was obvious there was still a spark between her and my dad. After seeing me safe and secure, she'd left with a promise to return. I'd campaigned hard for her to come back sooner. *Spend the summer with me in Tokyo. You won't be teaching anyway. Say you will. Say you will. SAY YOU WILL.* Of course, she did. She arrived the first week of July. Dad and I picked her up at the airport. As soon as I saw her, I skipped over. "Oof," she said as I squeezed the life out of her. We disengaged and Dad swept into a bow. She did the same.

"Mak," she said breathily, using his college nickname, short for Makotonomiya.

"Hanako," he said, his smile reserved. "I am deeply pleased to see you again."

By the time we hit the outskirts of Tokyo, Mom's hand had inched across the car seat to hold Dad's. Their little spark had become a tiny flame. She'd intended to stay at a nearby hotel, but the press quickly became unbearable. Safety was a concern. Hers and mine. It was decided, mostly by Dad, that she should move to the palace. A guest suite was prepared in a separate wing. She extended her trip from two weeks to three, then finally, to the rest of the summer.

There you have it.

Ever since, my parents have been full-on, absolute love-sick delinquents—a raging inferno. Morning walks in the garden. Cozy evening meals in corner booths. I even caught them in the pantry canoodling. And now this, a midnight rendezvous. Well, not quite midnight, eight p.m., close enough. All in all, it's been a trip watching my pragmatic mother blush, swoon, and throw caution to the wind. I'm happy for her. And for me.

We've settled into a routine. Mom, Dad, and I have breakfast together. It's what I've always dreamed of. Sitting down at the table, discussing our day—where we'll be going, who we'll be seeing, what needs to be done, then rushing off to our separate lives. My father and I to our imperial duties. Mom to read or relax since she's on vacation. We come back together for dinner most nights. Staying long after the table has been cleared, Mom and Dad regale me with stories from their school days. How they met at a senior mixer. How Dad fetched a chair for Mom because he was concerned her feet might be hurting. "It was her shoes. The thick soles, I thought she had the same painful condition as my great-uncle who wore similar heels," Dad confessed with a dry smile.

"They were platforms." Mom frowned. "I bought them because they made me taller."

I grinned broadly, the words *go* and *on* shining in my eyes.

Dad turned to her. "You were very cross with me."

"I thought you were being deliberately rude. You insulted me, then wouldn't look me in the eye," Mom replied, leaning into him. I've noticed they naturally drift toward each other, like a tide to its beach.

"I was trying to be chivalrous and not stare at you. I found you . . . absolutely fascinating," he said with wonder.

Moments like these are a balm to an ever-present ache. I blink and see the family portrait I drew in the second grade. There was Mom, me, and a purple amorphous blob as my father. I swallow. I'd thought knowing who my father *was* would be enough. But it's not. There is still a void. I want us. I want the whole family.

The ache has doubled since yesterday. Mom booked a ticket home. She leaves in five days. She has to be back before school starts at College of the Siskiyous, where she teaches biology. I'm trying not to dwell on her departure. How much I'll miss her. How much Dad will miss her.

Now, Mom's eyes light on something behind me. "Akio," she says warmly, a little too saccharine. "Hi. Nice to see you."

I turn. He is at the mouth of the hall. For a moment, I

stare. Bask in him. Six feet of perfection. Broad-shouldered. Cheekbones carved from granite. Piercing deep-set hooded eyes that burn right through me. Truly, Japan's finest. *Akio*. His favorite movie is *Die Hard*. He exclusively reads nonfiction. And he most definitely has a future measuring the grass in his yard to ensure each blade is precisely five inches high. *Sigh*. I don't know why, but I find all this enormously appealing. Once upon a time, Akio was my bodyguard. Now he's just mine.

Growl.

Tamagotchi stands in front of me and bares his teeth. His hatred for Akio is directly proportional to my love for him. *Love*. Do I love Akio? I don't know. I know I care for him. And I know Akio feels like home. Safe. Comfortable. Secure. No matter where I go or what I do, I am a boomerang; it's him I think of; it's him I want to return to. Is that love?

Tamagotchi shifts his weight forward. His hackles rise. Akio narrows his eyes at the dog.

Mom scoops up Tamagotchi. "Shush. You're an awful dog," she croons to him in a sweet voice. He squirms, but she keeps a hold.

Akio sweeps into a bow. "Ms. Tanaka." Slowly he rises and moves forward, his steps quiet. Stealthy.

"Well," Mom says. "I'll just leave you two here. Have a nice evening." She escapes with Tamagotchi around a bend in the hall.

Akio stops an inch short of me. "Are you certain that dog has had all his shots? And is your mother okay?"

"Tamagotchi is fine. And so is my mom," I say, smoothing

my hands over his lapels. He owns less formal clothing, but he wears a jacket and collared shirt every time he visits me in the palace.

Somehow, I maneuver him into my room. We pause near a lacquered credenza inlaid with gold chrysanthemums. On the top are frames, including a picture of the girls and me. Yes, Hansani has a full mouth of shiny braces. Yes, we're wearing matching denim outfits. And yes, my hair is permed.

There is also a waka poem Akio penned for me.

Now I understand
It is all so clear to me
Against wind, rain, sleet
I stopped believing in love
Until I saw the leaves fall

Poetry is kind of our thing. Originally, we were mortal enemies. Akio drove me *nuts* with his schedules, his overall gothic-novel vibe, and his eight inches of height over me. But now, our couple dynamic is fun-loving princess and gruff former bodyguard turned promising pilot who only shows his soft side to those closest to him. It really works for me.

I regard Akio slyly, getting right up in his space and nipping at his chin. "Are you here to have your way with me?" I ask.

He gives me a smoldering once-over. "With Reina watching?" He dips his head to the dark garden, where Reina canvasses the area. My new bodyguard wears a black suit and once confessed she rendered a man unconscious using his ponytail alone—it's why she keeps her hair short.

I purse my lips. "Kinky, but no." Should have had the foresight to close the curtains. I sigh, step away from him to a small table by the window. Two chairs are on either side of it, and on top, a Go game board. I grip the back of a seat. "Rematch?"

His lips curl in a faint smile. "You're on." He shrugs out of his jacket and empties his pockets next to the game board. Phone. Keys. Wallet.

"It's my turn to be first," I say, pulling a wooden bowl of black stones toward me.

Akio inclines his head and positions the bowl of white stones near him. "Loser always goes first the next game."

I have never won against him. *So far.* Most of our summer has been spent at this table, dueling for territory. Akio's dark eyes glinting while he carefully strategized, then taunting when he won. But tonight, his reign of terror ends. Tonight, I am out for blood.

He rolls up his sleeves. His forearms are thick and veined. "Music?" he asks, scrolling through his phone.

"As long as you promise not to sing."

Akio's speaking voice is deep and melodic. His singing voice, the opposite—a cross between a barking seal and the shriek of a seagull.

His expression is playful, almost boyish. "No promises."

"No music, then."

"All right," he agrees somberly.

Playing commences. My opening moves are aggressive.

Akio rubs a white stone between his fingers. "Going right in for the attack?" he murmurs.

"Less talking, more playing," I volley back.

He clucks his tongue, but amusement lights his eyes. "Always the first to go all-in."

In eight moves, I've captured two of Akio's stones and occupied their liberties. His good humor has fled and he drops forward, brow furrowed—a samurai plotting. Six more moves, and Akio has captured five of my stones for his prisoner pile. I tease him throughout. *You sure you want to do that? I am inside your mind right now. Tsk, that's the worst move you could make.* There is a stark difference in our playing styles. Akio is methodical. Controlled. I am unrestrained. Risky. He is the pull, and I am the push.

We are done an hour and a half later. It's a close game. Black, twenty-four points. White, twenty-three points. An over-the-top grin lifts my cheeks.

"Mairimashita." *I lost,* he says with a slight bow of his head.

"Arigatō gozaimashita." *Thank you,* I respond politely, accepting his surrender.

"Arigatō gozaimashita," he returns. Formalities done, he leans back in his chair, legs splayed, a baffled look on his face. What just happened?

I pucker my lower lip, skirt around the table, and settle into Akio's lap, draping my arms loosely around his neck. "You're devastated," I say. "I know how much you love to win."

His hand cups my waist. "I do like to win." He pauses.

His thumb lazily strokes my hip. "But I like it better when you win."

"That"—I inhale—"is a good answer."

"Radish," he says.

I warm at his nickname for me. Originally it had been my code name. I thought he'd been making fun of me after I'd accepted a radish chrysanthemum from an airport chef. I'd confessed to Akio I hated it. And what had he said? *A radish is a very formidable vegetable,* he'd stated quietly, with an intent stare. *They're my favorite, in fact.*

Now, he's peering at me the same way. "Reina is gone." His voice isn't a whisper, but it's just as soft.

We tilt toward each other. A new silence settles between us, burgeoning with an air of expectation, like right before a thunderstorm. He kisses me, nose nudging against mine. My mouth opens, soft and ready. *Willing.* My body, this close to Akio's, produces a quiet heat. We are fusion, two atoms colliding.

Forget Mount Shasta, my hometown, where the Rainbow Gatherers converge June through August to bask naked in the sun, live communally, and wear flowers in their hair. This year the summer of love is in Tokyo.

2

The next day at ten a.m. sharp, the imperial family and court descend upon the University of Tokyo campus for a tour. Mr. Fuchigami is to my right and a baby-faced graduate student, our guide, is on my left. An entire entourage trails in our wake. A mixed bag of Mom, Dad, Dad's equerry, Dad's chamberlain, the dean of students, and his assistant. Plus Reina and a gaggle of imperial guards. We're rolling deep. Akio, whom I brought as an emotional-support animal, has drifted to the back.

The campus is a blend of modern architecture and old stone buildings. Mr. Fuchigami is all hyped up like a kid on cupcakes as we're led into a dormitory. "This is a brand-new building," says my chamberlain. "It is very nice, don't you agree, Your Highness?"

I smile placidly. "It's lovely."

Mom, Dad, and the rest are riding separately. Something about weight limits and no two imperial family members in the same elevator, you know, in case a cable breaks and it plummets to the ground. But Reina and Akio are with me.

For the duration of the ride, the graduate student highlights community events—mixers, organized karaoke nights, even a flag club. "I was a member as an undergraduate," the graduate student confides with a sly smile. "I admit, it can get a little wild. The year I left, we voted to introduce fictional flags starting with those in the Starfleet." At my blank look, he presses on. "*Star Trek*. I'm a big fan."

Akio coughs into his fist. I catch Reina's smile right before she drops her focus to the laminate floor.

"What fun," Mr. Fuchigami says with light in his eyes.

The elevator doors split open. We reunite with the rest of the group—Mom, Dad, the dean of students, and others—and squeeze into a hall.

"Wait here," Reina commands. Then she muscles her way inside the open dorm room. I smile at the tour guide like this is all normal. "Akio-san," she murmurs, inviting him in. Together they inspect the shoebox space, opening and closing the closet, flicking the light off and on, twisting the lock on the door back and forth.

They confer with each other, discussing the security features and risks—concrete walls and double-paned windows, but not bulletproof. What a shame. Behind me, my mother and father have the same amused expression. Akio places a hand on the doorknob and knocks on the wood. "Hollow," he states.

Reina nods. She runs a manicured finger over the faux wood. "Wouldn't keep an intruder out."

A muscle twitches in Akio's jaw. His eyes gleam with intelligence. "How many break-ins were reported last year?" He steps to the tour guide, interrogating him like the hero he is.

"I don't know." The tour guide hesitates, a nervous knit in his brow. "I'd have to inquire."

"What about incidents resulting in police reports?" Reina asks.

"Um, I'm not sure." The tour guide's face flushes red, the color of the cherry tomatoes we used to grow in our garden in Mount Shasta.

"And security guards?" asks Akio.

Akio and Reina are totally letting their I'm-a-contract-killer vibe run wild right now. Together they face down the much shorter tour guide, staring at him for one long, uncomfortable minute while he searches for an answer.

Nothing. He's got nothing.

The dean steps forward, hands opening in a congenial manner. "The campus is very safe, I assure you."

"I'd still like to know the answers," my father says, centuries of imperial blood in his tone.

Good lord. I shut my eyes, then open them. The dean is mid-bow. "Of course, Your Highness. I will have those numbers to you this afternoon," he states with abject deference.

"Once the princess has decided on a school, imperial guards will meet with campus security and police. She'll have her own detail, but we like to cooperate as much as possible with the local authorities," Reina proclaims.

The dean inclines his head and promises to follow all imperial protocols. He turns to address me. "Your Highness, I hope you will find University of Tokyo akin to coming home since your father and his father matriculated here for their undergraduate degrees. I am certain you will desire the legacy to continue."

Deep breath. I paste on a robotic smile and link my hands together, bowing my head. "It would be an honor," I say, voice steady. But on the inside, my stomach turns over.

The dean invites me to explore at my leisure and falls into conversation with my parents.

I wander the narrow room. It smells musty and like something else I can't place—a combination of the ghost of dirty clothes and overcooked food. All in all, it's pretty standard with a small closet, bed, and desk. However, it's been spruced up for the imperial visit. A welcome banner hangs from the wall. There are brochures from programs on campus—they run the gambit on esoteric and harmless subjects. My father majored in medieval transportation. Imperials are discouraged from studying anything too controversial: no political science majors or even those with career tracks. We are not allowed to earn an income. Even if I wanted to be premed like Noora, pre-pharmacy like Glory, or a pro bono environmental lawyer like Hansani, it would be forbidden. Being a princess is a lifestyle choice. Suddenly, it hits me hard, what it will be like if I choose this path. The limitations. The high expectations.

The window has a nice view of the campus. I part the flimsy curtain and study the students scurrying across the quad, chins held high with purpose. Could this be mine for the next four years? Do I *want* this to be mine? A gap year is still on the table, as far as I'm concerned. I try to imagine what that might be like, returning to the States. And doing what?

"Out of curiosity . . ." Akio is next to me. "Still don't like trackers in your phone?"

I let the curtain fall back. "I'm not going to dignify that with a response."

When I first arrived in Japan, Akio placed a tracker in

my cell phone. So not okay. Even though it was standard practice, I said never again—it's my hill, and I'll die on it.

His face twists with dissatisfaction. "And you haven't recently acquired any close combat training?"

I outright laugh.

Suddenly, conversation in the hall halts. All eyes are on me, and they are full of questions. Mom: *What's so funny?* Dad: *Are you happy with the room?* The dean: *Do you like the university?* Mr. Fuchigami: *I have the application right here. Would you like my help filling it out?*

I need some space.

"Mom," I say. "I read that the new Economics building here is state-of-the-art and LEED gold certified. The rooftop rainwater collection device supplies seventy percent of the water to the building. Why don't you go take a look?"

My mother's face lights up and my father's face warms. Mom lives for sustainability, and it's becoming clear that Dad lives for her.

"I'd love to, but . . ." She glances at me. "Really? Are you sure? This isn't my tour. Would that be okay?" Now she's looking at my father. In turn, my father looks to the dean.

The dean bows low. "Of course, of course. My apologies that we didn't think to prepare a visit to the Economics building. Right this way, please." He opens his hand and gestures for my parents to proceed him.

"You sure you won't mind, Zoom Zoom?" Mom asks me over her shoulder. She's already halfway to the elevator.

Go, I mouth.

They leave. The tour guide, Reina, and part of the imperial security detail stay behind, loitering in the hall. I cross the carpet and nod at Akio, who closes the door behind us. Some of the pressure in my temples eases in the quiet, in the stillness. I lean against the window and inhale the stale air.

Akio saunters to me. "What do you think?" he asks quietly, searching my face.

I have to admit now that I feel a certain pressure from Akio, too. This need for me to settle somewhere, on something. To make some choices about my life. What *is* the life I've dreamed of? Growing up in America, when I was younger, I didn't see many kids who looked like me in books, in video games, on television. What I did see were stereotypes—good at math, studying, working hard. Narrow versions of myself. Now, my world has expanded. I can have things at the touch of my fingertips. But there are still rules to abide by. Princess rules. What I can do and can't. Like my major. I may choose it but within certain parameters. Does life always come with constraints? Is that part of growing up?

"Are you sweating?" He reaches for a handkerchief but I shake my head.

"Akio." I stare at the bed. There is a new tag on the mattress. "Did you always know you wanted to be a pilot?"

He considers my words for a moment. "Well, when I was five, I wanted to be a T. rex, so no. But once my father bought me my first toy plane, I knew." I picture Akio's childhood room. Littered with airplanes. His journey hasn't always been a straight line, but somehow, he's arrived. He regards me. "What did you want to be as a child?"

"Once I pretended to be a tub of sour cream for a whole week." I smile. He smiles back.

"The truth is, I'm having a hard time deciding what to do. I mean, what am I really passionate about beyond eating and sleeping?" I joke again, but it falls flat. I sigh.

"Maybe you should start by narrowing it down by what you don't want to do." He picks up a brochure, reads, then flashes the pamphlet to me. "Any interest in the fascinating but very slow-paced field of mollusks?" He rocks back on his heels. "Pun intended."

I scrunch my nose. "Pass." Geez, I can't even laugh at a good pun.

"You sure?" He quirks a brow. "I am almost certain your great-uncle received his doctorate in the study of sea urchins." I say no again. He places the brochure facedown. "You're doing well. Check one off the list." He picks up another brochure. "Egyptology? One of the required classes is 'Ancient Babylonian Magic and Medicine.' That's actually kind of interesting."

"Too many curses and mummies," I declare.

"Very wise," he murmurs, setting the Egyptology brochure on top of the mollusks one. "Ah, here's one on mortuary science."

"That's not real." I snatch it from him. It's a brochure for the English department.

He merely shrugs. "You just need to figure out where your proclivities lie."

I smirk. "Where my proclivities lie?"

"Radish." His voice is deep and lush, a rasp of velvet against my skin. He stands in front of me, grasps my hand, then squeezes it and lets go. A fleeting touch but reassuring all the same.

"I'm not even sure if I should go to school," I say with an exaggerated frown.

He smiles. "You'll figure it out. I believe in you. Follow your heart."

You lead with your heart. He told me so before. It's my natural inclination and has never failed me before. But what does my heart want? Where is it going?

Tour over, we stop outside the Economics building to meet up with Mom and Dad. A swarm of imperial guards surrounds us. My feet are tired and aching. I'm ready to go home.

"What about you, Kobayashi-san?" the tour guide inquires of Akio. "Are you interested in University of Tokyo as well?"

"No." He buttons his suit jacket and scans the quad. "I recently resigned from the imperial guard and joined the Air Self-Defense Force. I am attending Officer Candidate School in Nara."

Along with Mom leaving, Akio will be going back to school soon. It's a double whammy. Fall is looking rather lonely.

The tour guide's mouth screws down in disappointment. "It's true what the tabloids say, then. You're just a cadet?"

I wince. Really?

"Yes. Just a cadet," Akio answers, his voice neutral.

Mom and Dad emerge from the Economics building. Cameras flash. We've drawn a crowd. My father and I come together and wander to the side, distracting the royal watchers from Mom and Akio. We stand together and let the photographs commence. Instantly, we're pummeled with clicks and flashes and questions. *Princess Izumi, have you filled out your application to University of Tokyo? Crown Prince Toshihito, are you pleased your daughter will be enrolling at the same university as you?*

We ignore them all.

"I'm glad we have a moment alone," Dad says so only I can hear.

"Oh?" I smile and wave at a mother holding up her toddler in a plaid jumper. She grasps his chubby wrist and parrots a wave back at me. His face scrunches, his eyes well with tears, and he lets out an almighty wail. *Right.*

"I have decided to ask your mother to marry me," he says simply.

I forget what I'm doing and stare up at my father, mouth agape. "Seriously?" More cameras flash and click.

"Seriously." His dark eyes twinkle in the late-afternoon sun. He's amused himself. Lately, both my parents have been adapting my favorite phrases—*dumpster fire, chaos demon, I am a soulless void.* It is slightly terrifying but mostly gratifying being the butt of their inside jokes.

"That's fast," I say. Dad and Mom dated in college. Years passed before they saw each other again. Now they've only been back together a handful of weeks. Is he doing this to prevent her from leaving?

Dad's mouth tugs downward. "You don't approve?"

"No, that's not it," I hurry to say.

I'm at a crossroads. I want this so bad. And I think

Mom might, too. Only I'm not sure. I blink, seeing my family portrait torn and scattered in the wind.

Before I have a chance to explain, Dad speaks up. "It's not fast. At least, not for me. I have been thinking of your mother for years. Waiting. And I don't want to wait anymore. But listen . . ." His voice drops. "I won't ask her without your blessing. We've felt like a family these last few weeks. It is my greatest hope to make it permanent."

Mine too. One thing I am sure of: Mom loves Dad. Dad loves Mom. Some things just are. "Of course. You have my blessing."

"Seriously?" he echoes back at me.

I touch my chest, right over my heart, where it beats wildly with the sudden promise of it all—love, family, a second chance at happily ever after. God, I want Mom to say yes. To choose us. To stay in Tokyo. "Seriously."

"Excellent. Tomorrow then."

Wow. Talk about not wasting time. "Where are you going to do it?" I ask. "I think you should use the—"

"Greenhouse," he cuts me off.

"Exactly," I agree. I grin and shift back to our audience and the paparazzi, finding an awning speckled with bird droppings above their heads to focus on.

The greenhouse. It was the first thing my father showed me when I arrived. I didn't know it then, but he had built it for my mother, filling it with her favorite flowers—orchids. I should've known he'd want to marry her now that they've found each other again. She has always bloomed in his heart.

3

Nearly twenty-four hours later, I shake a bag of dog treats into a pair of Mom's favorite shoes. "Mom, trust me, I'm doing you a favor," I whisper to her, even though she's not present. I pat the pleather slip-ons, bidding them a fond farewell—her taste in footwear hasn't improved since her college days.

I stick two fingers in my mouth and whistle for Tamagotchi. He tears around a corner and whips by me, sniffing out the fake bacon and cheese. I hurry to find Mom in her room, reading a book about foraging. Pretending to be out of breath, I splutter, "Mom. Quick! Tamagotchi has a pair of your shoes."

"No!" She slams the book down and gives chase.

I slip away into the backyard. The sun is high and bakes my cheeks red. When I arrive at the greenhouse, my father is already waiting.

"How did it go?" he asks.

"Good. She'll be distracted for a little bit." Staff in crisp uniforms perch on ladders, stringing up lights. "I thought we were going to do this." I touch a tiny twinkle light.

"I told them we wanted to do it ourselves, but Mr. Soga"—the grand chamberlain—"insisted staff be present to help and to stand on any ladders."

I shrug. It's to be expected, I guess, for the grand chamberlain to have opinions about this sort of thing. We set to work—uncoiling lights, placing lanterns, arranging everything just so. As we light the last candle, a dozen men in white-tie tuxedos appear carrying instruments—the imperial orchestra will play behind the trees a little ways away. Evening is coming, and everything in the garden is cast in a reddish-golden waning light. It's a whole mood.

I veer to go, but my father stalls me. "Wait, Izumi. I have a gift for you." He disappears inside the greenhouse and reappears with a book, and hands it to me.

I read the title aloud. *"One Thousand Things to Know About University."*

He taps the cover. "It is filled with very practical knowledge. I am looking forward to you having a more realistic university experience than I did. Did you know most students buy their own textbooks? My chamberlains had the authors annotate and personally deliver them to me."

I have nothing to say. We really grew up worlds apart. I hug the book to my chest. "Wow. Thanks."

"It seemed like you enjoyed the tour yesterday," he says.

In the last few months living in Tokyo, I have become semi-fluent in the Japanese way of asking a question without asking a question. His statement, *It seemed like you enjoyed the tour yesterday,* really means, *Did you like the tour yesterday? Are you still considering a gap year? Please tell me you aren't. Please just commit to a university so we can formally announce it and the chamberlains will stop harassing me.*

"I did," is all I say. I grow quiet. Dad is waiting for me to offer more. I have nothing. My heart is silent. It doesn't know what to do. Maybe I should take a gap year after all. Maybe I need time to discover myself. Who am I beyond a princess? Beyond Izumi from Mount Shasta? What defines me?

He scratches his forehead. He does this when something displeases him, like when he's confused by his recently acquired teenage daughter. His gold watch with a crown emblem blinks at me. "I can have Mr. Fuchigami set up a tour of Gakushūin University for next week if you'd like."

Gakushūin was established to educate the imperial aristocracy. My perfect twin cousins attend there. I hope to see more of them like I hope to be caught by the *Tokyo Tattler* with toilet paper trailing from my waistband.

"Let me think on University of Tokyo for a bit," I say, buying time. I play with the book, my brain full of storms. Sometimes I still don't feel like I belong in Japan. Having been raised in the States, I will always be a kind of outsider here. But I don't feel like I belong in Mount Shasta, either. Where do I want to make my life? "I better get going. Mom will be here soon." I skip away before Dad can say anything else about university.

I come across Mom on my way back to the palace. "You might want to kiss Tamagotchi goodbye," she huffs out. "He's going to the pound tomorrow."

Some of her hair has escaped its ponytail and stands out in frenzied spikes. Her jeans and top are wrinkled. Clearly, she's been in a tussle. It's unclear who won. My money is on Tamagotchi. He's scrappy. "I will cuddle him extra close tonight." I step to her and undo the rubber band holding her hair up. I kind of comb it and fluff it around her shoulders. *Better.* I slip the rubber band into my pocket.

"Where are you coming from? Your father asked me

to meet him at the greenhouse, have you seen him? I'm late because of *your* dog. What's that?" she says, all in a flurry. When I started getting busy with school and friends around four years ago, she'd evolved into a rapid-fire question machine. It's amazing how much communication she fit in while we passed in the hallway. *What time will you be home tonight? Do you need anything from the grocery store? Are you waiting for magical trash fairies to clean your room?*

I ignore her other questions and focus on the last. "A gift from Dad." I flash her the book. "Did you know that his textbooks were hand-delivered by the authors and signed?"

She rubs her temples. "I didn't, but that's about right."

When I found out my father was the Crown Prince, Mom told me a bit about him and what he was like when they were in college. It was my first glimpse of the man my mother loved. *He didn't know how to iron a shirt, do laundry, or make a cup of soup. He drank like a fish, loved microbeers. And he was funny. He had this dry sense of humor and a wicked wit. You wouldn't know you were at the receiving end of one of his barbs until you were bleeding and he was gone.* At the memory, my eyes crinkle at the corners. I step away. "See you."

"Wait." She pauses. I do too. "Is Akio coming over again tonight?"

I nod. "Yes. Later. He's visiting some old imperial guard buddies right now."

"I see." She rubs her lips together. "You two have had a lot of late nights together. Should we have another conversation about being safe?"

My eyes widen. "No." So much no. Nope. Never. We had "the talk" years ago. Mom borrowed models from the biology department. It was horrifying. Ever seen your mother handle an anatomically correct male dummy with expert precision? I have. Anyway, time to run away now. "I should go. Dad's waiting for you. Great chat." I scurry off like a small woodland creature and don't slow until the palace is in view.

In the empty kitchen, I settle at the counter across from a shiny French gourmet stove with red knobs. There's the fragrance of freshly baked bread and a plate of dorayaki on the island. I glance out to the garden.

Is Dad getting down on one knee yet? I can picture it. Mom's hair gleaming in the waning light. The sound of Dad's low voice as he asks those four simple words: *Will you marry me?* What will her answer be? Yes? No? She rejected him once before, when she found out she was pregnant with me. Made the decision to raise me alone. Left him without a word. Because she wanted another life for us. What life does she want for us now? For herself?

I tap out a text to Noora and the girls.

Me

My dad is proposing RN.

I stare at the screen, giddy and nervous, waiting for them to answer. It's almost seven o'clock in the evening here, so it's six a.m. in New York, where Noora is. And three a.m. where Glory and Hansani are. Noora is the only one to respond.

Inhuman shriek What? No. Stop.
This is madness. This totally
derails my plan to become your
best friend/stepmother. I had a
whole speech about how I would
never replace your real mother but
hoped we could stay friends.

Me

Sorry. Not sorry.

A soft voice floats from the kitchen entry. "Sumimasen,
Izumi-sama." I turn to see Mariko, my lady-in-waiting.

I smile and rise from my seat to greet her. "You're back."

She hovers in the doorway. "O hisashiburi desu. O
genki desu ka?" *Long time, no see. How are you?*

"I'm fine," I say. "Come sit. How was your trip?" I wave
her in and pat the seat next to me.

Mariko missed the university tour and was gone overnight to visit her folks. I found Mariko—short, slender,
and neat to a T—vaguely terrifying when I first arrived.
She is in charge of dressing me, keeping my schedule, and
other assorted tasks. Her father is a poet laureate, and she
probably has a million better things to do than hang out
with me. Yet she stays. I am eternally grateful she is a permanent part of my solar system.

"Good, they say hello," she says, perching on a stool.
"Mr. Fuchigami asked I give you these. An emissary from
the university delivered them." She deposits a handful of

pamphlets in front of me. They are all from University of Tokyo, various programs I might be interested in.

I set them away, as far across the counter as I can reach. She has also brought a copy of the *Tokyo Tattler*, which she spreads open in front of her. Technically there is a media ban on royal property, but Mariko occasionally sneaks the papers in. Most of the staff look the other way. It's become an idle hobby of ours, reading the headlines, laughing at them.

"You're on the front page again, but under the fold," she says with a disappointed sigh. Her most recent life highlight was my picture, above the fold, in a dress she chose— "HIH Princess Izumi Stuns in Hanae Mori Gown." "It's an article on you and your choice of school."

I nibble on a piece of dorayaki and glance at the article. The photograph is a little grainy. It's of my father and me right after the tour.

Mariko reads the headline out loud. "'Her Imperial Highness Princess Izumi Smiles During University of Tokyo Tour but Does Not Commit.'" Mariko clears her throat. "'Yesterday, HIH Princess Izumi toured the University of Tokyo campus. Her bodyguard turned beau, Akio Kobayashi, accompanied her, and their body language was anything but cozy.'" The papers vacillate between reporting watered-down press releases, semi-truths, and outright lies. They love the idea of Akio and me breaking up. Heartache always sells. "'Could there be trouble in paradise?'" She stares at me a long beat, and I shake my head, quietly refuting the claim. She goes on, "'Palace officials are hopeful that's the case. They'd much rather have the princess focusing on school and her imperial duties, and believe Kobayashi to be a distraction. They and, rumor has it, her father, the Crown Prince, are desperate for her to make a decision about what she'll do next spring.'"

My palms begin to sweat. The back of my neck prickles. Mariko doesn't notice. It's all internal.

"'Since the Japanese school year begins in April, the princess has technically already missed a year, which puts her behind her peers and cousins, HIH Princesses Akiko and Noriko.'" The mention of the twins, who glide effortlessly through imperial life, is a knife-twist to the gut. They wear the princess mantle with ease and gusto. "'But this is to be expected, since the American school year differs from the Japanese. What is not to be expected is Princess Izumi taking an *intentional* year off. "She's considering not going to college right away if at all," a palace insider says.'" Mariko scans ahead and stops. "That's enough for today."

"What?" I wipe crumbs from the corner of my mouth. My Japanese reading proficiency is slowly improving, but I rely on other people to translate something quickly. "Go on." I keep my voice light. I wonder what made her pause.

She gives a brisk shake of her head. "I don't know if I should."

"It's okay," I say. "Really."

Here is what I have learned in half a year of dealing with the tabloids and life in general. I ask myself two questions: Am I dead? Did someone I love die? If the answer is no to both, I know I am fine. Maybe bruised a little, but okay. For the most part, the tabloids focus on trivial subjects. They can be a bit rough. It is their reminder the imperial family is subject *to* them, not above them. Mr. Fuchigami says the press is merely trying to enjoy my life in an aspirational way. It's a symbiotic relationship, he says. They keep the public interest in the imperial family alive. I suppose he's right. It's the price of admission.

Mariko purses her lips, then picks up the paper and reads again. "'According to a Mount Shasta public school employee, the princess barely graduated high school. Although she did well in her English and social studies coursework, her math and science scores were particularly dire.'"

"I earned a very respectable B-minus in algebra," I state, defensive. I don't mention my C-minus in chemistry.

The paper crinkles under her hands as she reads more. "'Regardless, this less-than-average student is receiving private tours of Japan's most revered institutions. University of Tokyo spent weeks preparing for the princess's visit. All of the fluorescent lights were changed out at the dorm before she toured to ensure none would flicker while the Crown Prince and his daughter were present. Reportedly, the dean of students had to scramble to accommodate an unscheduled visit to the newly renovated Economics building. "We would be thrilled if the princess attended our humble institution," he remarked, refusing to comment when pressed about the princess's grades or the side trip to the Economics building. Some are more critical of the princess. "Are we expected to celebrate the princess for her mediocrity?" imperial blogger Junko Inogashira asks.'"

I dig into another dorayaki, gnashing my teeth and

taking out my frustration on the sweet bean treat. It's true that I was an average, maybe below-average, student. But is there something I am unaware of? Do you really have to abide by a set of certain rules? Do you really have to be special to be loved?

Mariko sets the paper down, hooks a finger over the plate edge, and slides it to her. "The rest is speculation on what you'll wear to the emperor's luncheon in a few weeks. They wonder if you'll wear pants, which means . . . you owe me one thousand yen." She bites delicately into a piece of dorayaki.

"The bet was if the tabloids would report on me wearing pants again, not speculating if I would," I clarify.

She shrugs. "Same-same. I prefer cash, but I will also accept PayPay."

"It's unbecoming for a lady-in-waiting to take a bet." I draw the dorayaki plate closer to me.

She slides the plate back to her. "Then it's also probably just as unbecoming for a princess to make a bet."

I open my mouth but snap it closed as Mom and Dad materialize in what I can only describe as a cloud of happiness. Mom is grinning ear to ear. Dad looks equally pleased.

I stand and go to them, elation spiking in my chest, and clutch Mom's hands. "I'm assuming good news?"

Mom nods, liquid in her eyes.

When was the last time I saw her cry? When I had found out my father was the Crown Prince of Japan, and I was boarding the plane to meet him. She had shoved me. *This is me kicking you out of the nest.*

It occurs to me now that we're both poised to take flight, though I don't know what path I'll be choosing—dutiful princess or wanderer. I hug her, letting all my emotions show in the tightness of my arms, in the width of my smile—the three of us in one happy, dizzy bubble. A family at last.

4

Two weeks pass in a happy blur. Mom takes a leave of absence from her job. News of my parents' engagement ripples quietly through the imperial estate. We go to Uncle Nobuhito's house for an informal celebration among close family. Champagne is uncorked, and toasts go around wishing my parents all the best. My chest swells with happiness. Noora texts me at weird hours of the night, often with recommendations for the guest list—Oprah, ONE OK ROCK, a dog with over one hundred thousand followers on Instagram. I help Akio pack for his return to school. Tamagotchi develops a bald spot on his back. He is diagnosed with late-onset alopecia, and the royal vet prescribes a special cream to be rubbed on his body three times a day. More university brochures arrive. I use my parents' engagement and Akio's imminent departure as a ruse for more time. *There is so much to consider*, I tell Mr. Fuchigami with a wide-eyed innocence I'm sure he doesn't buy. I try not to think too hard about it all. Akio and I play Go. We're tied eight to eight. This morning we're planning one more game. Winner will be determined for all time (unless I lose, then I will demand a rematch).

I have just finished a breakfast of rice, miso soup, natto, and yakizakana when I hear voices from my father's office. It's not abnormal. The palace usually hums with activity, with stewards, chamberlains, and various staff coming and going. What is abnormal is the tenor—the low-pitched whinny of a sad song.

Odd.

The door is open a crack, and Dad sees me hovering. "Izumi," he calls.

I push into the office and pad in, catching sight of two figures first. The grand steward, Mr. Tajima, stands with the grand chamberlain, Mr. Soga. Mr. Fuchigami, my chamberlain, rounds out the trio of visitors.

All three of their mouths are flat unhappy lines. Next, my eyes fall to my father. He is sitting behind his desk, severe but unruffled. And last, there is my mother, in a chair. She wrings her hands and offers me a weak smile.

"Morning," she says, her temperament cloudy. "Did you have breakfast?"

"What's going on?" I ask.

Dad draws in a deep breath. "The Imperial Household Council held an unofficial vote late last evening." He leans forward, plucks a heavy silver pen from his desk, and fists it.

I blink twice. "The Imperial House Council?"

Mr. Fuchigami smooths down his navy tie. "The Imperial House Council is the ten-member body responsible for overseeing statutory matters regarding Japan's imperial house. It is led by the prime minister . . ." He pauses to draw in a weighty breath. The tabloids have long reported on the tepid relationship between my father and the prime minister. For a change, they are right.

Unfortunately, I haven't helped much. I accidentally insulted the prime minister at his wedding, asking after his sister when it's well known the two aren't on speaking terms. My stomach flips, remembering the humiliation. Being so fresh in Japan, being so thin-skinned, I'd bolted from the event. Ever since, I've managed to avoid the prime minister. When I see him on rare occasions, we're polite and nod at each other daringly, as one does an ancient enemy. *Another battle again, so soon?*

Mr. Fuchigami continues, "The Imperial Household Council must approve of certain matters before advancement: any marriage of any male member of the imperial family, forfeiture of imperial status, and changing the order of succession. Prince Nobuhito and Prince Yasuhito voted in favor of your parents' match," he says. "However, the others voiced . . . hesitations."

I trudge farther into the room, taking up residence behind my mother. I place a hand on her stiff shoulder. She is like frozen porcelain ready to crack. "What sort of hesitations?"

Mr. Fuchigami suddenly looks as if he'd rather be arranging a funeral. The tension in the room ratchets up a notch.

Mr. Soga clears his throat. He inhales and says, "Among other things, Hanako-san's accomplishments have come into question. She graduated summa cum laude from Harvard, but the council wonders why she accepted a position at such a low-ranking institution."

My jaw clenches. What an unfair and asinine thing to think. Mom chose to raise me in Mount Shasta, a small town the opposite of Tokyo. Even if she had been wrong in not telling my father about me, she's always tried to do right. And sometimes I remember fondly and very warmly being an anonymous person in the world. I wouldn't change my childhood for anything.

Mom straightens, and my hand falls away from her. "I am proud of my time and tenure at College of the Siskiyous," she says with a bite, and pride surges under my skin. So what if the Imperial Household Council doesn't approve? Growing up, it was just Mom and me. We never had to ask permission for anything. "They didn't have a functional biology department until I arrived. *I* built that program," she declares.

"Of course." Dad's eyes warm as he focuses on her. Then he transfers his gaze to the steward and chamberlain, a scowl emanating. "It is silly and unbelievable the Imperial Household Council would use Hanako's job as a sticking point. Quite frankly, I'm offended, and I really don't care to have this discussion any longer." He flicks a hand.

All three of the palace officials swallow and bow. "Absolutely, Your Highness. We will reconvene at a later time," Mr. Soga says evenly.

They shuffle out.

Dad stands and skirts around the desk. "Hanako?" He pulls up a chair and sits in front of her.

"Mak," she says softly with a shake of her head.

"Sumimasen." A butler appears in the doorway, sweeping into a low bow. "Mr. Kobayashi just arrived."

I thank him and squeeze Mom's shoulder. "Talk later," I promise. I slip away, and Tamagotchi trots after me. Akio is in the living room.

"Hey," he says warmly, tenderly.

My jaw clenches. I'm still sorting through everything.

A little confused. A lot bewildered. Uncoiling the dread in my stomach.

"Hey," he says again, voice bending with concern.

"Let's go outside," I say. We put on our shoes, and he follows me out the door.

"Radish," he says once we're on the grass. Tamagotchi sniffs and lifts his leg to mark an azalea bush, the empress's favorite.

I peer at my feet, at the rounded toe of my navy heel. "What do you know about the Imperial Household Council?"

"Quite a bit," he says.

I don't need to explain, then. "They held a meeting and voted against my parents' match." I rub my forehead. Akio is silent. "I don't understand. Why does what they say matter so much?"

Akio's face is hard. "No imperial family member has ever been wed without it."

I blow out a breath. "That serious, then."

"Hai," he confirms, and it sounds like the chop of a knife. He knows how bad I want this. He knows my secret dreams. How incomplete my childhood felt without a father, a family.

There isn't a chance to agonize over it. Voices drift from the front of the house. "The Crown Prince is insensible where it concerns Hanako-san," the grand chamberlain says. I press my finger against my lips at Akio and creep closer.

Akio exhales slowly, but I feel him behind me. I peek around the corner of the house. The chamberlains, including Mr. Fuchigami, and steward stand next to an idling black sedan.

"He believes everyone should adore Hanako-san as he does," the grand steward says with a shake of his head. My poor father, the fool for love.

"Izumi," Akio whispers. I grab his hand to hush him.

"He is protecting her too much," the grand chamberlain says. "The Imperial Household Council will comb through Hanako-san's life. Every move she makes henceforth will be scrutinized."

"Their daughter's romance with the bodyguard doesn't help," the grand steward murmurs.

Akio's hand falls limp in my hand. In a flash, I remember the tour guide from a few days ago. *You're just a cadet?* When news of our relationship broke, it was all over the tabloids, how Akio wasn't good enough for a princess, how he had betrayed his family lineage, spurning his role as an imperial guard to join the Air Self-Defense Force and enter Officer Candidate School. He was painted as a shameless opportunist. But I thought the tabloids were past that. That Tokyo was past it. There is even Akio and Izumi fan fiction. Mariko reads it, but I don't. Well, maybe I've scanned the one where he is a werewolf and we live together in a magical forest full of fairies and talking toads.

I squeeze Akio's hand. I don't care what they say about Akio. Any of it.

"What say you, Mr. Fuchigami?"

I risk another glance around the corner.

Mr. Fuchigami shifts his weight. "Princess Izumi is still adjusting to imperial life," is all he says.

"She hasn't chosen a school or major. Could she still be considering a year off? That decision will count against her mother, her job as a parent," the grand chamberlain adds.

The grand steward nods sagely. "Agreed. Young people may have loved her interview in the *Women Now!* article, but it doesn't mean the Imperial Household Council approved."

"Yes." Mr. Fuchigami scratches his brow. "I know. They viewed it as obvious self-promotion." Does he regret helping me with that? He was the one who set up the interview. It's not his fault—I asked him to. "And now, if anything, it has worked against her mother's favor."

"Exactly," the grand chamberlain declares. "In addition, they do not like Hanako-san's wariness of the imperial life. How she chafes against the palace restrictions."

"She is very modern," allows Mr. Fuchigami.

"The press will interpret it as snobbish. Especially with her American political sentiments," the grand chamberlain says.

I narrow my eyes, feeling super punchy right now. The conversation. The air of superiority. The disdain for my mother and me. It's all too much.

"Yes, many fear she will be a corrupting influence. I wish the Crown Prince had chosen someone with a more pliable character or from a better family," says the grand steward. "Many won't approve of such"—a pause—"social cross-pollination."

Their words are muted by the arrival of another vehicle. Car doors slam, and silence descends. Wind rustles the

trees. The summer air feels hotter somehow, more suffo-
cating.

I swear that I hear Akio swallow. We're still holding
hands, but his touch is wooden. Akio pulls back, and his
face is indecipherable. He doesn't speak.

"That was awful. What they said about you and me and
my mom. It's not true," I rush out.

A beat passes. Akio nods slowly. "Of course it's not
true." He presses his lips together and runs a hand through
his hair. "You should probably go check on your mom."

"What about our game?" I ask lightly, poking him in the
ribs. "Running scared?"

Akio forces a smile and catches my hand. A cloud drifts
over the sun. He kisses my fingertips and murmurs, "Radish."

"Rain check?" I do feel the gravitational pull to be close
to my mom right now.

"Tomorrow," he says firmly, and my cool, broody guard
who can withstand anything is back.

I peck his cheek. "Tomorrow," I say, and it's a promise.

The painful tightness in my throat eases. Things are always brighter in the morning.

5

I spy on my mom through a crack in her bedroom door. Her head is bent and she holds a silver-framed photo in her hands. I can't tell of who or what. A lock of her hair blocks the image and some of her expression, but what I observe is sadness—in the slope of her shoulders, the downturn of her mouth, the way her body is folded in like a piece of origami. In just a couple of hours, the mood around the palace has plummeted from glorious to glum.

I paste a smile on my face and use my body to push in the sliding door. The movement is the opposite of elegant. The tray and tea set I carry clinks, hot water bubbling up and spilling from the spout.

"Izumi," Mom starts. She sets the photograph down. Now I see. It's of me—my official imperial portrait snapped right before the emperor's birthday. I'm standing by a window in the imperial palace, afternoon sunlight pooling at my ankles.

"I brought tea," I say brightly. I place the tray on the table near the photo. I chew my lip and hesitate a moment, try to mask my worried expression. "You okay?" I ask, even though I can tell she isn't.

Her eyes are tired. "Honestly? I don't know. The meeting . . . it wasn't the news I had hoped for," she says grimly. "The last few weeks here have been so easy. I guess . . . I just expected for everything else to fall into place. Is that ignorant of me?"

"No, of course not." I smile and change to a chipper tone. "So you have to win a few hearts. That shouldn't be too hard. Remember when you convinced your entire faculty to buy three boxes of Girl Scout cookies each when I was selling them?" I wanted that prize T-shirt so hard, and now we use it as an extra rag when we wash Tamagotchi. I learned two lessons from that: Mom is a fighter, and nothing lasts forever. I mull it over. The possibilities. What she, what *we* do now.

Mom smiles. "I do."

I flash her a grin. "When is the real council meeting again?"

She scrunches her forehead. "I think Mr. Tajima said late December."

"We have time, then. It's only the end of August now. That's four months to turn things around. I mean, if the Virginia opossum can have a litter in twelve days, we can convince the council you and Dad should be able to get married." I sip my tea, pretend for us both that it's not a big deal. She and I have faced down bigger foes before. Like the time our water heater and furnace both went out in the middle of winter. Our basement flooded, then the floor froze. Mom had to open a credit card to pay for it all. It was a lean season, mostly peanut butter and jelly sandwiches instead of Christmas ham. But still, we managed. We strung up lights and made presents for each other—a handmade ornament for Mom and a bouquet of dried flowers for me. It's one of my favorite memories. We created our own warmth. No matter what, there has always been a happy glow around us fueled by her courage, her will to go on.

Mom's gaze falls to the photo. She studies it for a moment, tracing the folds of the gown with her finger. "When you were younger, I had this resentment for anything princessy, you know?"

I nod. "I remember." She eschewed gendered toys. She bought me blocks and trains and animals and dressed me in gender-neutral yellow.

"I had my own biases, I suppose," she says, abashed. "My experiences with your father, falling in love with a prince, bent my perspective. I wasn't sure if, being a princess, you could ever be a part of something important outside of the institution." I keep my face straight although I'm wincing inside. "And I hate this feeling that I need to be more feminine or just *more*. That I am not enough as I am."

"It's not forever," I declare. How do I convince her not all is lost? "Sometimes working within a system is the only way to change it." Sometimes you have to burn things down, and sometimes you have to dismantle starting from the inside—tearing wallpaper off, ripping up carpet, scraping popcorn off the ceilings.

"True," she says. We share a smile. But Mom's quickly fades. The sadness is back. And my Japanese-princess-born-in-a-small-town heart can't take it.

She sighs and focuses on the window, at the garden stretching beyond. There are at least half a dozen horticulturists out there, pruning trees, raking nonexistent leaves. Our backyard in Mount Shasta is high with overgrown grass. I remember Mom on summer days out there on the weekend, sweat pouring from her brow as she pushed a mower or pulled up weeds, only to do it again the next weekend when everything grew back—such a fighter. I am too. We Tanakas don't give up.

She could have had all this eighteen years ago. When I first found out about who my father was, I blamed her for how I grew up. I called my mom selfish, accused her of looking after her own self-interests and not mine. But I see things clearly now. No matter what anyone says, she chose the rougher road because she thought it was best for us both. So yeah, not mad. I know who I am. I know where I come from. I don't know where I am going, but I'm tabling it for now. Mom is more important.

"I don't want to hide who I am to be the person I'm expected to be," Mom admits quietly. She stares at me now. The tilt of her chin is a kind of a challenge—what do you say to that?

I lick my lips. "Maybe it's only for a little while, to gain approval from the council." Mom has only been here a short time. She isn't familiar with playing imperial games. Maybe we are chess pieces, but we certainly have some free will, don't we? Some say in our futures. The board is ours. Right?

Mom places her cup in the saucer. "I guess I'm grappling with my own ideologies about being a member of an imperial family." Of course she is. I am too. What does it mean to be a princess? Is there a place for them in the world anymore? Is there a place for me? She crosses her arms. "To be honest, the reason I left when I was pregnant was because I was scared. It's hard to admit." She pauses, gathering strength, resolve. "But I was pregnant, alone, and afraid," she states with finality. "I wanted to protect you, but also myself. The imperial life frightened me."

I tilt my head at her. "Are you scared now?"

She looks me directly in the eye. Shakes her head once. "I'm daunted but unafraid."

"Do you want to marry Dad?" I ask.

"I do," she says unflinchingly. "With my whole heart."

My mind wanders, skipping through more childhood memories. Mom buying me new school clothes, then staying up late to repair her work suits with a needle and thread. Mom missing a faculty party or dinner with friends to be at my soccer games. I never scored a single goal. But she still came. She showed up. All the ways she's given to me but never takes for herself. It's Mom's turn to have it all.

I straighten, my resolve matching hers. "Then I'll help you any way I can."

"But how?" she asks bleakly.

I chew my lip. "I don't know yet." But I kind of do. The gravity of the moment sucks me in. This is big. It is more than helping her pick out dresses, or learn Japanese, or calligraphy. The makeover includes me, too. Mentally I run down the checklist the chamberlains provided. Akio is nonnegotiable, but that just means I'll have to shine brighter in other areas. Like in school. Suddenly, my indecision fades. I am going to apply to university in Japan. Mr. Fuchigami will be delighted. "We're going to make the Imperial Household Council change their minds. You'll see."

Mom shuffles over on the settee. "Come here." She pats the space beside her and opens her arms.

"*Mom*," I say. The door is still open. Anyone could walk by, walk in. See us. I am much too old to be caught cuddling with my mother.

She shakes her arms. "Come here," she insists.

I roll my eyes and groan, but stand and move to sit next to her. She yanks me in until I'm resting on her chest, and her cheek is pressed against my head. Same as when we were waiting to get the furnace fixed and shivering under a mound of blankets, Tamagotchi buried there too, licking my toes. Tears leaked from the corners of her eyes and soaked my hair. She said she was just crying because she was tired. I get it now. She *was* tired. Life was hard. But it doesn't have to be anymore. She's found her prince, literally. And I'm going to help hand-deliver her happily ever after. Mine, too.

"We're going to do this," I state. *I promise*, I silently vow. And maybe somehow, I believe I came between my parents once before. What if Mom hadn't gotten pregnant? Would she still have run? Would she have stayed with Dad? Would they have continued long distance when he returned to Japan? Maybe. Maybe not. All I know is this is her second chance.

She holds me for a moment. I let her. It's kind of nice now that I'm here. I have discovered the older you get, the fewer hugs there are.

"Your father thought the empress might give me some lessons on court etiquette. I'll give him the go-ahead to inquire." She squeezes me, then kisses the top of my head. "Nobody will ever love you as much as I do," she proclaims.

My face screws up, and I grouse, "I feel like that's really unhealthy to say to me, and also, you shouldn't want that."

"It's true, though." She releases me, and I smooth my hair back down.

The staff member who carries Tamagotchi over mud puddles pauses outside the door and smiles at us before moving along.

6

Akio returns late the next afternoon. Our time together has dwindled to a mere forty-eight hours. He's leaving for Nara in two days.

"One more game of Go?" I ask outside the palace. "I have so much to tell you."

We haven't had a chance to speak since the conversation with Mom. This morning, he's been with his family and I had the All-Japan High School Sign Language Speech Contest.

"Let's walk instead, then," he says. "I have something I want to speak with you about, too."

We make our way to the Imperial Palace East Garden. "What did you want to talk about?" My steps are bouncy and light. The night air clings, hot and sticky on my arms.

"You first," he says, ambling beside me.

I delve into it. Telling Akio all about the plan. "So that's it," I say, a little out of breath. For every one stride Akio takes, I have to take two. . . . Okay, three. "Mom and I are both going to forge ahead and win the Imperial Household Council's approval. She will enlist the empress's help. I will enroll in an elite school. Somewhere in Tokyo."

Akio slows. "University?" he asks. "Is that what you want?"

A security guard passes us and bows low. I incline my

head out of habit. The garden closed an hour ago. Akio and I are alone, aside from Reina, who is around somewhere.

"University is . . . fukuzatsu. It's complicated," I say. "But it's what my mom needs me to do." That and more I haven't even thought of yet. I stop and place a hand on my chest as if making a sacred vow. "From here on out, I will be the perfect princess." I give him a bright, reassuring smile. It's all okay now.

He brushes a thumb over my lips. "Your parents' marriage is this important to you."

I nod. "You know it is." We amble on, and I explain more. "My mom, she hasn't had an easy go. I want them to be married for myself. But for her, too. It's her time to be happy." I slip a piece of ramune candy from my dress into my mouth, letting it melt on my tongue. Sweets are a part of my fundamental essence. That and skirts with pockets. Observe how I've married the two.

Akio nudges me. "My grandfather used to carry candy around in his pocket."

I nudge him back. "Are you saying I remind you of an elderly gentleman?" There is little left of the original Edo Castle here. Near us, a sign marks the location where Asano drew his sword against Kira—the triggering event for the forty-seven rōnin.

Akio's mouth is a tight line for a moment. He smiles sadly. "I'm going to miss you."

Nara is only a few hours by train from Tokyo, though, and I plan to visit as much as my schedule allows.

"In that case, maybe I *will* immortalize myself in one-eighth scale."

Months ago, I toured a startup specializing in personal clones. For 108,000 yen, roughly one thousand dollars, a clerk will create a 3D model of your head, then print it and attach it to the body of a doll. I'd teased Akio with a pocket-sized Izumi. He'd been appropriately horrified.

A swallow bounces his throat. "Radish," he says softly. "This isn't going to work."

I stand inches from him. "All right. No clones, then."

We're on a wooden bridge now. It arches over a pond, thick with lily pads and koi. We had our first kiss in a similar garden in Kyoto. It was dark, and much later, the magical hours between midnight and sunrise. I couldn't sleep—too high on Kyoto—and Akio had invited me for a stroll. We discussed the concept of gimu—a lifelong obligation to family or country. Akio's father was an imperial guard, and his father before him. It was Akio's legacy. But Akio didn't want it. He left the guard to become a pilot. That night we gave into ninjō, the human emotion that conflicts with gimu.

He shifts away. "No. That's not what I mean. This is what I wanted to speak with you about. I wasn't completely sure. But hearing you talk about your parents' marriage, I believe this is the right decision." His eyes bore into mine. "We can't see each other anymore."

My heartbeat slows. "Sorry?"

He prowls down the bridge ahead of me and grips the wooden balustrade. Below, a koi fish darts close to the surface, body coiling like a dragon before it dives deep into the cool water. "You heard what the chamberlains and steward said. A perfect princess doesn't have a bodyguard boyfriend."

A memory surfaces of the *Women Now!* article. I thought

I could take on the tabloids by telling my story in an exclusive interview. It worked. Japan forgave my affair with the bodyguard. They embraced me, for a time. They saw my intentions have always been good. But I'd been wrong. The free press bows to no one for long. And neither does the Imperial House Council. I suddenly feel very out of control.

Still. "You're not my guard anymore," I say feebly.

Hot wind ripples through the garden and musses his hair. He straightens and moves to me. "Our relationship jeopardizes your parents' future."

"Okay," I say. He's right. "There is some truth to what you say. What if we put things on hold for now? Yeah." I nod, convincing myself. "Yeah, we'll stop seeing each other for a little while, then when my parents have approval, we'll be together again."

Akio regards me, and I don't like the look in his eye. The pity in his smile. As if I'm an orphan, insisting to the other children that my parents will be here anytime to pick me up. *Anytime now, just wait and see.*

He shakes his head. "We can't. Someone will find out. There will be another scandal. We *are* the scandal. It will never end. This is for the best."

"Don't do this," I say, feeling a pinprick just beneath my rib cage. I want to stomp my foot, want to ball my fists and hit something. "Don't be like the Imperial Household Agency deciding what's best for me. Don't give up on us." There is sadness, but anger, too. I swallow against a gigantic knot in my throat as if a clot of rice is stuck.

"It's already done," he says flatly.

I focus on the tower ruins behind him. They've been

meticulously renovated—crumbling stones replaced by laser-cut rocks. An hour ago, children were climbing to the top. Their laughter soaked up by the summer heat. But it's empty space now. Lonely and bleak. Like I'll be without Akio.

I turn my gaze to my feet. "If you walk away, don't come back." I say dumb things when I'm angry. It's no exception now. I'm threatening what I want to keep.

"Okay." In his voice, there is a new finality.

I peer up and see him through a watery haze. See his perfect face, the unforgiving slices of his cheekbones. "Akio, please," I shake out. Minutes-long moments pass. "Don't." *Say something. Tell me you don't mean it.*

"Radish." His eyes are red-rimmed and liquid. It's a small comfort knowing he's hurting, too. Dusk spreads its purple wings. The color of the sky bleeds from orange to deep indigo. He thumbs my cheeks, hands drifting down to my shoulders. He buttons my cardigan. "It's getting cold out." His tone is clipped, resolute. He kisses my cheek, my forehead, and lingers. "How could I have expected to stay in your golden orbit forever? I should have known. We've been playing a losing game the whole time."

I stiffen and turn my cheek. He inhales hard and releases me. Stepping back, he executes a formal bow. "Your Highness."

I squeeze my eyes shut so I don't have to watch him walk away. A little sob wrenches from me. I wrap my arms around myself, trying to keep it all contained. When I look again, he's gone. Vanished. Like he'd never even been here.

TOKYO TATTLER

Imperial Household Council holds secret meeting

September 1, 2022

An unusual amount of traffic was spotted around the Imperial Household Agency building late last evening. *Tokyo Tattler* sources say Their Royal Highnesses Prince Nobuhito and Prince Yasuhito alighted from vehicles, along with the Prime Minister, the Speaker and Vice Speaker of the House, and the Chief Justice of the supreme court. Altogether, the *Tattler* counted ten. What do all these men have in common? They are all members of the Imperial Household Council.

The Imperial Household Agency has been tight-lipped as to why the council was convening in secret. But sources tell the *Tattler* the Imperial Household Council assembled to do an off-the-record pre-vote regarding the Crown Prince's engagement to his American love, Hanako Tanaka.

The pre-vote did not go well, according to sources.

Only two voted in favor of the marriage—both members of the imperial family. "The other council members are concerned with Ms. Tanaka's lack of pedigree and commitment to the monarchy," our imperial insider tells us.

In the past, chamberlains have discreetly placed calls to the Kasumi Kaikan, Japan's floral families, to create a database of eligible women for the Crown Prince to marry. Criteria included: younger than the prince but not by more than six years, three to five inches shorter than the prince, well educated, and in good health. One woman was cut due to a family history of webbed toes. How does Ms. Tanaka compare to Japan's most eligible?

"She does not compare at all," imperial blogger Junko Inogashira says. "She's a Christmas cake, far past her due date."

Ms. Tanaka's age *is* a serious consideration. Japan is facing a royal succession crisis. One of Emperor Takehito's sons must produce a male heir to continue the imperial lineage.

The Imperial Household Agency had high hopes when Prince Nobuhito married celebrated soap actress Midori Ito, but after the birth of her twin girls, the princess withdrew from the public eye. Inside sources tell us she refuses to have more children. "Prince Nobuhito and Princess Midori sleep in separate rooms, and more often than not, separate homes," an imperial insider tells us.

Little is publicly known about Ms. Tanaka, but what is known makes the Imperial Household Council uneasy. "It is no secret Ms. Tanaka is a feminist, and not only that, she has extreme views on environmental conservation."

The imperial family must remain neutral. Any political stance is anathema to the institution, which must respect *all* its citizens' opinions. The only protection for the monarchy is apoliticism. Sources say the imperial palace has launched its own investigation into Ms. Tanaka.

We will have to wait to see what happens next. In the meantime, all eyes are on Ms.

Tanaka and her daughter. Sources tell the *Tattler* that while the Imperial Household Council couldn't control Princess Izumi's entrance into the imperial family, they are dead-set on doing so with Ms. Tanaka's.

7

I manage to make it back to my room in one piece. Mom and Dad are out for the evening; the palace has dwindled to a skeleton staff. I slide my bedroom door shut and touch my forehead to the cool wood. A tear escapes. Then another. My heart thunders. My shoulders shake. A sob wrenches free and I crawl into bed to lie awake. Through the window, the moon is high in the sky. Tamagotchi wiggles under the covers and I pull him to me, confessing that I will love him until I die.

He squirms away and hides under the bed. Then I am still. Somehow, I manage to fall asleep and when I wake up, day is breaking. Morning light crawls like hands across the ceiling. The imperial family is said to be descendants of the sun goddess Amaterasu, but I'm cold inside. The sun doesn't shine for me today. My throat goes painfully tight. *Akio.*

I roll to my side. My phone rests on the nightstand. A desperate, sick hope has me reaching for it. Checking if he's texted or called. *I'm sorry. I didn't mean any of it. Please call me.* Nothing. What now? What does a girl with a broken heart do? She texts her best friend, of course.

Me

Talk?

My phone rings, Noora's name flashing on the screen. I shift so I'm sitting upright. I pull my knees to my chest, rest my chin on top of them. I answer, and her face lights up the screen.

"Hey." It's afternoon where she is, and she's in her dorm room. I recognize the aggressively sticky-noted calendar and standard-issue bleached wood furniture.

"Hey." I wiggle my toes in the sheets. The tears start again. I sniffle.

"Zoom Zoom?" Concern bends her voice. She's wearing a hoodie, and I can just see the tops of letters spelling out *Columbia*. I'm wearing my favorite T-shirt, from Mount Shasta High School with the school's mascot, a bear. My second-favorite T-shirt is one I stole from Hansani that says LOVE IS MY SUPERPOWER in glitter. "What's the matter?"

"Akio broke up with me." I duck my head and use the edge of my T-shirt to wipe my nose. I'm such a disaster.

"What? Why?" she says, surprised. Then her eyes narrow. "Say the word, and I'll cut off his dangle and sew it back on his ass like a little tail."

"Wow." My smile is dry. "That's so graphic and well thought out."

She huffs and flops back on her bed, holding the phone above her. Her dark hair fans out like a crown. Noora should have been the princess. She would have done it right. "You know I'd do jail time for you."

"He said our relationship jeopardized my parents' marriage." Then I launch into an explanation all about the

Imperial House Council, the pre-vote, overhearing the conversation between the chamberlains and steward, my plan to be the perfect princess . . . Akio's final words—*We've been playing a losing game the whole time.*

Her face twists. "Oh my god, he White-Fanged you."

"What?"

"You know, that thing when you drive someone you care about away because you don't want to see them get hurt."

I let the phone rest on my knees and slide my hands under the covers to play with my toes. *You don't get to decide what's best for me,* I'd said to him.

"You're right. That's such bullshit," I hiss. I am not a wild dog.

"Total and utter bullshit," she said. "That loving, caring bastard."

I frown and sniff. "Maybe it's for the best, then. If he can't stick it out now . . ." I trail off. Hating that I kind of hate him right now. Unforgivably, tears fill my eyes again.

A few seconds tick by. "How are you feeling now?"

"Sad. Pissed," I say. "You might want to get off the phone with me soon. This is going to be a nine out of ten on the ugly-cry scale."

"Please," she says. "I was there when you had too much to drink at Joseph Finch's house party and puked your guts out in his parents' bathroom." Joseph Finch was the only guy in our class with a full mustache. They didn't check his ID at the Berryvale market. That was back then. When my biggest worries were weekend plans, homework, and if I had enough money to buy a milkshake *and* fries at the Black Bear Diner.

"Noora?" I ask.

"Here." She raises her hand like we're still in school.

"What do you think of college? I mean, how is it?"

"Aside from the fact I share a bathroom with twenty girls, the radiator in my dorm is broken, and classes haven't started yet but I'm mainlining coffee and stress-eating Bundt cake like it's my job?" She pauses, twirls a piece of hair around her finger. "It's awesome. I don't know. It feels like I was lost, and now I'm found. Remember how you always talked about not fitting into Mount Shasta? I didn't get it then, but now, I do. I fit in here."

I'm glad Noora has found her spot. I still feel like a fish out of water in Japan and Mount Shasta. But it's not about finding a place you belong, it's about making one. At least, for me it is. I decide not to say so and focus on something else. "Bundt cake, huh?"

She nods with vigor. "A place down the street sells them. Every day I spend at least twenty minutes deciding between four different-flavored bite-sized Bundts *or* one large same-flavored Bundt."

I scoff. "An impossible choice." She just smiles. And to that, I say, "I'm happy for you."

She grins. "I am happy for myself. Feeling better? You look a little less ready to curl into the fetal position and die."

"I am." Tamagotchi crawls from under the bed. Footsteps sound outside my door. The palace is stretching, waking up. "But I should go."

"What are you going to do?" She waves a hand, encompassing it all. The breakup. My parents' engagement. My plan to enroll in university and mold myself into the perfect princess, someone whom the Imperial Household Council would approve.

For a moment, I don't speak, don't move. What else is there to do than persevere? "I'm going to carry on."

Noora's lips curl in approval. "Embrace the anger," she advises, soft and warm. "It will motivate you and burn away the hurt."

"You're right," I say.

We hang up. I open my phone and stare at the most recent photographs of Akio I snapped. Images still imprinted on my brain, I switch to the note app.

Less than eighteen hours
you have been gone, and I have
died a thousand times.
Is this the meaning of love?
To fall? To wreck? To ravage?

My phone alerts with a text a few minutes later.

Noora
Still okay?

Me
No, but I will be.

Noora
Let me know if you change your mind about cutting off his dangle.

Will do.

Carry on.

Carry the fuck on.

And there we leave it. With me, heartbroken but determined.

Mr. Fuchigami frowns as I pick up my teacup and sip delicately. His dark, caterpillar-like eyebrows knit together. He repeats my question. "How do you win over the Imperial Household Council?"

It's afternoon. Sunlight floods the palace dining room. I think about Amaterasu again. Ask her to light my way. I sit across from Mr. Fuchigami. Mariko is also present and smiles at me as a butler steps forward and refills her cup.

How to tell Mr. Fuchigami I know I need to reform my image without actually telling him I heard him say the exact thing outside of the palace? "I want to give my parents the best chances possible. I don't want to be the wrench in their happily ever after for any reason." I sit straight, legs crossed at the ankles, hands folded in my lap.

He taps his fingers against the table. I smile encouragingly at him, even though it feels as if someone has thrown a bucket on me and washed all my color away. Mr. Fuchigami is paramount to my plan working. He knows the imperial engine inside and out. He will help me grease the wheels. I'm still learning. How courtiers, like Mr. Fuchigami, advise and coordinate. How the princes and princesses are supposed to perform. The parts we all have to play.

He turns the saucer of his cup clockwise, then counterclockwise. "In that case, we should probably discuss your future plans. As in, you need one."

My pulse slows, then quickens. "Agreed." A pause. "That's why I've decided I'd like to go to college in Japan." I don't miss the flash of hope in Mr. Fuchigami's eyes. Quickly, in my head I run through the university options. I could go anywhere in the country. "But I'm not sure I should leave Mom and Dad right now." More Mom. She needs me. Or maybe I need her? Whatever. I'll unpack that later.

Mariko sets her cup down with a delicate *click*. "It wouldn't be right away. The new school year starts in April. It's only September. Plus, if you attend University of Tokyo, you would be close to home, less than a twenty-minute drive. Or you could remain living at the palace while going to school as well."

Mr. Fuchigami nods, the thin, loose skin of his cheeks trembling. "Yes, I don't think it would be wise for you to begin midyear. We need time to prepare you."

"What kind of preparations are those?" I ask. I eye a plate of dorayaki, but I'm not hungry. Mom always knows I am sick when I've lost my appetite.

"Japanese schools are incredibly competitive. For example, University of Tokyo has a twenty-seven percent acceptance rate. Though they are eager to have you, you will still have to go through the regular application requirements." He lists off the hoops I will have to jump through: a review of high school transcripts, including certificate of graduation, entrance exams, other documents of evidence of achievements, two letters of reference, and an interview. My heart plummets. Of course, I didn't believe college would be easy. But this is just getting in. It's a lot. Intimidating. Is it any wonder why I'd considered a gap year?

"My high school grades aren't great," I confess.

"Yes," Mr. Fuchigami says, with a hint of reproach. "There isn't much to be done in that regard, but if we strengthen the other requirements—achievements, exam scores, the interview, etcetera, that should be enough." He flips open a leather folio and writes something on the legal pad inside it. "I will engage a tutor for you. Someone who will help get you in shape academically, prepare you for equivalency exams. They can also assist with your language studies."

I exhale. "Thank you."

"You'll need to declare an intended course of study now," Mariko cuts in. In Japan, students determine their major right away.

Mr. Fuchigami murmurs his agreement. His pen is poised, ready to jot down the course of the rest of my life. Like it's that easy. At my blank look, he says, "I wonder if you might consider science with a concentration in botany? It would be a nice nod to your mother's profession and fits in excellently with majors previous princesses have chosen."

I don't have to think about it. "Okay. Done. I will be studying botany at University of Tokyo." I've learned a lot through Mom purely by osmosis already. So what if it doesn't make me all hot and bothered?

Mr. Fuchigami smiles in vague approval and writes it down. "We should also discuss your relationships outside of your family."

"You mean Akio and me?" My stomach sours. "He's leaving soon and . . . I, uh, well, we aren't seeing each other anymore."

"What?" Mariko all but shouts. Mr. Fuchigami rebukes her with a glower. "Sorry," she mumbles. "It's just . . . you two have fought so hard to be together. How—"

"It's fine." I gloss over it. I stare at the wall, at the antique Noh mask my father said gave him nightmares as a child. If we start talking about Akio again, I may cry. Wet glue is holding me together. I shake off the creeping sadness. Instead, I focus on the goal. Carry. On.

Mr. Fuchigami scribbles at a mile a minute. "I'd be happy to form a committee to find a suitable companion," he says, eyes on the page. "We could start with sons of former nobility, someone with their roots deep in the old capital. Relatives of politicians are out, of course, for obvious reasons. The imperial family must be above politics. Perhaps a focus group to find the ideal match."

"No," I say abruptly. Mr. Fuchigami stops writing and peers at me. "No committees or focus groups." He gives me a look as if he's painfully constipated, which would explain so much. "No dating or setups." I may technically be free, but I can't fathom dating anyone else right now. My heart is still battered and bruised. Getting over Akio will take time.

Mr. Fuchigami crosses off what he just wrote.

"We will say Izumi-sama is focusing on her studies," Mariko says.

I nod at her and smile, silently thanking her for being in my corner. She dips her chin back. It used to be Mr. Fuchigami and her in cahoots, but now it's us.

"That will work for a time," Mr. Fuchigami agrees, but still clearly disappointed. "You will also need to choose a hobby for your royal profile," he says. "This will add to your extracurricular requirements for admission and will show the press and council you are taking your imperial role seriously."

I shake my head, trying to think of a hobby I might like. "I don't know. . . ."

"Is there anything you enjoyed doing in America?" Mariko prompts.

Mr. Fuchigami and Mariko are waiting for my answer. I shrug. "I took wrestling as an elective one year, but then I quit because I feared I might become too physically dominant." I can't hide my grin.

Mariko smiles into her lap. The frown lines on Mr. Fuchigami's forehead deepen. Someday I will make him laugh. Today is not the day.

"We'll circle back to a hobby," he says. "Now." He places his pen down and interlaces his hands, making direct eye contact with me. I've seen my father do this with his chamberlains when he wants his point taken. "Regardless of suitors, there are still certain circles you should be moving in. While I can find a tutor for academics and such, you will need additional support . . . someone, or *someones*," he emphasizes, "who knows the ins and outs of the imperial life.

Who can mentor you, show you how to navigate it all—someone you can emulate, someone who the press loves." I close my eyes and pray he won't say it. "Your cousins, Noriko and Akiko, would be excellent mentors."

When he lays down the gauntlet, I wonder if it's possible to puke up my own organs. There is a full circle in hell of the things I'd rather be doing than hanging out with Akiko and Noriko.

My gaze flicks to Mariko. It's all there in my eyes. *Remember when they hazed me during the silkworm photoshoot by dumping a caterpillar on me?* It doesn't sound so bad now, but trust me, it was very traumatic. Especially since I was fresh off the plane from California and was trying so hard to be perfect, to be correct. *Also, remember . . .* I widen my eyes at Mariko . . . *when they set me up at the prime minister's wedding, then called me gaijin?* Which translates to *foreigner* in Japanese, and not in a good way. They were so mean to me, I even thought they were behind selling photographs of me to the tabloids. Turns out, it was my cousin Yoshi. It still burns remembering it. How he'd set me up to be caught in compromising positions in exchange for money. He'd wanted to move off the imperial estate. I was the means to his end—financial independence from the family. I've had little luck finding allies on the imperial side of my family.

Mr. Fuchigami knows none of this and sings the twins' praises. "The princesses always have the imperial best interests at heart. They are agreeable, very eager to please. You could learn a lot from them."

I cross my arms and stare at Mr. Fuchigami for a moment,

feeling small and childish for not agreeing right away. "All right."

"Excellent." Mr. Fuchigami is pleased. He closes his leather portfolio with a happy flourish. "I will set it all up, then."

He leaves, and Mariko scoots into the seat next to me. "A lot happened just now."

"You're telling me."

"Are you really okay with the Shining Twins mentoring you?" she asks.

She means Akiko and Noriko. I told her the nickname a while ago. She'd never seen the movie. We watched it together in Japanese, which was somehow even more terrifying. She had to sleep with a night-light on for a month. I'm not sure she's forgiven me yet.

"Of course," I say, crisp and clean.

It's all for the cause. Right? *Right.* This is for my mom and dad. This is for us. For our family.

Two weeks later, I hug my laptop close to my chest and jog up the steps of the Imperial Library, a gray monolith on the outskirts of the imperial estate. It's still hot here, despite it being September and the first month of autumn. The air is humid and reeks of ozone. Rain is predicted for later in the day. There is some strange alchemy to weather forecasting in Japan and the times are usually spot-on. There is a gust of wind and I duck my head as I pass through the double doors.

Oomph.

I collide with a large, immovable object. Keeping hold of the laptop, I fall back onto my butt, one hand bracing my fall. White sheets of paper catch in the air, then filter down like a spray of confetti.

"Oh my god, I'm so sorry." I scramble to my knees and start collecting the papers filled with handwritten music in blue ink. The person I ran into stoops down. I can only see the top of his head, a flop of dark hair, as he scoops the papers up, too.

We rise together. Me with paper and laptop in hand. We bow our heads and exchange apologies—mōushiwake gozaimasen. Then we straighten, facing each other.

The boy is cute, hair tousled like a pirate's, and eyes crinkled with a perpetual smile. He's tall, taller than Akio, and lean, with a swimmer's body. He wears a Ramones T-shirt, jeans ripped at the knees, and a motorcycle jacket. Around his neck hangs a pair of motorcycle goggles. It's uncomfortably quiet for a moment.

I clear my throat and thrust the sheet music at him. "Here."

If it's possible, he smiles even wider, a pair of perfect dimples creasing his cheeks. "Your Highness." He executes the formal ninety-degree bow I am all too familiar with.

"Please, don't." I discreetly check the lobby. We're the only two around. Beyond brass turnstiles, shelves stretch, high and heavy and overstuffed with books. Nestled between the stacks are large wooden tables with green lights. Columns support the arched ceiling. It smells musty, whatever is endemic to institutions this old. Mr. Fuchigami sent me here to meet my new tutor.

"Are you familiar with the building?" I ask, raising up on my toes to peer over his shoulder, thinking maybe the boy works here. "I'm supposed to meet someone."

"This is my first time here," he says. The boy scratches his head. "Do you have a description of the person? Perhaps I can help you find them?"

Mr. Fuchigami didn't give me much information, which is kind of unlike him. "His name is . . ." I shuffle my laptop down and peer at the printed piece of paper my chamberlain slipped me before coming here. "Nakamura-sensei. He's supposed to be tutoring me. I imagine he's wearing a tweed blazer, complains about the weather a lot, sleeps with books, maybe sneezes from the dust in the library . . ." I rattle off.

"Ah, I see." The boy laughs. He casually slips a pencil behind his ear. "That's me."

"Sorry?" I'm still expecting a Mr. Fuchigami doppelgänger to round the corner.

"Nakamura Eriku to mōshimasu. Hajimemashite. Yoroshiku onegai shimasu. I'm your tutor." He bows formally and rises with another smile, crooked and charming. Then he screws up his nose in a faux sneeze. "*Achoo.*"

Eriku and I sit next to each other at one of the long tables on the second floor, deep in the stacks. We pretty much had our choice of where to sit. Turns out, the Imperial Household Agency reserved the library for our exclusive use the next four hours.

I pop my laptop open. Nodding toward the entrance I say, "I'm sorry about what I said back there."

"No worries," Eriku says. I don't think I have ever met anyone who smiles this much. Even the way he talks is like a grin, the tone happy and light. He has total golden retriever energy. "You wouldn't believe how often I get mistaken for old tweed-wearing professors. Happens all the time."

"It's just that I was expecting someone . . ." I open and close my hand.

"Older, stiffer, wiser?" he offers.

I frown. "Yes. Well . . . no. Sorry."

"Water under the bridge," he says.

He has a laptop. Maybe the first laptop ever invented. The thing is as heavy as a brick and has a giant screen. He pushes the power button on, and it slowly sputters to life. "My computer takes a little while to warm up. Come on, ganbatte." *Do your best,* he cajoles, patting the side of the laptop as if it's a turtle inching across a finish line.

"Um, my chamberlain, Mr. Fuchigami, didn't tell me very much about you. . . ." I say.

He drums the table with his fingers, and an image of one of those perpetual-motion machines flashes in my mind. The laptop is still booting. There is a bar on the window tracking its progress. Twenty percent complete. "Well, you know my name—Eriku, which my parents chose because it sounded more American and they wanted me to speak English someday. What else, *what else?*" He taps his lips. "I play the piano." He opens his hands like that explains it all. There you have it. Enough said. No more questions at this time, please. Thanks for coming to my TED talk.

Right. "Mr. Fuchigami indicated you would be able to help me with getting into University of Tokyo."

"Yes, I definitely can. I am currently a student at UTokyo. And prior to that I completed two undergraduate degrees, computer science and English literature. Both in America at Yale University. Go Bulldogs!" He pumps a fist.

I suck in my cheeks. "Would you mind if I asked your age?"

He beams. "Turned nineteen last month."

I'm eighteen. We're near the same age but clearly not the same place in life. "You started university when you were . . ." I screw up my face and count backward, trying to work out the math.

"Thirteen." He grins. "My parents shipped me off to the

States. It's impossible to skip grades in Japan. Don't want anyone to be treated differently, you know?"

I lick my lips. Mom made me watch reruns of some old show once about a kid who became a doctor but still lived at home. Eriku is like that. "You're a genius."

He scratches his head. "Not quite. Genius-level IQ is one-forty or above. Mine isn't near that ballpark, or it wasn't. I really don't know. The last time I was tested I was eleven. Then it was in the one-thirties, I think." He gives a small, nervous laugh. His laptop makes a strange wheezing noise, and the screen appears with a picture of a Saint Bernard. It's a close-up of the dog's droopy face, a thin line of drool hanging from its left jowl. "That's Momo-chan," he says. *Momo* means *peach* in Japanese. "She is the love of my life."

I swivel my laptop toward him, showing him my screen. It's a photograph of Tamagotchi. His teeth are bared, and the picture is a little dark—flashing lights give him seizures. "Tamagotchi. The love of my life."

We share a smile, lock eyes for a moment. I hear the gentle *plink* of drops on the roof, against the windows. The rain has come at last.

"We should get started," he says, gaze still on me, smile still set. Then he breaks away, focusing on his computer, clicking the internet open. "I thought we could have a kind of soft launch today and fill out your application. Then we'll move on to the actual entrance exams and studying for them."

I inhale a deep breath and nod while Eriku speaks. Since I grew up in America, I will be taking the Japanese University Admission exam, the EJU, for international students, in place of the National Center Test, a more hyped-up version of the SATs.

On the University of Tokyo website we create a log-in for me and open the application. While Eriku taps away, I stare at the picture of Tamagotchi on my computer. It used to be a photograph of Akio and me. It wasn't a special occasion or anything; I had handed my phone to Reina to capture us in the moment. In it, I stared directly at the camera, just so effing happy it makes me a little sick remembering. Akio focuses on me, a rare soft expression on his face. Of course, I had to change it to Tamagotchi instead. Two nights ago, I'd deleted all remnants of Akio in an angry red haze. Photographs. Texts. Even stuffed the poem he'd written me in a drawer. Out of sight, out of mind. No more looking backward, only forward from now on.

That night, it's my turn to choose dinner. I know exactly what I want—McDonald's. French fries and Bai Big Macs are plated and served on priceless china inlaid with golden chrysanthemums. Melon soda and chocolate shakes are dumped into crystal goblets. The whole palace smells like fried food. Outside the window, the garden is melancholy— muddy puddles, water dropping from the branches, weighing the leaves down.

I dig in while telling my parents about Eriku.

"Nakamura-sensei," Dad murmurs. He is using a knife and fork on his hamburger. "I've been hearing the name Nakamura often recently, but can't remember in which context."

I bite into my burger, wiping a glob of ketchup from the corner of my mouth. If the tabloids could see us now. "He's a genius. Maybe he's been in the papers or something." Probably invented some machine in second grade that recycles urine into water then cake batter.

"Maybe," Dad says.

Mom nibbles on a french fry and appraises me. "Well, I'm proud of you, honey," she says. "Deciding to go to school is a big deal. And at such a prestigious university." Her hair is shiny and styled. Her cheeks are healthily flushed. She holds up a goblet full of Coke. The last two weeks she has turned things around, gone from glum to glorious, relishing in the new challenge. She seems more like herself. "Cheers to University of Tokyo."

I wave a hand. She'll jinx it with her unflappable confidence in me. "I haven't gotten in yet."

She waves a hand back at me. "Details. You'll get in. Look at the two of us." She gestures at me, then her. "You're off to university, and I'm having tea with the empress tomorrow. I never would have imagined . . ."

I scrunch my nose. "I know, I never really saw myself at an elite university in Japan." Or anywhere, for that matter.

"I did, or at least I hoped." Her eyes glow. "I didn't want to say anything while you were searching, but you had me worried for a while."

"Me too," Dad says.

My insides turn cold. "What?"

"We just want to see you doing something to fulfill all of your potential," Mom clarifies. She lays a hand over Dad's.

Of course they wanted me to go to university. They met at Harvard, after all.

I put down the french fry I was about to eat. "Oh. Well, you did a good job of hiding it."

"We didn't want to put any more pressure on you," Dad says. "Mr. Fuchigami informed me you will be pursuing coursework in botany."

Mom's lips part in happy amazement. "Botany?" she echoes.

"We have another Hanako in our midst," Dad says, raising Mom's hand to his mouth and kissing the knuckles. Dad would totally make a clone of Mom. A little compost pile and crown of orchids as accessories.

She looks at me quizzically. "All those years, I thought I was putting you to sleep when I talked plants."

Before she can press me more, I say, "So, tea with the empress . . ."

We chat a bit longer about Mom's new schedule. It's nearly as full as mine. She's spending most of her days at the Archives and Mausoleums Department learning court etiquette. Her enthusiasm hits me square in the chest. I like to think I take after her, leading with my heart, barreling forward in the face of adversity. Here goes.

A chamberlain appears and asks for a word with my father. As soon as they've gone, Mom lasers in on me. "Real talk now. *Botany?*" She looks at me as if she knows where I have all the bodies buried.

I wipe my mouth with a cloth napkin embroidered with the imperial chrysanthemum. "Must be in my blood."

She tilts her head. "Uh-huh."

"It's a good major. Solid. Something I know about and is right for a member of the imperial family."

"But does it feel *right* for you?"

I chew my lips, focus on my plate. "Of course it does. Why wouldn't it?"

"Just asking." She studies me for a moment. "And how are you doing otherwise?"

It's her not-so-subtle way of inquiring about Akio, about our breakup. It didn't take her long to notice my gloomy mood and Akio's absence. I told her we weren't seeing each other anymore, mumbling about it being mutual and not the right time for us. He's off to Air Self-Defense Force Officer Candidate School (he left twelve days ago, in fact—not that I'm keeping track or anything). I'm off to university in the spring. You know how these things go.

"I'm fine," I say, light and easy. No way am I telling Mom the nitty-gritty details. I don't want her to know she's the whole reason behind everything I'm doing. The reason behind Akio breaking up with me. *Our relationship jeopardizes your parents' future.*

"Losing your first love is always hard," she says.

Just through the doorway is the living room. Akio and I touched the first time there. It was right before the prime minister's wedding, and prom back at home. I asked him to dance. He'd been reluctant then, unable to remove his bodyguard mantle. But I managed to draw him out toward me. I remember his hands on my hips. How he spun me in a dizzying circle. How I'd confessed, quietly and with desperation, that I thought he didn't like me. Then how he'd softly admitted it was the opposite. "I probably like you too much," he'd said.

Now, I ball up my napkin and toss it on my plate. "We weren't in love." I force a smile. "Tell me another story. About you and Dad in college," I say, and Mom is already grinning.

"Have I told you about the one when he *tried* making me soup while I was sick?" she asks.

Yes. But I say, "No." I am such a sucker for their stories. Lapping them up like Tamagotchi does his toes.

She leans in. "I had a terrible cold . . ."

9

"Your cousins are very excited to see you," Mr. Fuchigami says as we rise higher and higher in the glass-encased elevator. We're at Mitsukoshi, a department store founded in 1673. Like many things in Japan, the building with red awnings has withstood three hundred years of history. It's a shopper's paradise. This evening it closed early, but it's still fully staffed to accommodate us. Employees dressed in smart navy suits scurry about below us like busy ants.

"I'm sure," I respond. And by that I mean, I am sure they are as excited as a snake when it spies a mouse. *Dinnertime. Yum.*

I study the ghost of my reflection in the glass elevator. Slightly larger bottom lip. Round shoulders. Blunt-cut bangs. A little A-line dress with blue flowers. Nothing impressive. I shift focus to the atrium the floors open to. It's airy and light, sumptuously designed in creams. A towering sculpture stretching close to thirty-six feet dominates the space.

The department store general manager accompanying us follows my gaze. "It is a pleasure coming to work every day and beholding such a treasure," she says, accent curving her speech. The *treasure* is a sculpture of a Tennyo, a Buddhist divine kind of spiritual being. "It took Sato-san and his apprentices almost a decade to complete."

The elevator dings and we step out onto polished white marble floors and racks of clothes with designer labels posted elegantly above them. *Prada. Chloe. Oscar de la Renta.* It's still a little intimidating being surrounded by so much finery.

The department store manager continues. The click of her heels matches the rhythm of her speech. "The sculpture is carved from five-hundred-year-old cypress wood and decorated with gold, platinum, and assorted jewels. This way, please." We slide past the pristine racks to a large, open dressing room.

The Shining Twins perch on an upholstered blush-colored sofa. Am I really shopping with my Stephen King–esque cousins? If the metaphor wasn't apt before, it is now. I am definitely picturing the linen-papered walls running down in blood. Their imperial guards, a set of guys who chug Red Bulls and flip cars to stay in shape, are present. Reina has assured me multiple times that she "could take both of them," to which I readily agreed. I have no doubt in Reina's ability to throw down. Also along for the trip is their chamberlain. Lastly, a saleslady holds a silver tray with flutes of champagne. Chocolate-covered strawberries and assorted cakes are arranged with expert precision on a tiered tray on a coffee table. The department store manager makes introductions to the saleslady, then leaves us in her "excellent care."

Mr. Fuchigami bows low to the Shining Twins. They greet each other, chat, and exchange pleasantries. Soon enough, the conversation dwindles.

"I'm sure you three have much to discuss," Mr. Fuchigami says.

For the most part, the Shining Twins and I avoid eye contact, but I do see them smile placidly at my chamberlain. Boring and infuriatingly perfect, they think they are better than everyone else.

The saleslady offers glasses of champagne, stooping low for the Shining Twins to pluck them off the tray. They incline their heads at her, and she preens under their attention. They have a magnetism about them, pulling people into their sphere. In comparison, I'm more of a donkey in a muddy meadow, if you know what I mean.

"Yes," the Shining Twins' chamberlain says, rubbing his hands together. "We will leave you to it."

"Of course," Akiko says, prim and proper.

"We'll take good care of our cousin," Noriko promises.

It's always like this. Akiko leads and Noriko follows.

The chamberlains bow and are gone. The saleslady offers me a glass with a bright smile. I accept it with a meek thank-you and take a healthy drink. The Shining Twins exchange a look. I wander to the opposite couch and sit down, crossing my legs so tightly I'm sure I've cut off circulation.

The saleslady invites us up to a platform surrounded by mirrors. Her hand brushes Akiko's, and she titters, "Kirei. Your skin is so soft."

Akiko brushes the bangs from her forehead and her perfectly glossed lips part into a smile. "Sō desu ka?" *You think so?*

Wow. So fantastic for her.

A few minutes pass while the saleslady uses a long tape to take our measurements. She jots down the numbers and promises to return with clothing options. We are here today because the Shining Twins are supposed to help me pick out a dress to wear to an upcoming banquet for a visiting sultan.

"Cousin," Akiko practically purrs in cultured speech that takes years to perfect. We're back on the couches, and they've turned toward me, heads tilted in unison like a pair of mole rats. "It's been too long."

Not long enough, I think. A decade could pass. I nibble a chocolate strawberry. The twins make me feel insignificant. Like I don't mean anything.

"Yes, we haven't had the pleasure of each other's company for . . . how long has it been?" Noriko turns to her sister. She has a little mole under her left eye. That's how I tell them apart.

Akiko taps her chin in a graceful way I find maddening. "Well, let me see, we were jogging on the imperial grounds, and Izumi accused us of selling her story and pictures to the tabloids."

"Yes, that's correct," Noriko says, eyes widening, then narrowing. "As if we would ever be that desperate." She leans forward and plucks an almond from the tray, cracking it between her molars.

I do feel kind of bad about accusing them of Yoshi's terrible choice. But not bad enough to apologize. Especially when they are so perfectly awful. Instead of meeting their gazes, I whip out my phone like a shield and furiously check for messages, any sort of lifeline, while we wait for the saleslady. Noora has texted.

Noora

Red alert. Hansani just informed
me she is taking a class on how
to weave baskets out of invasive
species.

Hansani's future is in environmental law. She cares more about the world than she does herself.

Me

Ha. I'm shopping with my
cousins. Pray for me. FaceTime
tomorrow—if I survive?

Morning in Tokyo is late evening in New York, so it's the best time for us to connect. When my day is starting and Noora's is ending.

Noora

Want to so bad but going out to
dinner with new roomies tomorrow
night, then I'm chatting with Glory.
We're going to compare some
notes, can you believe we're taking
two of the same classes? Two!

Noora and Glory always had a love-hate relationship. But now it's more love-love, a bubble of intimacy blown around their shared college objectives—premed and pre-pharmacy.

At the sound of wheels on carpet, I look up. The saleslady rolls in a rack of dresses. She gives us a preview, showing off what she picked and why. A red chiffon number from Alexander Wang's most recent collection. A silk taffeta Stella McCartney dress with tulle skirt. An ombre from Yuasa, an up-and-coming designer modernizing the kimono. The twins nod at a couple of gowns, and I absently do, too. Noriko wonders if there are more colors of a certain dress. The saleslady bows and darts away again. Off to find Noriko's request.

Truth? I'm at a loss. Mariko has always helped me with my wardrobe up until now. Between the two of us, I've managed to wear things that are comfortable but still "appropriate." She's certainly kept me from ridicule. But no press isn't always good press. I've never made a best-dressed list. In the war of appearances, the Shining Twins are the winners. And to the victors go the spoils—better, more positive magazine articles, public accolades. Sales are always up for them. The Imperial Household Council would definitely buy in to my cousins.

I shoot them a look. Akiko's self-confidence is intoxicating. And Noriko *is* charming. A few moments ago, she was standing shoulder to shoulder with the saleslady as if they are the best of friends. I tick off a list in my head—tutoring, applying for university, leaving Akio behind—all the things I've done so far and what I've sacrificed for my parents' love story. I've even signed up to study *plants*.

Dammit. Dammit. Dammit. I need the Shining Twins. I set down my champagne flute with a decisive *clink*. Might as well get this out of the way. "Look, I know we haven't been on the best terms. . . ."

Akiko straightens, keen interest in her eyes.

Noriko turns from the rack.

Now I have their attention. "Tell me what I'm supposed to wear on Friday. Onegaishimasu." *Please,* I say, adopting a humble tone and gesturing inelegantly at myself. "I've never attended a welcome banquet for a sultan before." To be honest, it's more than a dress I need. But baby steps. Rome wasn't conquered in a day.

And . . . nothing. Great and vast silence. Somewhere, in the distance, I hear the seconds of a clock ticking away. Akiko cants her head at me.

"Ugh," I say, frustrated. "Forget it. I'll choose something myself." I move to stand.

"Relax," Akiko says with an eye roll. "We'll help you find a dress." She rises and I plop back down. As she crosses to the rack, she murmurs something about me being dramatic and listening to too much Bon Iver (no such thing). Akiko and Noriko discuss my skin tone and body shape as they thumb through options.

Noriko holds up a beautiful nude dress with navy beads. "Too mature," she says, putting it back. I stare at them.

Akiko holds up another dress, sage with ruffles. "This is from last season."

I stare some more; even rubbing my eyes at one point as they go about their business. Shaking their heads at a couple choices. Outright laughing at a few.

Noriko plucks the second from the last dress on the rack. "This one." She beams, proud of her choice.

Akiko stares at it, taking it in for a moment. She brings it to me, and I stand as she holds it against my frame. It's black and sleeveless with a deep V-neck and a cinched waist. Gold threads are delicately woven through the sheer material, creating a celestial pattern.

"Yes," Akiko whispers with a gleam in her eye. "It's perfect."

At home, Mariko unzips the garment bag in my closet. She removes the dress and hangs it on a silver hook so it's on display. Stepping back, she examines it. "Hmm. You say your cousins helped you choose it?"

I nod and lean against the marble island. "What do you think?"

I really have no idea. I know what I like, and I know I like this, but there are so many rules for how to dress properly here. Transparent sleeves are reserved solely for evening wear. But stay away from scooped necklines no matter the time of day. Silver accessories are preferred over gold, which is *much* too common.

She peers at the tag. "It's by Tadashi Shoji. He is a well-known and respected designer." She grows thoughtful. "It would be seen as favorable if you wore something from a Japanese label, I suppose. There is a certain glamour and ease to the dress." She slides the silk between her fingers, still considering all the angles.

"It's really beautiful. . . ." I stare longingly at it, remembering dressing up as a little girl, twirling around in an old taffeta skirt. When did clothing become so complicated? When did I start feeling pressure to look a certain way? It started before I became a princess, I know. But the stakes are even higher now.

"But I'm afraid it's not appropriate," she finishes for me. We stop, lock eyes. "You don't think so?" I ask.

"Honestly, Izumi-sama? I'm not sure. But I don't trust them. Do you?"

I thought I did, at least for a short while this afternoon. But not now. Not with Mariko casting so many shadows of doubt on them. "Yeah, they were so nice about it. It made me a little suspicious, I guess," I admit.

"You were right to be. It's too modern. Too cutting-edge. And it's sleeveless," she says, scowling as if personally offended. She sets the dress back in the garment bag and zips it up with zest. "Good thing I have a backup ready." She hangs the dress my cousins picked in the farthest corner of the closet and shows me what she has chosen—a jade embroidered evening gown. Mariko and I make eye contact in the mirror. "It's not as special as the Shoji, but it's the safer bet."

I try on Mariko's choice. The fabric is stiff and uncomfortable, but I am thankful for my lady-in-waiting. It is all too easy to picture a humiliating photograph of me in the tabloids. Been there, done that. It was a big deal back then and an even bigger deal now. Mom and Dad's marriage hangs in the balance.

In the mirror, I see the reflection of the black dress squeezed between gowns—its gold stitching catching and shimmering with light like stars in the sky. It's a shame for such a beautiful dress to go unworn. But there it will have to stay. I turn from it, smiling fully now, my soul at peace. The jade dress is definitely the more sensible course of action. It's not like I'm keeping score or anything, but if I were, I do believe I just pulled ahead of the Shining Twins.

TOKYO TATTLER

HIH Princess Izumi nursing a broken heart

September 29, 2022

A certain someone has been noticeably absent from the imperial estate recently. Akio Kobayashi, HIH Princess Izumi's erstwhile beau, has departed for the Air Self-Defense Force Officer Candidate School in Nara—but even so, it has been a little too quiet.

"He hasn't called or written any letters," a palace insider tells us.

It is odd, considering the two were attached at the hip just weeks before his departure. The chemistry between the couple is well-known. Our issue exposing their affair, including pictures of a torrid kiss before the emperor's birthday, was our bestselling yet. Afterward, the princess withdrew, keeping their relationship as private as possible, opting to spend their evenings together on the imperial estate.

But all that chemistry may have fizzled recently. "It's clear the couple has hit some sort of an impasse," another palace insider says. "The princess refuses to speak his name, and she stripped her room of all photographs of him."

It is likely the two have called it quits. A Mitsukoshi employee observed the princess while she shopped at the store's flagship location. "The princess was . . . off. A little distracted. And there were circles under her eyes, as if she hasn't been sleeping," the employee said. "Her cousins, HIH Princesses Akiko and Noriko, worked very hard to cheer their cousin up. They helped her choose the most beautiful dress for an upcoming event."

Kobayashi has been silent on the matter. When asked by fellow officer candidates and press about his romance, he has stayed mute. And the only pictures posted in his quarters are those of his parents.

No doubt all those dour chamberlains at the Imperial Household Agency are smiling ear to ear. "They wish to see Princess Izumi with someone more suitable, her age but with a better pedigree," our palace insider adds.

Meanwhile, her mother, American-born Hanako Tanaka, and father, HIH Crown Prince Toshihito, were spotted dining at the Mandarin Oriental's uber-exclusive Molecular Bar.

Apparently, the Imperial House Council's pre-vote isn't getting this couple down. "The Crown Prince is insisting their plans to wed forge ahead despite the fact that the Imperial Household Council has yet to give their consent," our palace insider states. "He wants to set the date and begin the proceedings as soon as possible. He lost [Hanako] once before, and he doesn't plan to a second time."

10

Eriku clicks a key on his ancient laptop, then hits it with his fist when the button sticks. At last, the slide advances. "Most recently, Japan's population has been shrinking."

On my own computer, I type out a note under the heading *Japan Current Events*. We have returned to the Imperial Library. It is our first official study session. The EJU covers multiple subject areas depending on course of study. I have to take: Japanese as a Foreign Language, Science (chemistry and biology), and Japan and the World.

This morning, we started with Japanese history as a primer for Japan and the World—to understand the present, we have to understand the past. In three hours, we covered the first recorded human habitation of the Japanese archipelago around 30,000 BCE to recent times. After a short break, we finished up history and eased our way into modern politics, economics, and society. I'm not sure how to keep everything straight in my head—language, geography, history, chemistry, biology. Between all I'm learning and all the events I'm expected to attend, including the sultan's banquet this weekend, my head is spinning. I rub my eyes, trying to bring my brain back online.

Eriku traces the curve of a graph shaped like an upside-down bell. "Japan has one of the world's most rapidly aging societies." He smiles. Hasn't stopped smiling since I greeted him four hours ago. I've never met anyone quite like him. Always amused and enjoying himself. He's also wearing a Queen T-shirt today. He bounces his knee, tapping out some ghost beat that sounds like the intro to "Another One Bites the Dust."

"In 2010, the population began to decline. The number of babies born in 2019 was thirty percent less than in 1989." He grins at me, despite the subject. "It is expected to worsen exponentially." He clicks again. The slide is of a classroom, but instead of students at the desks, there are overstuffed puppets. They stare vacantly straight ahead, static smiles waiting in eternity for their lesson to begin.

I inch forward in my seat to take a closer look.

"Population decline is most severe in rural areas. This is Nagoro village, Valley of Dolls." Another click. A snapshot of a puppet perched on a rock next to a river, his hat is tipped over his eyes, his arms crossed as if he's snoozing. A fishing pole is planted in the ground near his elbow. "Most residents have left for bigger cities in search of opportunities. An artist who grew up in the village returned and began populating the city with dolls. For every one departure or death, she adds another homunculus." He clicks through more slides. Pictures of the village. A biker on the side of the road repairing a flat tire. A couple leaning against each other, sharing a cup of tea. A woman in a kimono bent and gardening. It's eerie and sort of beautiful. It steals my breath. And it's sad, too. Makes my insides feel like sand, slipping away alongside these people.

I stare into the lifeless black felt eyes of one of the dolls. "Why is Japan's population shrinking so much?"

Eriku drums his fingers against the long table, and his brows draw tight. "Good question. If you ask the government, it's young people's fault. They do not have enough sex," he murmurs with a furious blush and embarrassed smile. "That, and many women are putting their careers first." He pauses. "But the truth is there are far fewer opportunities for young people, especially men. They simply can't afford to have families. Too much economic insecurity." He runs a hand through his already mussed hair. "After the war, Japan had a tradition of regular employment with dependable raises. It was understood if someone worked hard, they would keep their jobs until retirement, and now . . ."

"There are lower salaries and fewer benefits." Sounds familiar.

"Exactly." He smiles, impressed by me as though I've just read from the bullet-pointed slide he's clicked to. "And there's too much emphasis placed on men being breadwinners." He goes on to describe the impact. Fewer people in the countryside means dying arts and crafts.

I dash out a waka poem in the margin of my notebook.

Who will live here now
that you are gone? Whose hands will
stoke the fire? Forge the
steel? Dye the cloth? Whose hands will
tend the soil from which we grow?

He shuts his laptop with a decisive click, stretching his arms high up to the arched ceiling. "That's enough for now. If I don't get home to Momo-chan, she'll sleep all day and then be up all night watching the puppy channel, hopped up on kibble and wanting to wrestle, you know?"

"Absolutely." If I don't walk Tamagotchi every evening, he has a sudden, very acute case of the puppy runs right before bed. It's impossible to get him down afterward.

I start to clean up. Closing a book on a page with a portrait of a past emperor. My great-great-great-great-grandfather's head is shaved, his teeth are blackened, and he has long, lacquered fingernails. The look was all the rage those days. Next, I reach for a recent history textbook. And I am in it. The photograph was snapped a few months ago, during the emperor's birthday. The entire family is all present on a glass-enclosed balcony. I'm standing a little farther back, all the way to right, nearly in the shadows. My gaze shifts to Akiko and Noriko. Their chins are tilted up, their smiles bright and confident. I can't help but compare myself to them. How they fulfill the roles they're expected to with such ease and grace. Have they ever felt how I do? Like a tree stuck in an avalanche, ready to buckle under the weight of it all?

Eriku ducks into my vision. "Daijōubu desu ka?" *You all right?* he asks.

"Yes. Fine," I say back. "I was just thinking . . ." I stop short. "About . . . about expectations, and how much pressure that creates."

Eriku's forehead wrinkles. "Yes, I am certain all of us, to an extent, feel as if we have big shoes to fill."

I glance at him. "You feel that way?"

Eriku scratches at his jaw, he looks away, mulling it over. "Hai." He lapses into silence and I wait for him to go on.

Finally, he speaks. "My father . . . he is waiting for me to complete my degree in music. He is always going on about me dating the right person. Settling down and moving into the family business as soon as possible."

I whistle low. The mention of dating makes me think of Akio. I miss him. Miss the way he made me feel. As if I could conquer the world as easily as moving stones around a board. God, I can see him now. His mouth quirking into the teeniest, tiniest smile. I wonder what he's doing, who is he doing it with, at officer school. What he would say if he found out I was still sleeping in his sweatshirt like a regular old creeper. Actually, I know what he would say. He'd look at me in that particular way of his and say, "Radish." That's all, and I'd know exactly what he meant. I exhale hard, not liking how small, how needy I feel.

Eriku nods soberly. "My father has big dreams of a piano-playing prodigy with keen economic insights and political aspirations—we have a former prime minister in the family."

I uncross my ankles and bend toward him. "It's hard to feel as if your whole life has been predetermined," I say.

"Exactly," Eriku says, eyes half-lidded.

"I didn't feel that way as a kid, but I do now."

He taps his fingers against the table and his mouth twitches. "I never really had a childhood. Once my parents discovered what I could do, they placed me in every sort of extracurricular they could find. Since then, it's been . . ."

"Nonstop?" I venture.

He nods, chewing. "When I was younger, it was all math and space camp. They flirted briefly with me being an astronaut. But bad things happen to me on airplanes."

He pats his stomach, and a sad ghost of a smile touches his lips. "Can't handle the ascent and descent. Anyway, next came language lessons, competitive cup-stacking, piano . . . then degrees once I was old enough for school." He pauses. "Gaman, right?"

Gaman is one of those special words in Japanese that doesn't have an English equivalent. It is the art of perseverance through tough times. It is a part of duty. A sign of growing up. Maturity.

"Hai. Gaman," I agree, and I can't help but smile. It's nice to know I'm not the only traveler on this uncertain road.

11

I stare out the window of the imperial Rolls Royce, a buzzing in my veins. Despite dozens of events like these under my belt, I am still dazzled and a little bit nervous. Tonight is the sultan of Malaysia's welcome banquet, and Akasaka Palace is all lit up for it. Once upon a time, the palace modeled after Buckingham Palace and Versailles was the Crown Prince's residence, but it was converted into a state guesthouse in the 1960s. Now, it's a designated national treasure and is mainly used for high-profile events like this one.

Ahead, luxury vehicles crowd the drive. It is bumper-to-bumper Mercedes, Jaguars, Porsches, most flying their home countries' flags. Staff in white gloves open doors and pop umbrellas to protect guests from the misty night.

We pass through the majestic white-and-gold gate and I rest my head on the back of the seat, closing my eyes for a moment. Almost there. I stayed up super late last night studying for the EJU. While reviewing Japan's market economy, I fell asleep and woke up hours later with the note page stuck to my face. I'm drained, wishing I was home in bed. Still, the limo inches forward.

Reina is in the front seat. The car ahead brakes, and her cheek is cast in a red glow. She chatters something into the microphone of her earpiece. My parents are also attending. Dad had a private audience with the sultan and Mom tagged along to tour the building.

Mr. Fuchigami perches next to me. "Your cousins are in the car up ahead." I see their two dark heads through the car's windshield. I fiddle with the gloves in my lap. I'm wearing the jade embroidered evening gown rather than the celestial silk dress the Shining Twins chose. "There is some press present. But follow your cousins' lead."

At the front of the line, a couple disembarks from a Tesla. The woman wears a red gown and an ermine shrug draped around her shoulders. Her lips are painted a matching crimson, and diamonds the size of kyohō grapes hang from her ears. She looks like a classic old movie star. She hooks her arm through a man's. He is handsome and lanky in a vaguely familiar way. A third person, younger, then alights from the vehicle, dashing in a white tie tuxedo.

"Eriku," I say aloud in disbelief. I almost didn't recognize him. No band T-shirt. No earbuds. What is he doing here?

"Ah, your tutor," Mr. Fuchigami hums. I sit back in the seat and watch Eriku glide along behind his parents down the red carpet. "I hoped his father would bring him. The young Nakamura rarely attends such events," he adds.

I frown into my lap. Eriku indicated his family was well-off. But how well-off? I shake my head. I don't have time to think about it because the Shining Twins' car has pulled to a stop, which means I am next. I pull on my gloves as the twins disembark. They wear silk dupioni dresses, one in pink, one in yellow. Their smiles are bright, meant to be printed in the papers. They pick up their skirts and ascend the steps, stopping midway. They shift, sweeping their gowns behind them, and wave to the press and crowd outside the gates. The photographs will be fabulous. I can already tell. Raindrops falling around but not quite touching them, their bright and dazzling smiles shining.

My turn arrives, and the choreography is the same. Reina opens the door for me. I step out, chin high, gaze focused on the reliefs and statues topping the roof—samurai armor, drums, and phoenixes mixed with chariots, violins, and lions. I do as the Shining Twins did. Midway on the steps, I stop and turn. Only I rock back a little, faltering, and my heel catches on the step. Reina is near, and she steadies me. *Click. Flash.* Cameras capture me, my mouth parted in shock, hands bracing for the fall. Immediately blood rushes up my neck.

"Izumi-sama, daijōubu desu ka?" *Are you all right?* Reina asks, expression carefully bland and professional.

"Yes, sumimasen," I say, so self-conscious I could die. How will this literal misstep play out in the papers? With the Imperial Household Council? Does anyone care I am trying as hard as I can?

Reina melts into the background. I pause for a second or two and will my nerves to steady before making my way into the pre-reception ballroom. Red velvet curtains drape the walls and the ceiling is a glimpse into paradise—a painted sky with plumes of incense smoke billowing from censers. It's already hot and crowded, the din of multiple conversations overwhelming. And I'm still recovering from my near-fall.

I seek out a server with water, and my cousins sidle up, startling me. It's not unlike when a spider drops from the ceiling right in front of your face. Akiko cocks her head and apprises me, eyes flicking from my toes to the top of my head. "You didn't wear the dress we chose."

I look away. A man wearing a press badge spies us and starts navigating through the crowd. "Too many loose threads," I say finally.

"Oh." Noriko frowns. She almost, *almost* appears hurt. "I thought I chose so carefully. What a shame. I didn't see. . . ."

Akiko straightens and moves to block her twin. "Yes, it is a shame. Wouldn't want you to trip and fall on the threads. How embarrassing."

I close my eyes for a moment and wonder how I might time-travel away. The member of the press is right in front of us when I open them. He bows low and delivers the proper honorifics. My cousins make up excuses to leave, nodding at a nonexistent person under one of the massive crystal chandeliers. They're off, and I am stuck.

"Your Highness, do you have any comments on the future of your parents' relationship? Rumors are swirling the two are engaged but might face obstacles on receiving approval from Imperial Household Council." He has a little notebook open, pen poised and ready.

I consider the question. I paste a neutral smile on my face and answer. "I have no comment, really. My only hope is that my parents will be allowed to follow their hearts."

He thanks me and scoots away. I navigate my way into the crowd, searching for Mom and Dad. I'm waylaid by a viscount visiting from London. His name is Phillip, or George, or something, and he is very into sheep farming. Finally, I join my parents near a little bar table.

"Zoom Zoom," Mom says. "Thank God."

I hand her a glass of water. "Thought you might need this." Dinner won't be served for another hour. Hydration is of the utmost importance.

"Thank you." She guzzles the water. Her gown is cream and fitted, pin-tucked at the waist, and long-sleeved. The ivory coloring is warm against her skin, and her cheeks have a natural flush. She is elegant. Beautiful. Empress-worthy. This is the first official event she's attended. She'll be watched here, as I am, too. All to determine how she might look on my father's arm, fulfill the role of Crown Princess. This is her rehearsal.

"This is quite the event," Mom says, finishing her water.

"You're doing wonderfully," Dad praises her. But when is he not? He is entirely focused on her, the deep brown tones in his eyes crystal clear. She lights up his world.

"As it turns out, dressing up like a movie star is hard work," she says with a sigh. Then she stares up at my father and murmurs, "The things I do for love."

I tear my gaze from them and spot Eriku. He's been cornered by his father. His shoulders are slightly hunched and his head hangs low, like a chastised puppy.

"Izumi?" my father says, brow pulled in. "Is something the matter?"

I nod toward the two. "That's my tutor. Eriku Nakamura."

"Oh, he looks kind of sad," Mom says.

"Nakamura," Dad echoes. "Ah! Wakatta. Now I remember why the name sounded familiar. Eriku's father is a shipping magnate. Hanzo Nakamura. Last year, he purchased an offshore oil exploration company to minimize his fuel expenses. Since then, their family's holdings rival the imperial estate's. They have deep pockets and even deeper roots in Japan—they are descendants of a powerful daimyo."

"Wow," Mom says, voicing what I'm thinking.

"Eriku-kun is an only child if I remember correctly," Dad says. "And he's your tutor, you said?"

I nod, focusing on the father and son. Eriku's dad is clearly browbeating him. A lump rises in my throat. Finally, Mr. Nakamura finishes, and Eriku slinks away.

"I, um, I'm just going to go say hi," I tell my parents, then hurry after Eriku.

I find him in one of the hallways, leaning against the wall between a couple of columns. "Konbanwa," I say softly as I approach him.

"Oh, hey," he says, starting to bow.

"No, please don't." He stops mid-bend, then straightens. He slumps against the wall again, a dispassionate outsider. "This is nice," I say, my voice carrying in the cooler, quieter hall.

"Yeah, I had this sudden desperate need for fresh air or the closest thing to it."

I take up residence beside him, hands tucked behind my back. "I didn't know you would be here this evening."

He peers down at his shiny black dress shoes. The last time I saw him, he was wearing Converse with rainbow laces. "My dad forced me to come. Threatened to send Momo-chan to my aunt's if I didn't."

"Harsh," I say.

His mouth turns up like he wants to smile but just can't—his body won't let him. It's all too heavy. "It's pretty standard. I remember wanting a puppy so badly as a kid.

When I scored in the top one percent for IQs in my age group, he bought her for me from a breeder in Australia. He's been using her against me ever since."

"Super harsh." I feel a pang of sympathy for Eriku, then anger at his father. Why can't Mr. Nakamura see his son? How brightly he burns?

He bangs his fist back against the limestone wall. "I don't really want to talk about it."

"Do you want me to leave you alone?" I straighten.

"Not really."

I resume my position next to him. "So . . . how is Momo-chan?"

A dimple creases his cheek. "She took a ten-hour nap today."

"My kind of girl," I say earnestly. We smile together, then go quiet, hearing voices in the hall. They recede into the ballroom. I crane my neck to the ceiling. "You know, I went on a tour of this place way back when, but I don't think I've ever been to this section." Mirrors line the walls, our reflections traveling into infinity. The floor is a black-and-white checkerboard.

He loosens his tie. "Updating the neo-baroque architecture after the war cost over ten billion yen. It took more than five years to complete. . . ." he trails off. No heart for history this evening.

I elbow him. "You don't have to tutor me right now. You're off the clock."

"I'd give my entire inheritance to be in the Imperial Library instead of this party right now."

"This isn't exactly my idea of a good time, either," I say.

"Back home in Mount Shasta, on Saturday nights like this, I'd spend the weekends with my friends. We would wrap ourselves in heavy wool blankets and lie out on my back lawn to search the night sky." The universe was vast and open, and we'd wish on shooting stars. Mine was always to find my father. I thought it would be such a simple thing. You can't see very many stars in Tokyo. Light pollution obstructs them. I wonder if Noora, Hansani, and Glory and I will ever lie outside like that again. I wish I remembered the last time we did.

"That sounds nice," Eriku says.

I sigh. "It was nice." I felt untouchable then. So far removed from me now.

"Sometimes I wish I was still in the States, still going to school there." Eriku's hair falls forward, and he pushes it back. "I can never make him happy." Oh, he's talking about his father again. He splays his hands in a helpless gesture, and his voice is tortured. "I mean, I'm taking a double course load to finish my program early, but that wasn't enough. He wanted me to personally tutor you."

My brows dart in. "Your father asked you to tutor me?"

His lips twitch. "It was strange. When I started at the university, I wanted to take a job in the library as a clerk, and my father said no. It was beneath me. But he was insistent I tutor you. He set it all up. Of course, I said yes, because you don't say no to Mr. Nakamura or to the imperial family. . . ."

I tune Eriku out. Memories tumble through my mind. Meeting with Mr. Fuchigami after I'd overhead the chamberlains and Akio broke up with me. *I'd be happy to form a committee to find a suitable companion. We could start with*

*sons of former nobility, someone with their roots deep in the old
capital,* he had said right before I shut him down. Then, Mr.
Fuchigami's pleased expression as we pulled up this evening
and spotted Eriku. And lastly, my father a few minutes
ago. *Nakamura . . . Their family's holdings rival the imperial
estate. . . . They are descendants of a very powerful daimyo.*

"Eriku," I say, catching his arm. "This is a setup."

"Nani?" *What?*

I gesture between the two of us. "Your father wants you
to marry someone someday—the *right* someone. And my
chamberlain, Mr. Fuchigami, all but said the same thing to
me. Your dad and the Imperial Household Agency engi-
neered this whole thing."

"Ehhh!" he says, eyes widening. "That makes total sense.
A secret omiai."

I shake my head. "Sorry. What is an omiai?"

"Matchmaking," he says simply.

"Whoa," I say. Hot anger rises to the surface, and I feel
my cheeks flush. I'm so mad at Mr. Fuchigami right now.
Another choice that has been lifted from my hands. "I can't
even think about this."

"Ha, me neither," Eriku says. "You're great and all . . ."

"So are you, I mean. I'm just not . . ." I trail off, embarrassed.

"Interested . . ."

"At all," I finish.

We chuckle. The echo of our laughter bleeds away, and
we're left with cavernous silence.

But the wheels of my mind are turning. I toe the black-
and-white flooring, thinking about earlier, falling on the

steps. The papers would have liked it if I had someone other than an imperial guard to steady me. I imagine Eriku there, holding my elbow as I alighted the stairs, that grin of his in place. I feel sort of conniving even considering it. Mr. Fuchigami has gotten into my head. My thoughts shift to Akio. To the pain I felt when he walked away from me. How I'd love to show him, the world, that I am not decimated. He hurt me so bad. I open my mouth. Close it. Then open it again and speak tentatively. "What if . . . I mean, what would your father do if you were *actually* dating an imperial princess?" I ask.

"Oh man, I imagine his head might explode from the ecstasy," he jokes. Then he sees me. Sees I'm not laughing. "You're serious?" A corner of Eriku's mouth lifts as if he wants to smile but isn't sure if he should, like he may be on the receiving end of a practical joke.

I nod and swallow. "It could be mutually beneficial."

I can't believe I'm suggesting this, that I am about to make such a dark underworld deal in this shady alcove. I am doing so much to aid in my parents' engagement chances, but it's obvious I've dismissed the one thing that could catapult them over the top. It is as Mr. Fuchigami said, the right partner could be the missing puzzle piece to my perfect-princess makeover. I hate it when he's right.

Neither of us speaks for a moment. The suggestion dangles in the air, an enticing promise.

He turns to me, shoulder propped against the wall. "The press would lose their minds if we were seen out together."

"That's kind of the point," I say.

He studies me with a thoughtful curiosity. As if he's

trying to figure me out. I wonder if I should tell him about my parents and the engagement—the real reason I am taking the EJU and why I need him to complete the picture. *No, too soon.* I'm not ready to tell him about all that, how some of the lies the papers print about my mother, about me, still hurt. How I fear she will lose her second chance at happiness. How I want my parents to be married for myself, too. My secret dream of a family. "I'd like the media to focus on something other than me tripping or my poor academic record. You would be a good distraction for them. A positive distraction," I add.

He grins, dimples on show. He juts his chin out at me. A little arrogant. But mostly playful. "You want me to be your arm candy?"

"I do." I sweep into a faux bow. "Eriku Nakamura, would you do me the honor of being my fake boyfriend?"

Moonlight dances in from the upper windows, and the room shines with silver. Eriku rocks back on his heels. My pulse kicks up when he stares at me, mouth pursed. He runs a hand through his hair, shakes his head, and says, "I can't believe I'm about to say this. That I'm even considering it. But . . ." He sweeps into a bow. "Your Highness, it would be my honor."

12

The following morning, I stand in the cool air, waiting on the palace steps as a sleek Bentley rolls down the drive.

At my side, Reina audibly inhales. "That car isn't even on the market until next year."

I furrow my eyebrows. "How do you know that?"

She shrugs. "I like cars."

The Bentley slows to a stop, and the door opens. Out steps Eriku. Gone is the white tie tuxedo from the night before. He's clad again in ripped jeans and a Led Zeppelin T-shirt. But instead of the beat-up leather jacket he usually sports, he's wearing . . . a tweed blazer?

Delighted, I give him a finger-wave and jog down toward him.

"Hey," he says with his signature smile. He bows, then slouches against the open car door. The smell of the interior—woody notes and exquisite leather—mingles with the wet morning air.

"Hi," I say back. "I like your jacket. Nice touch."

I remember a time, not too long ago, grabbing Akio's lapels. Pulling him close. *Have you come to have your way with me?* I shake the memory loose. Forget it. Focus on what's in front of me. Carry on.

"Picked it out just for you," he declares proudly, running

his hands down the scratchy fabric. "Had to borrow it from my dad."

Well, that's not super endearing or anything. "No moped today?" I bob my head at the car.

"No," he replies. "I received a very intense dossier last evening outlining, among other things, acceptable modes of transportation. It stated absolutely nothing with two wheels."

When I announced Eriku would be coming today to take me on a date, Reina lost her mind. *I need at least twenty-four hours' notice to plan and execute a security detail. Seventy-two if you intend to leave the imperial estate.* Mr. Fuchigami intervened. *I am sure something can be arranged,* he had said. My chamberlain had never been so accommodating with Akio. He'd seemed so pleased, and I have to admit I'd felt a little stab of pride. Like I was finally doing something right.

"I bet you didn't know I came with paperwork," I say with a sigh.

"It's to be expected," he says. "Although . . ." His voice drops to a more serious tone. "I did have to sign a second nondisclosure agreement beyond the one I originally signed to tutor you. It was much longer. Forty-two pages. And it included a death waiver."

"Wait, really?"

He leans toward me, expression aglow with mischief. "Honto ni. It said I may not hold the imperial family accountable in case of accidental dismemberment. I mean, there's a reason it's listed." He pauses for gravity, then stage-whispers, teasing, "Because it's happened before." He ducks back into the car, reemerging with a fistful of assorted flowers. He thrusts them at me. "Here. These are for you."

I bring the blossoms close to my nose and inhale. Last night we ironed out the details, making a list of the dos and don'ts of our scheme. Number one is no one can ever know of said scheme. Not Reina. Not Mariko. Certainly not Mr. Fuchigami. The Imperial Household Agency runs a tight ship, but leaks do tend to spring up. And least of all our parents—which is weird, because I am used to telling my mom everything.

"The flowers are a thank-you," Eriku says, then lowers his voice. "You should have seen my father when he found out we were going on a date. Usually, he's about as animated as a head of cabbage. But he gave all the staff raises and promised to walk Momo-chan *himself* today."

Eriku rounds the car and opens the door for me. I slip into the Bentley, and he starts it up. The engine purrs. At the gate, an imperial vehicle pulls in front and behind us. Fake-dating rule number two: make a spectacle of it.

Eriku switches on the radio. The tune is soft and mellow and matches the day. "Good choice," I say.

Eriku's mouth hitches high. He splays a hand against his chest, right over his heart. "Ah, I wish it were that simple. But alas, the music chooses me."

I smile. Laying the flowers across my lap, I run a finger over a serrated leaf edge. "So, where are we going?"

Eriku then turns onto the highway, one hand on the wheel, the other shifting gears. "I actually put a lot of thought into it. It was hard to decide on a place where we'd have maximum exposure but also enjoy ourselves. Somewhere the public can take us in, yet there's a lot of crowd control."

We pass a billboard with a castle and a princess dressed in an ice-blue gown. I shift in my seat. No. Way. "Are we going to Tokyo Disney?"

He smiles. "Life is a song, princess. Let's go make some fake-dating music."

A VIP concierge in a black suit greets us at the Tokyo Disney entrance and escorts us around the park. Pathways have been cordoned off. Crowds surge against the barriers, snapping pictures—the clicks of their cameras like tiny insects as they gather to watch us eat breakfast at the Great American Waffle Co.

Eriku practically vibrates with excitement as he holds up the red plastic plate with a Mickey Mouse waffle the size of our heads to clink it against mine. "To a healthy start to the day."

We cheers. "The healthiest," I say before digging in. The waffle is served with a scoop of ice cream, pureed mango, and mousse—total breakfast of champions.

Before he's done with the first one, Eriku is ordering a second waffle. "My parents have had me on a very specific diet since I can remember. Brain food. When I was in the States, I ate whatever I wanted. I miss stadium food so much. It didn't matter the game, all I ever cared about was the concessions." I feel this last statement in my soul. He digs in with tremendous delight. Swallowing, he says, "I've been thinking we should have pet names for each other."

I lick a dap of syrup from the corner of my mouth. "Oh?"

He nods vigorously and drinks. "All couples have them."

Akio called me Radish. I swirl the whipped cream around my plate until it starts to melt. "I'm not sure. . . ."

Eriku sits back and pats his lean stomach. "I looked up some pet names. There's babe, baby, honey, honey bunny, bear, pumpkin . . . and once I watched a show in America where the woman called the man she was dating *Daddy.*" He trembles as if spooked. "It doesn't seem right, but if you want to try it—"

I wave a hand, silencing him. "No pet names, I think. Let's just stick with Eriku and Izumi for now."

"Oh, okay. I had a list of like forty more options. But Eriku and Izumi are fine, I guess." He sighs, disappointed, but perks up when I offer him the rest of my waffle.

The crowd trails us through the park as we play games at the Penny Arcade and ride Pirates of the Caribbean. Eriku insists on sampling all the foods available. In between Splash Mountain and Big Thunder Mountain, we eat Uki-waman, shrimp in a doughy bun in adorable Donald Duck packaging. We have curry rice and then a milk tea drink with berries on the bottom and whipped cream and nuts at the top for lunch. Which Eriku also orders seconds of.

By the time we're climbing the stairs to the top of the Swiss Family Treehouse, his complexion is waxy, and pale, a little green.

"You okay?" I ask at the top.

The attraction has been closed while we tour it. Imperial guards and Disneyland staff stand at the perimeter. We're alone and can finally let our guard down.

Eriku rubs his stomach. Dots of sweat form at his hair-line. "I think I overdid it."

"Was it the curry or the second milk tea?"

"Please don't mention food." His face whitens. "Warui da yo. Why did you make me eat so much?"

"Watashi ja nai yo. *I* didn't."

"Look at us, our first argument." He smiles crookedly, then groans.

"Hold on." I usher us past a roped-off area into one of the displays. "Please don't throw up on me."

"Oh my God, don't say 'throw up,' either," he says.

I help him to a seat in a rustic kitchen setting. "Breathe in, breathe out. Slow and steady," I advise. A cool breeze whips up from the moat. He does, and after a few minutes, his color returns. "Okay now?"

"Better." He gives me a weak, lopsided smile.

"Do you want me to get you a glass of water or some-thing?"

"No. But let's stay here for a moment." He places his elbows on the table, musses his hair with his long fingers. "Ugh, look at me. I can't even get a fake date right."

"Don't be so hard on yourself. This is the most fun I've had . . . in a long time," I say softly, surprising myself.

I try to remember the last time I'd felt such effortless joy. Even in the garden with Akio, before he'd broken my heart, I had been wary, scared of being discovered by the press. Ever since becoming a princess, all experiences have been weighted with expectations and worries about how I might be perceived. This all feels so effortless. Almost natural. I shake the thought away. Being with Akio was easy, was natural. *This* is fake. Even the trees I'm staring at are artificial. Like everything in the park, Eriku and I are manufactured. Something people want to see—pretty and perfect. A dream.

"It is?" He peers up, vulnerability threading through his expression.

Despite the direction of my thoughts, there *is* a realness to this moment. Our pictures will surely be in the papers tomorrow. There is a high likelihood Akio will see. Guilt slices through my abdomen. He'll see the way I smile at Eriku. The lightness to my step. Does it make me an asshole to say I kind of hope he does? I'm still so mad at him. I stare at my lap. "It's nice right now, not to feel so much pressure. To feel like I'm doing something right by just having fun with you."

"Agreed." He's sitting more upright now. "I have another caveat I'd like to add to our fake-dating scheme."

"You do?"

He's grim, overserious. "Now that you've had a taste of dating me . . . the wrinkled band T-shirts, the champion overeating, and near throw-up, I can imagine it's very difficult to *not* be attracted to me." I try to contain my smile, and he does, too. "Therefore, you must promise not to fall in love with me."

I smile. "Does that happen often?"

He leans in close as if to tell me a secret. "Imperial princesses asking me to fake-date them, then succumbing to my charms and falling, totally, irrevocably in love with me? More than you think."

"I believe my heart is safe." Permanently on the shelf since Akio.

He nods. "All right, then . . ." He peers up at me from under a flop of bangs, a hopeful puppy. "Boo-boo?"

Laughter bursts from my mouth. "No. Just no."

TOKYO TATTLER

HIH Princess Izumi out on the town with new love interest

October 25, 2022

When asked about her parents' engagement and the Imperial Household Council's hesitation to approve it recently, HIH Princess Izumi said she hoped they "will be able to follow their hearts."

Imperial fans balked at this sentiment. "She doesn't care about the imperial family at all," imperial blogger Junko Inogashira says. "She only cares about her individual desires."

However, Princess Izumi has recovered from her blunder in spectacular fashion. Visitors to Tokyo Disney received a treat when Princess Izumi showed up on a date with shipping heir Eriku Nakamura. "The two were quite chummy," said a park-goer. "They were very in sync. Leaning into each other, smiling, even tasting each other's food. It was cute."

"I love them together," Junko Inogashira says. "This is the type of person the princess should be dating."

There you have it, Tokyo. If anyone is keeping score between suitors for Princess Izumi, it's Akio Kobyashi—0, Eriku Nakamura—1.

13

Two nights later, I'm on a second date with Eriku at Florilége, one of Asia's top five eateries, nestled in the Aoyama neighborhood. The chef started his career at a three-star Michelin restaurant, then quit to open this one. It's a kind of theatrical eating with the kitchen located in the dining room center, and a sixteen-seat counter surrounding it. Also, there are large containers of plants—wild herbs that will be freshly plucked and used in the food.

But . . . I glance around the dim room. "Where is everyone?" I ask. Reina stands guard at the door, and the chef and his assistants work quietly away, chopping vegetables in a synchronized motion. Other than that, it's empty. Eriku and I are the only customers.

"I rented the place out." Eriku hazards a smile. "Or rather, my father did. I know we agreed on public outings, but he insisted. . . . Sorry."

I unfold the crisp white napkin and place it on my lap. "It's fine. It's kind of nice, actually." I rub my ear. "I think I lost some hearing today with the screaming crowds."

Earlier, we went on a very public walk through Yoyogi Park. I blink, remembering the frenzy. The hands reaching for us through the wall of imperial guards. Some held copies of the *Tokyo Tattler* with Eriku's and my picture splashed over the front. The headline about our day in Disneyland. I wonder how the *Tattler*'s circulation is in Nara. If Akio saw the pictures.

I sip my water and try to forget how my broken heart still doesn't beat quite right. "Does your father do this for all the girls you date?"

Eriku's mouth thins. He shakes his head. "No. Mr. Nakamura has never approved of the girls I've dated before. My parents discourage all distractions, actually . . . friends, girls, etcetera."

The chef slips two plates of perfectly arranged snap peas in front of us. He bows low and explains the menu, Japanese-French fusion. Staring down at the small plates with an even smaller amount of food, Eriku and I smile conspiratorially at each other. We had a whole discussion about Japanese versus American serving portions—which are pretty much double, and sometimes triple. I mean, Black Bear Diner uses platters as plates.

After placing our palms together, we say "Itadakimasu!" and eat the snap peas as slowly as possible, savoring the flavors. An olive amuse-bouche arrives next, and after that, comté cheese served with an abalone liver ragout.

"Everyone says my father and I are so much alike. We may look similar, but we don't have the same heart," Eriku says as he finishes. His manners are impeccable. He sits at the counter eating expensive food with the same ease and confidence I've seen my father exude. This is his world.

I play with my napkin. "Have you ever stood up to him? I mean, not that you should or have to, but have you ever told him how you feel?"

Eriku flexes his hands and licks his lips. "I haven't," he

says. "I'm too afraid. Even though I don't like him a lot of the time, there is still this little kid inside me who wants him to *like* me. Sometimes I feel so thirsty for his approval, I'd drink mud. Then other times, I'm like, screw him, I'll do what I want. But I'm also not sure what I want. That's the problem with everyone always telling me what to do. I don't know who I am without them." Eriku pauses, then goes on, "Now, I'm in limbo. Dad's waiting for me to graduate and start my business career with him, but I just wish I had a little space to stop and think, to figure out what I actually—" He cuts off as another plate is served—foie gras with hazelnut meringues. "I don't know why I put up with my dad. Maybe I'm just a sucker for loneliness and self-doubt," he says in a half chuckle.

I remember him smiling when he was sick at Tokyo Disney. Eriku is someone who laughs through pain. "I feel like I'll never live up to my cousins," I blurt. Eriku has shared so much. I want to share something, too. Something to show him he's not alone. He's not the only one who feels a little lost. A little less than. Small.

His eyes flicker. "Princesses Akiko and Noriko?"

"Yes, the twins." I consider whether or not I should say more. But then I remember Eriku signed an NDA. Meaning I can talk to him like my therapist recently quit, and I have a lot to get off my chest. "It's worse because since I arrived here, they haven't always been very kind." I recap everything they've done, from planting a silkworm in my dress and ruining an expensive photo shoot to calling me gaijin to most recently trying to trick me and sabotage my wardrobe.

He nods, finishing his bite of guinea hen with spinach in a sesame red wine sauce. "Consider how those girls grew up. I wasn't in school with them, but I am aware of Gakushūin and the imperial court's inner workings. It's a cutthroat world. They were born with knives in their hands."

"It just . . . it doesn't make sense," I say a little too loudly with a shake of my head. The chef and his assistants glance up, and I quiet, angling closer to Eriku. "Their mother has been treated awfully by the press. The imperial family hasn't been much better. Her husband, my uncle, all but ignores them. But Akiko and Noriko love their mother and fuss and fret over her. You would think it would make them . . . I don't know, softer."

Eriku disagrees. "Or harder. Perhaps they see the way their mother has been treated. How the papers twist facts. How their father refuses to acknowledge it or them. That would make anyone wary and distrustful of new people."

It's true. They are as vicious as Roman rule. "You're making me feel bad for them."

"Consider the role models they've had. They have succeeded by being the opposite of their mother and father— people they perceive as weak and ambivalent."

I rub my forehead. "This is a lot to unpack."

He gives me his biggest and brightest smile. "I'd like to meet them someday. They sound so mean. I imagine it makes you feel alive."

"Ew," I say.

Eriku chuckles, chagrined. "You're right. It's probably

just me trying to re-create the problematic relationship I have with my father."

While we eat dessert—glazed strawberries, dark chocolate, and a passionfruit mousse—I tell him about my friends from home. Eriku is especially interested in our neighbor Jones's lifestyle, how disconnected he is from society and how he marches to the beat of his own drum. Literally. Jones loves a good drum circle.

"He lives off the grid?" he asks.

I wipe the corner of my mouth, a swipe of chocolate coming away on the white napkin. "I think so. He doesn't get mail. Or have a cell phone. I don't even think he has a last name. His entire property is solar-powered and completely self-sustaining."

When we've finished our meal, we bid the chef goodbye and Reina intercepts us at the door. "There is a crowd outside now, including some press. Straight from the restaurant and into the car," she instructs.

I nod, used to following directions now. I can hear the royal watchers through the door, their excited chatter.

Eriku turns his palm up, offering me his hand. "Should we give them what they came for?"

He waits patiently for me. The last hand I held was Akio's. After a beat, I slip my fingers between his. His grip is firm, tight . . . reassuring. Different than Akio's, but not unpleasant.

Pictures are snapped as we race toward the Bentley in a flurry of imperial guards. The crowd's murmurs are a buzz of static electricity. The hairs on my arms raise. Eriku quickly unlocks the doors with his fob, and Reina opens the passenger door for me. I dive in, Eriku right behind me.

As we pull away, Eriku glances behind him. "That will definitely be in the papers tomorrow."

We grin at each other. Mission accomplished.

14

I stand on a velvet pedestal as a seamstress in all black slips a heavy, cool kimono over my shoulders and undergarments. Mom is beside me—another seamstress drapes her in a kimono as well.

We both inhale, seeing ourselves in the three-paneled mirror. I run my hands down the fabric and trace the intricate pattern. The maple leaves are hand-painted, outlined in gold and silver on a peach background. Mom's kimono is light orange and ombre the color of the sunset, with cranes alighting from the hem. The gowns are yūzen kimonos, part of a dying art in Japan. Master makers struggle to pass the traditions on—there are no students to teach. All of a sudden, I remember Eriku showing me the slides of Nagoro village. The stuffed puppets frozen in time, populating a deserted landscape.

"You got in late last night," Mom remarks, brushing hair out of her face.

Because I have lived with her the last eighteen years, I recognize a searching statement when I hear one.

"Uh-huh," is all I say. I watch the seamstresses at the open trunks, choosing obi.

Eriku and I went to a movie last night, to a cutting-edge luxury theater in Tokyo, a place that offers augmented environmental effects. The seats jerked. Air jets blasted in tandem with the action. Again, Eriku ate like it was his last day on Earth—melon Fanta, popcorn, two hot dogs. It's all coming up roses.

"Who were you out with again?" She tilts her head like she doesn't know. Like she wasn't there when Eriku came to the door and asked for me.

"Eriku."

Mom nods thoughtfully. "That's right. He brought you cotton candy," she muses.

Eriku likes to bring me gifts. Cotton candy. Beigoma spinning tops. Kusudama origami. I pivot to her. "Is there something you want to ask me?"

She straightens. "No. Of course not. It's your business. I wouldn't assume to intrude," she states emphatically. Then, "Though you have been seeing *a lot* of him lately. Tutoring during the day, then the evenings . . ." She pauses. "Things seem to be moving fast, that's all."

"Mom," I say. "Relax."

Have I been a little out of control? Maybe we're laying it on a little too thick. It's easy to lie to the public, harder to lie to my mother. We don't keep secrets from each other. Hiding that my father was the Crown Prince of Japan my whole life notwithstanding. But just like her, I'm doing what I think is best. For both of us.

I brush away any bad, ominous feelings. After my parents are happily married, and once Eriku and I have a somewhat public yet amicable breakup, I'll tell her everything.

"We have a lot in common. We've been enjoying each other's company."

She murmurs in agreement. "I can see that. You two are a lot alike."

"You think so too?" I ask, surprised.

Mom inhales and nods. "From what you've told me, you two have the same character. The same spirit." Aside from Zoom Zoom, Mom used to call me Sticky Bun. And Eriku is pretty much a human cinnamon roll. So, I get it. Yeah.

The seamstresses return with obi choices, holding up bolts of fabric against the kimonos. We go silent while they discuss options. They return to the trunks to put the rejects away.

"Do you really like him?" Mom asks quietly.

"Mom," I say.

I do like him. Not in the way she means. But it's impossible not to feel happy around Eriku. He's Christmas morning; a day at the beach; the first time I glimpsed Tamagotchi. Joy, joy, and more joy. A smile in the face of harsh realities.

She leans in and teases me with, "I think you like him." Her smile is bemused. A couple of seconds tick by, and she doesn't drop the insane grin.

I scrunch my nose. "Stop looking at me like that."

She shrugs and turns back to the mirror. "I can't. I created you. I am biologically predisposed to find everything you do charming and fascinating." I make eye contact with her in the mirror and pull my lips in and widen my eyes. I look like a frightened horse, and it's awful, but Mom sighs, a moony expression on her face. "See. That just made me love you more."

"You need to take it down to a two," I say, dry as a desert.

She holds her chest, kimono sleeves pooling at her el-

bows. "What can I say? I am trash for you. Basic trash."
There is no stopping her when she gets like this. Happy and
silly and so extra-extra, and truth? It's my favorite Mom
mood. I kind of live for it, but she must never know—it's
best not to encourage her.

I gape up at the ceiling. "Oh my God. Where did you
learn that?"

"I overheard you say it to Noora." Her brows dart in.
"Am I not using it correctly? Your father and I had a whole
discussion about it. He felt very firmly it was derogatory.
But when you say it to Noora, it sounds so positive. Trash,"
she tries again. "I am trash for you."

I groan and shake my head. "Stop," I say. "It doesn't
sound right. . . . When you say it . . . it just sounds kind of
sad." I pause. "Sorry."

"Well, that is hurtful, but I instantly forgive you." She
shrugs it off. "Anyway, I'm glad you're having a good time
with Eriku. It's nice to see you smiling so much."

The seamstresses return and fuss over us again. I decide
to divert the conversation to Mom. "Tell me how everything is going with you. What have you learned lately in the
archives and mausoleums department?"

Mom folds her hair behind her ear, her face still playful.
"Did you know that the imperial family has been purchas-
ing from the same seaweed supplier for over three hundred
years?"

"No way," I say. One of the seamstresses taps my tabi-
clad foot. I lift, and she slips on a zōri sandal. She taps my
other foot. I lift, and she does the same, my movements
wooden, puppetlike. I feel like a doll being dressed.

"And those gold-and-black soup bowls we ate out of last night?" she asks under her breath. "The ones painted with the chrysanthemum motif? A set of five sells for over three thousand dollars. Three. Thousand. Dollars."

We chat about everything Mom has learned while the seamstresses finish up our fitting. The kimonos are gathered at the waist, then tied with a datejime to secure them. Our collars are arranged so everything lies flat, neatly pressed. It all must be just so. The seamstresses dart away for another moment.

"So it's all going okay, then? I mean with the empress and . . . Dad?" I ask.

"Everything is fine. Great, actually. The empress has been so warm and congenial. And your father says he loves how I am meeting the challenge. Then he . . . well, you probably don't need to know what he did. . . ." She drifts off.

I stare anywhere but at her. "Yes," I agree. "I'd like to talk about this again never."

But inside, I'm all warm and gooey. Ready to do whatever I have to, to keep this feeling, this family—*my* family—intact and going.

Mom plays it cool. She winks at me. "Anyway, all is good in the hood."

"Add that to your list of things to never say again."

We lapse into silence as the seamstresses finish up. With nimble-fingered hands they tie the obi around each of our waists, cinching tightly and securing them in the back in a stiff, elaborate bow. They step away and gesture at the mirror. "Dōzo." Go *ahead*, they say.

We do. "Wow," Mom says.

"Sugoi," I say.

She half turns to peer at her backside. "Not too bad for two girls from Mount Shasta."

I couldn't agree more. Our hair is down now, but it will be up at the empress's annual garden party in a couple of weeks. Over two thousand invitations have been sent out. Guests will range from astronauts to Olympians to screenwriters to governors. The prime minister and all the Imperial Household Council members will be there. Mom is attending as my honored guest. It's our opportunity to make a big impression, a better impression.

I shift, feeling the weight of the kimono, the cool silk sliding against my skin, a millennium of tradition. Mom admires herself in the mirror, too. We are a sight. All at once, our mouths part, and we smile together.

15

The weather cools. I double down on my goals. Eriku and I study all day in the Imperial Library, skating through politics, economics, and society topics and into the sciences. We practice Japanese. Today he's had the brilliant idea to teach me chemistry in Japanese—two birds, one stone. He waits for me to answer his question. "Wakaranai." I have no answer. Only confusion, so much confusion in such a large space.

Eriku gives me a warm look. "Perhaps chemistry *and* Japanese was a stretch." He pauses. I palm my face and groan. "Look," he says quietly and waits for me to meet his eyes. "These standardized tests are very predictable. I've taken enough to know what you will be asked and what you will not. All you need to learn is a few important concepts. Easy."

I shoot him a look. "I feel like you have a lot of misplaced confidence in me."

"Ganbatte. Here." He slips a package of yuzu gummies from his pocket and opens it, offering me one. I stare at the neon-colored candy. The package crinkles as he starts to pull back. "Is it weird? That I carry candy around in my pocket? My dad hates it."

"No, it's not that." I wrap my hand around his wrist, then let it go. I slide through a memory. Wandering with

Akio, munching on my own stowaway candy. "I'm pretty sure we're not supposed to eat in here . . . but thank you." I pluck the package of yuzu gummies from Eriku's palm and pop one in my mouth. "Umai!" I moan. "Now I know where all your energy comes from." I am fueled by sugar and love. The rest of the afternoon, I eat yuzu gummies, and by the end of our session, I know the ins and outs of ionic, metallic, and covalent bonds.

After that, he brings a new sweet every day. "It will help with your memory," he asserts. "Scents and flavors create specialized neurological pathways." He flips open a textbook. "Today is Tokyo Banana and intermolecular force." It goes on. Meito Cola Mochi Candy paired with changes of substances. Hokkaido melon with mascarpone-cheese-flavored Kit Kats and inorganic chemistry. We finish with Eiwa coffee-flavored marshmallows and organic chemistry.

Biology is next and we breeze through it. We take over the palace kitchen one day and make animal cell cakes. During breaks between ecosystems and biomes, I show him a video of a woodchuck riding a golden retriever's back across a river. And after that, a funny message strand from the girls.

Noora
Ugh, I went to the library today,
but I couldn't get in. They were . . .

Glory
Don't say it.

Hansani

Say it. Say. It.

Noora

Totally booked.

Glory

You said it.

In the evenings and on weekends, we throw ourselves into public events. Eriku dresses in a custom-tailored Brunello Cucinelli suit and escorts me to the sixty-seventh exhibition of Japanese traditional industrial art, where we rub elbows with a son of a Persian Gulf sheikh who is investing heavily in Bitcoin. We watch the Wheelchair Basketball World Championships. We drink beers in Eriku's family's private box while cheering on the Yomiuri Giants. We attend a performance of the Vienna Boys Choir. And backstage at the concert, behind a dark curtain, Eriku shrugs out of his jacket and clamps a flower between his teeth.

"Dance," he asks, thrusting a hand out to me.

"I thought you'd never ask." I place my palm in his.

He twirls me around until I'm dizzy and we fall back into the wall. Chest heaving, he slumps next to me. "Don't take this the wrong way, but you are a terrible, terrible dancer. The worst I have ever seen. Like a decapitated chicken." I collapse into a fit of giggles when he tries to examine my calves.

Two and a half weeks later, the day before the empress's garden party, I sit for the EJU. The auditorium is packed with hopeful international students. It smells like paper and body odor. The instructor announces when to begin, and the sound of flipping paper echoes like a bad omen. I nearly chew my lip off during the exam.

Eriku waits for me outside the nondescript building. "Well?" he asks as I emerge through the double doors with a flurry of imperial guards.

My head is swimming. "I really don't know. I think I did okay on the language, biology, and current events portion, but I might have spontaneously forgotten everything during the chemistry questions."

"You know what we need?" Eriku asks.

I squint up at him. "To find a small island with no postal codes so I can live out the rest of my days without learning of my failure?"

"That is very specific. I wonder if I should be concerned?" he asks, tapping his lips, then bats the thought away. "Actually, no time for that. I have two surprises for you."

Eriku spirits me away to a partially underground baroque coffeehouse. Giant slabs of rock divide the room, and sparkling fixtures better suited for the *Titanic* light up the cavernous space. We order ice cream sundaes and cups of strong tea served on plates with the Budapest landscape painted on them.

"This is my surprise?" I ask, a little bemused. The shop is empty, cleared by imperial guards and Eriku's black credit card, but there are basement windows. Paparazzi lie on their stomachs, snapping pictures of us.

Eriku drums his fingers on the table—*rat-a-tat-tat*. "Wait for it," he says.

The waitress appears and sets down waffle-cone bowls filled with a swirl of vanilla ice cream and topped with . . . "Is that gold?" I ask.

He nods. "I had it specially brought in from Kanazawa. First surprise complete," he says.

The waitress hovers for a moment, all of her attention focused on Eriku. She preens, smooths a hand down her glossy hair while asking if he needs anything else. *Anything at all.* At first, I'm confused. Is she flirting with him? She *is* flirting with him. Eriku thanks her, his smile bright as always.

As she trots off, I study Eriku. The dimples. The floppy hair. The restless, rock star–like spirit. There is something that makes you want to hold on to him, like catching a rare butterfly.

I bend toward him and jerk my head toward the barista. "I think she likes you."

Eriku dips his spoon into the ice cream, excavating a bite. "Ha."

"I'm serious." I glance at her again, then quickly away when we make eye contact. I pretend to admire an old Yamaha electric organ under a Tutankhamun mask and then come back to Eriku.

He places his hands to his chest. "Watashi no kokoro wa anata no mono desu." *My heart belongs to you,* he says loud enough for the barista to hear, and I swear, *I swear* she sighs wistfully. He gives me a goofy grin and commences eating again. "Tell me more about the exam."

I cast a frown at him, then proceed to say how badly I fear it went. What will I do if I fail? Cry, most likely. The ice cream has melted into a thick goo at the bottom of the dishes when Eriku receives a text. He checks his phone. "Your second surprise is ready. Let's go."

He stands and I rise—the air inside the café changes. Imperial guards rouse and cameras click and flash outside the windows. Lately, the headlines have been glowing. "Princess Izumi and Shipping Magnate Heir Eriku Nakamura Tear Up Tokyo." "Empress Wooed by Crown Prince's American Love." "Eriku," I say. "Do you mind if we call it a day? I'm not really in the mood. . . ." I trail off, gesturing numbly at the paparazzi.

He stops short and considers me. "No cameras where we're going." He touches my wrist. His eyes land on me and light up in a way I find slightly unnerving. "This is just for you."

That effectively snaps my mouth shut. Eriku tromps up the stairs. Halfway up, he turns to me and smiles, giving me a mischievous and bold look—a dare. "You coming?" he asks.

I swallow, intrigued. Okay, I'll bite. I press my lips together, bow my head, and follow him out the door.

I lie on my back, Eriku beside me, and under us is a scratchy Pendleton wool blanket (specially made and shipped from the company's headquarters). My eyes stay focused on the night sky, following as a shooting star blazes a path. Because central Tokyo is too bright at night, Eriku chose the Cosmo Planetarium in Shibuya. Nearby a little table has been set with hot chocolate and other sweet treats. The place is ours for the evening. Reina stands by the door, her back turned, her black suit blending into the inky darkness. And since no one is around, this isn't a fake date or a study session—this really is just for me. Led Zeppelin's "Stairway to Heaven" plays on the speakers—which is for Eriku.

"You used to do this all the time?" he asks with a sort of confused wonder.

"All the time. With my friends, we would lie outside and see how many shooting stars or constellations we could spot." I can't believe he arranged all this. I'm still processing it. How nice Eriku is, how well we get along. How I haven't thought about Akio in a while. The corners of my mouth tug downward. What does that mean? Am I over him?

"Huh," Eriku says. He points up, fingers tracing the path of the Milky Way.

"Maybe it's a small-town thing," I say. Then I launch into all my favorite things to do by season in Mount Shasta. Placing signs around trees in the fall that read: *It's okay to hug me.* Snowboarding in the winter. Running through the forest in the summer, barefoot and naked when I was much, much younger. Just so wild and free.

"Naked?" He swallows, his Adam's apple bobbing up and down.

I blush and ignore the question. For a few moments, we're silent.

Eriku turns to his side, propping his head up with a hand. His lashes lower. "Tell me more about Mount Shasta."

I copy his movement, shifting so we're a bit closer. I consider what I haven't covered. "It's pretty great. Although

I didn't always feel that way when I was living there. Being one of the few Asian people in Mount Shasta had its drawbacks. I never felt like I fit in."

He blinks. "Do you feel like you fit in Japan?"

"Sometimes, yes. Sometimes, no." It's hard to shake the feeling of otherness, telling me I am a tourist in my own life. *Growing up in America, Princess Izumi will never be truly Japanese,* an imperial biographer recently wrote. I faced the same in Mount Shasta. *Izumi will never be truly American.*

Truth? Sometimes I question if I should even *be* a princess of Japan. If I am laying claim to something that isn't mine. Maybe I will never be Japanese enough. My throat is scratchy, and I curl my fingers into my palms. *No.* This is my right. I was raised in America, but my father is the Crown Prince, and Japanese values are still a deep pool within me. Entrenched in my blood. People can say what they want. That I am not enough. They can talk, but I stay silent, quietly digging deeper, pulling up my roots, satiating my thirst.

He waits for me to go on. And I'm not sure how to explain it. If I even want to be that vulnerable with Eriku. "It feels . . . It feels as if I am always doing something wrong. When I first got here, I made all these cultural faux pas. I even insulted the prime minister at his wedding."

Eriku smiles. "I probably would have paid to see that."

"It's one of those moments that, if I had a time machine, I'd travel back to and undo." Let it spool around me, then rethread it into something new, something better. I swallow. "It's kind of why I'm doing all this." I gesture between him and me. "The fake-dating, I mean. It's more than eas-ing some pressure off of me. It's also to sway the Imperial Household Council into approving my parents' marriage. I'm sure you've seen the papers. The rumors are true. The Imperial Household Council conducted a pre-vote a cou-ple of months back and didn't approve my father's marriage to my mom. And I am part of the reason why." There are so many rules. Don't wear this. Do wear that. Don't date him. Do date him. I am supposed to care, but not show that I care. Don't be sad. Don't be too happy. Smile more. Smile less. . . . I flop back, hands on my stomach. Twin sets of stars streak against the sky. I shake my head ruefully. "Sometimes it's too much."

"I'm sorry," he says, and that's it. But it's all there in his voice. He means it. He wishes it wasn't so. The sincerity makes me ache. And it makes me realize Eriku is more than a fake boyfriend. He's my friend.

I inhale, feeling the rise of my stomach, and let it out. Let it all go and pretend I am in Mount Shasta. Safe and happy and free. But then I am pulled back to the present, to the boy beside me who can't stop drumming his fingers against the floor, who traces the constellations like a conductor, who smiles through pain, whose heart is at least twice the size as most humans'. "You're good people, Eriku," I quietly admit.

"Same," he says into the dark.

16

The next day, I wait to greet the empress and emperor. The weather is cool and the sky, blue—a perfect fall day with the scent of dried leaves and wet earth spicing the air. I am just warm enough in my kimono, the sleeves gently flapping in the breeze. My hair is sleek, slicked back in a pleated bun with a fringe of curls framing my face.

Dad leans over and whispers something to Mom, making her smile just before she's escorted to the garden party—she won't be part of the formal duties. Chamberlains descend and usher us into a line. Almost the entire imperial family is here today. My cousins down the way are in coordinated turquoise kimono. They stand with their father, my uncle Nobuhito. Their mother, my aunt Midori, isn't present.

The emperor and empress appear and I bow low as they walk by me. My grandfather is nearing ninety and wears every minute in his body—shoulders hunched forward and shuffled steps as if each one is a supreme effort. But my grandmother, the empress, appears ageless—though happy wrinkles span from her eyes and mouth. Her hair is snow-white and streaked with silver; it catches the light as she walks with a regal countenance, inclining her head at the family she's made. As I rise, I deliver the correct honorifics, and she blesses me with a warm smile.

Once each family member has paid their respects, it is

time to join the garden party. The guests have already arrived and we'll greet them as a group, with the emperor and
empress leading. We stand on a little hill for a moment,
waving at the crowd as they bow. Soon enough, my duties
are done. I spy Eriku and make a beeline toward him.

"Konnichiwa," I say, my steps slightly hindered by the
kimono. The garden party is bright and bouncy, and it
matches my mood.

Eriku smiles and bows. "Hey, you." White tents dot the
lawn, and across the way, his parents chat up an astronaut.

I motion to the astronaut. "Does that make you sad,
seeing what you might have been?"

"I am so, so sad." Eriku faux-pouts. "Please take me
away from here so I may weep in peace." He gestures to the
path and says, "Walk?"

I nod. We stroll about the garden. And I have to work
hard not to waver in the platform sandals, especially with
the uneven lawn. Swans float in the pond. The imperial orchestra is playing. And there is happy chatter everywhere
as the two thousand guests enjoy the scenery. Pretty soon,
we find ourselves at the edge of the party, then in a section that has been cordoned off to visitors. There is an old
teahouse nearby, its roof near collapsing.

We stand under a manicured pine tree, and the din of
the garden party is swallowed by the sound of nature—
insects, wind in the trees, a temple bell ringing far away.
Eriku plucks a needle off a branch and tears it into pieces,
letting it fall like confetti at his feet.

"Your father has moved on from the astronaut," I say,
watching Mr. Nakamura from afar as he approaches an

English duke in a morning coat. "*Ooh,*" I say in one elongated vowel. "I think the duke has an actual monocle pinned to his vest. He does!"

I pivot to Eriku. He's leaning against the pine tree, watching me with a softness in his eyes that reaches down inside me. The look is warm and reassuring, the feel of a hand gently cradling your cheek. I stare at him for one overlong second. The flop of hair spilling across his forehead like an inky wave. The dimples in his cheeks. The way he tilts his head as if he's waiting for me to answer a question. Oh, wow. Suddenly, I am seeing him in a whole new way. My stomach bottoms out.

I blink, opening my mouth, unsure what I'm going to say, but I have to say something. "I . . ." I start on a rasp.

"Your Highness." Reina materializes out of nowhere, a quickness to her step. "There has been a minor security issue. You need to come with me."

Eriku's eyes flicker as Reina ushers me away. "Sumimasen," I murmur.

I leave Eriku there, watching me as I go, so many unsaid things between us.

A scant few minutes later, the entire family is sequestered in a small windowless room in the imperial palace. The air is musty and humid. Probably climate-controlled for the artifacts in it.

Imperial guards surround us, hands folded neatly over their bodies. I've backed myself into a corner near some old vase with a fish-scale pattern. My parents stand with the emperor and empress. Mom casts me a worried glance. She scans my body, obviously checking to see if I am okay. Perusal complete and satisfactory, she speaks to the empress.

The grand chamberlain confers with an imperial guard. We all go still, waiting for an update. "Just a few more minutes," he announces. "All is well. A tourist decided to swim in one of the moats. He has been removed, but we are having trouble locating his . . . clothing." The grand chamberlain's cheeks are heightened with color.

The empress titters behind her hand, and the mood instantly lightens. I press my back into the wall, flipping through memories of the garden, of the tense moment between Eriku and me. Ugh, my stomach barrels up my throat. I'm sure I misread the flare of heat in his eyes.

Positive. In fact, I'm not even going to think about it anymore. But then he's back in my mind, his smile warming my insides.

My agonizing is interrupted by the Shining Twins. Heads together, they grin like a pair of cats while they stare at a phone.

"It didn't take him long to move on," Akiko says loud enough so I can hear. "Look at that girl. She's very plain-looking. If someone replaced me with her, I'd be insulted."

"Deeply offended," Noriko says.

Who has two thumbs and can't keep her nose out of other people's business? This girl. I shift closer to the Shining Twins and will them to tilt the phone. It's open to the *Tokyo Tattler* website. My heart stops when I realize who is in the grainy picture. I recognize the way he carries himself—straight and assured. *Akio.*

And he's not alone. There is a woman, too. They are in the city. It's night, and they're crossing a street. Akio is reaching back, holding her hand, pulling her along.

My eyes are suddenly full of tears. "Let me see that." I grab for the phone.

"No. Yada." Akiko jerks back.

I teeter on my sandals. Then I am tripping over my feet, the kimono strangling my legs, and I have no chance of staying upright. Down I go, and too late, I notice the vase is in my line of destruction. Akiko's and Noriko's mouths part in surprise. The rest of the imperial family turns toward us at all the commotion. I crash into the column supporting the vase, and it topples over. An imperial guard dives for it, but his hands come up empty, inches short. The vase shatters on impact.

I can't believe this is happening. I scrunch my eyes closed, unwilling to watch my literal downfall.

I hit the floor with a thud.

Izumi down. I repeat, Izumi down. It takes me a moment to look up. The room is heart-stoppingly silent, and the wreckage of the vase is in my direct line of vision, pieces jutting from the floor like bitten-off mountaintops.

The Shining Twins stare down at me and say in unison, "Izumi did it."

17

I wait outside the empress's office with the Shining Twins. *Return to the party. I will deal with them,* she had said to the emperor before leading our parents and us to her tuberose-scented private office. She invited my mom, dad, and uncle in, then instructed the three cousins to wait here. Then she slid the door shut in our faces. Or rather, a staff person did, but the message was clear. Winter is totally coming.

"This is all your fault," Akiko whispers at me.

Noriko piles it on. "Why do you have to be so clumsy?"

I press the heels of my hands into my eyes until I see bright white spots. I don't get it. Why won't the twins accept me? Now that I think about it, they are a big reason why I feel like an outsider. An imposter here. "Don't you ever get tired? Of being so mean? First, you call me a gaijin." A fresh wave of humiliation hits me, remembering how they'd spat the word at me at the prime minister's wedding reception. "Then you tried to trick me with that dress."

Noriko squints at me. "What dress?"

"For the sultan of Malaysia's welcome banquet," I hiss, staring at them. "You know what? Never mind. I forgive you. You can't help being so awful when that's what you've been raised with. You're products of your environment." It's a bad idea to rattle the wasp nest, but I don't care.

Noriko shakes her head. "That dress—"

Akiko puts a hand on her sister's arm, stopping her.

I sit back in the chair and cross my arms, wrinkling the kimono even more. "You two are so much like the tabloids that bully your mother, and you don't even know it."

There is a gasp. I can't tell from which one, Akiko or Noriko. But I can tell you how many effs I give right now. Zero.

The door slides open. A staff member bows to us and extends an arm, inviting us in. "Dōzo. Her Majesty is waiting for you."

Three empty seats have been arranged in front of the empress's desk. Our parents and chamberlains are there, too. We stand in front of the chairs, the twins and I, and bow deeply, profusely apologizing. Taihen mōshiwake gozaimasen. Oyurushi kudasai. *I am very sorry. Please forgive me.*

The empress pins us to the spot with a single sharp gaze. "You may sit." We sink into the chairs. My jaw is tight with residual anger and now fear. Behind the empress's desk are katana swords and photographs of her—in one, she is a young woman in full fencing attire. She used to be an excellent swordswoman in her day but quit when she married— her duty was to the country and imperial family. It was an honor, she has said about shedding those parts of herself. I focus on the gleaming metal of one of the swords.

A staff member knocks, and one of the empress's ladies-in-waiting allows him to enter. He carries a silver tray, the broken pieces of the vase atop it. He sets it on her desk, sweeps into a formal bow, and leaves. For one agonizing moment, she studies the pieces, picking through them with a sniff.

Finally, she opens a hand, sweeping above the remnants and says, "This vase has been in the imperial family for two hundred years. It is Famille-rose porcelain and was a gift from China." She picks up a piece. "Here is the mark from the reign of the Qianlong emperor. Not only is it a fine piece in terms of craftsmanship, but it also represents Japan's enduring relationship with China. It is an exceptional rarity both in provenance and price. Only one other exists like it in the world." The empress pauses and nods to the grand chamberlain.

"Yes, it sold at Sotheby's last year for two million euros," he interjects.

"Two million euros," she repeats, accompanied by a withering glower. "And now it's gone because you couldn't keep your hands to yourself. Imperial princesses fighting," she scoffs. "I saw the whole thing." She looks at the Shining Twins. "Teasing your cousin with a phone." She gazes at me. "Grabbing at your cousins like a toddler." She shakes her head like it is all too much, unbearable. I stare at the shattered vase and briefly relive my humiliating fall. "Your chamberlains have informed me they were unaware of any discord between you. Despite it being their duty to know the temperaments and weather patterns of their charges." At this, Mr. Fuchigami and the Shining Twins' chamberlain bow their heads. The shame game with the empress is strong. She purses her lips at the chamberlains, then shifts her attention to us. "Are you aware you are members of a vast imperial line and, as such, represent that line? That whatever you do or say or how you act reflects on that line? And therefore, you must be above petty disagreements and childish squabbles?" She waves a hand. "I simply cannot allow this."

I clench my jaw. I've done plenty to piss my mother off. There was the time Mom spent an entire day making a pot roast I refused to eat because I had decided to try vegetarianism for a while. Or the time I hid in the town library when I was five because I thought it would be funny—Mom didn't think so. Or when I took the last egg roll, and Mom reprimanded me. *You should have asked if I wanted it,* she had said. I dead-eyed her, then let the half-chewed bite fall out of my mouth onto the plate and pushed it toward her. *Have at it,* I said. Years thirteen through fourteen and a half were a dark time—I was bratty and sullen, vacillating between angry, happy, and sad tears. Anyway, all those times, I thought she might open the gates of hell and release some sort of demon curse on me. But I've never messed up this bad. Even insulting the prime minister hadn't been as cataclysmic.

Two million euros.

The empress motions the grand chamberlain forward. He holds a leather folio in his hands. "Her Majesty and I have arrived at a solution. We believe it will behoove you three to spend some time outside of the imperial estate together with a mentor." A glance at the Shining Twins shows me their eyes narrowing, heavy with suspicion. "You are familiar with Ise Jingū," he says.

Of course, I know of it. Ise Jingū is located in the heart of a sacred forest in the Mie Prefecture. It is the most important Shinto shrine in Japan and is dedicated to the goddess Amaterasu. It is more than two thousand years old, and every twenty years, the shrine buildings and bridge are ritually rebuilt. All part of the belief of death, renewal, and the impermanence of all things.

"Your third cousin, Princess Fumiko, is the chief Shinto priestess there, and she will be an excellent mentor. Not only will it be an enriching cultural experience, but it will also . . ." The grand chamberlain trails off.

"You will have plenty of time to reflect on your behavior," the empress fills in. Her fingers curve into knobby fists. "Let me make myself clear. There will be no more fighting. No more bickering. No more tussles." She pauses. "It is either this or work at the Imperial Hospital. Your great-aunt is convalescing there for her bowel condition. I am sure she would enjoy the company." The empress pauses, and shifts to look at me.

I press my lips together, rendered mute under the weight of her scrutiny. I feel my father place a reassuring hand on my shoulder. My mom places her hand on my other shoulder. "I'm sure Izumi would like to apologize profusely and welcomes the opportunity to spend time with our cousin Fumiko," my dad says evenly.

He squeezes my shoulder, and I squeak out, "Hai. I am very sorry and very thankful for this gift of time with Fumiko."

The twins chime in voicing their apologies again, too.

"Excellent." The empress rises, and so do we all. She halts between our parents—Mom, Dad, and Uncle Nobuhito. "I let you boys run too wild," she says. Back in the day, my dad was kind of a player and so was his brother. There are many stories about the two sneaking off palace grounds and into clubs together. "Hanako-san, I have decided you will come on tour with me to the Ibaraki Prefecture to get an idea of the breadth of work the imperial family carries out."

"Oh," Mom says, then smiles brightly. "That would be wonderful and such an honor."

"Excellent," my grandmother says, "You will enjoy our time together," she declares.

Then she's gone, kimono swishing as she leaves.

Mariko is waiting for me in my room. She peels the kimono from my body as I tell her about the awful photograph of Akio, the broken vase, and how I will be heading soon to Ise Jingū. "Princess Fumiko, did you say?" Mariko wonders out loud to me. The kimono rests over her arm.

"She has dedicated her life to the imperial family and Shintoism," I say, sliding pins from my hair.

Mariko's brow furrows, and she bats my hands away. "Let me. I don't know anything about Princess Fumiko. Sorry." She pauses. "I can't go with you?"

I jerk my head *no,* and Mariko pulls on my hair. "Ow. Just the Shining Twins and me. Five days of bonding."

"I'll start packing, then." Mariko finishes with my hair and disappears into the closet. I lean against the doorjamb and watch as she pulls a monogrammed suitcase from a shelf, places it on the island, and opens it. She begins sorting through clothes, neatly refolding the pieces before placing them in the bag. "Izumi-sama?" she says, noticing me, my mood.

Now that the dust has settled, my mind wanders to Akio.

"I guess I secretly hoped Akio would move away, but not move on, you know?"

She frowns and skirts around the island to stand in front of me. "How can I help?"

I look away, lick my lips. "I really don't know." Hot tears form in my eyes.

"I'm here if you want to talk. Or vent. Or both," she says.

I sniffle and peer at the heart-shaped lump underneath my bedcovers. There is really nothing she can do. Nothing anyone can do. I decide to divert the conversation. "Will you walk Tamagotchi while I'm gone?" I ask.

"No," she says, turning back to the island.

"Oh, and he needs his special cream rubbed on three times a day. You have to be careful because it will stain. Learned that the hard way."

"No again," she hums, retrieving a pair of my jeans from the drawers.

"What about letting him sleep with you at night? Don't be freaked out if he licks your toes. It's kind of his thing."

Mariko's eyes flutter shut as if asking the Lord for patience. "I've just lost my appetite."

My phone chimes with a text. I check it.

Eriku

Daijōbu desu ka? *Everything okay?*

I answer, *Daijōbu desu*. Fine. And leave it at that.

TOKYO TATTLER

Princess infighting

November 11, 2022

Guests were shocked when the entire imperial family was escorted off the property by security during the empress's annual garden party. An American tourist thought it would be funny to swim naked in the imperial moat (see picture). While the emperor returned to the party, much of the family did not. HIH Princesses Izumi, Noriko, Akiko, their parents, and Her Majesty the empress were notably missing.

What happened during the hour they were all away?

"The three princesses got into some sort of scuffle," a palace insider tells the *Tattler*. "The empress met with them and their parents in her office, and when she emerged, she was visibly displeased." Now, the entire imperial estate is in an uproar as the princesses prepare to depart on a mysterious trip— *alone*. Their destination is unknown.

"It's very hush-hush," our palace insider says. "Nobody knows where they are going except a select few. But it's clear they are being sent away." The empress is very concerned as of late about the durability of the imperial institution. While she may reportedly be supportive of her eldest son and heir marrying an American commoner, she demands *everyone* adhere to certain codes of conduct. This certainly doesn't help Princess Izumi's parents' cause seeking approval for their engagement from the Imperial Household Council.

"They are watching carefully," our palace insider states. With the princess's latest behavior, the chances of official approval have been reduced to an even narrower margin. Nozomi wa usui na—can anyone say razor-thin?

18

Fog clouds the train's windows. I wipe away the condensation. The Japanese countryside whips by in a blur of green and gray. I sit as far from the Shining Twins as possible, which means opposite ends of the private car. Reina and my cousins' imperial guards are situated between us, reading books in the plush purple velvet seats. One train transfer in Nagoya down and a little less than two hours until we reach the shrine.

It is not the first time I have been on a train like this, speeding toward the countryside. It is the imperial family's modus operandi when dealing with potential scandal—if you run, the story can't catch you.

I was sent to Kyoto after insulting the prime minister at his wedding and the Shining Twins called me gaijin. All ended well, though. I learned a lot during my time in the first capital of Japan. Even managed to steal a kiss from Akio. Anyway, it is true what they say about history repeating itself.

My phone dings with a text.

Noora

Totally excited to visit you in a
few weeks! Question, will I need
an alias? If so, I'd like to go by

Jerome McBeaverfish. Gah. So
excited.

Noora

I feel like I haven't spoken to you in
years. Call me. Call me. CALL ME.

Me

Can't. On the train.

Speaking on the phone isn't allowed on trains. I glance
at my cousins. The air in the car is tense with an extra helping of blame. Nothing is ever their fault. I add another text.

Me

Plus hostiles are present.

Noora

What? Are you okay? OMG.

Me

The Shining Twins. It's a long
story. But I'm headed to the
wilderness to atone, and my
cousins are with me. We're
bonding.

Noora

Woof. Sounds like a kick to the
crotch. Call me when you can?

Will do.

I close out of the texts, nibble my lip, and open the web browser. I don't have to type in the address because it's already bookmarked. The *Tattler* article opens, and I scroll down. It's always the pictures I look at first. The three dark and grainy photographs, taken at night by a telephoto lens, snapped seconds apart. Akio and a woman, their heads bent as they cross the street. He's a stride in front of her. They are both in uniform, navy pants and light blue short-sleeved shirts with shoulder epaulets. The next photograph, he's reaching back. The last one, they are clasping hands, Akio pulling her along the busy street. I study the woman. Her cheek is lifted with the curve of a smile. I know that look on a woman's face—keen interest and bubbly excitement. *Where will the evening go? Perhaps it will end in a kiss?*

My stomach churns. I want to curl up in a ball and cry. I painstakingly translated the article as well. There wasn't much more information. After all, pictures speak a thousand words, don't they? But it did tell me that the woman is a female companion in his class and speculated that they'd been together for some time. I grip the phone harder in my hands. Is this my fault? Did Akio see the photographs and articles about Eriku and me and find someone to move on with himself? I wish I could talk to him, tell him the truth about Eriku and me, about our fake dates. *I could never get over you that quickly. I was angry and hurt. So hurt. But I would never rebound that fast. My relationship with Eriku is all for show.* Except . . .

Is that true?

I shake my head and dismiss the thought. I look once more at the mystery woman. I bet she and Akio have loads in common. The rusty taste of heartbreak fills my mouth. A movie reel of moments plays in my mind: Akio glaring at Tamagotchi. Akio sitting across from me, a Go game board between us. Akio standing outside the palace gates, waiting for me. *Planned on taking as long as it needed to see a princess,* he'd confessed after he'd quit the guard.

We'd been separated before. Weathered storms together. But we'd always held a space for each other in our hearts. In the past couple of months, I'd gotten used to the particular ache of missing Akio—a dull, ever-present throb. But seeing him with someone else, the hurt shifts to something deeper, sharper, more painful.

My eyes are hot and sticky with liquid. I catch the Shining Twins in my peripheral vision. With some sixth sense, Akiko pops her head up from her phone and stares at me as if she is trying to decide the best way to dismember me. I swipe away the tears. I will *not* let them see me cry. Brave front, and all that. I plan on not speaking to them. I will not engage. This is my solemn vow.

The brakes whine and hiss as the train comes to a stop. The doors swing open. Reina and the other imperial guards exit. As we disembark, there aren't the crowds I'm used to. A few stragglers at the station notice the train car and gather. One person snaps a picture.

A woman wearing a fine gray suit and cashmere overcoat moves forward to greet us. "Konbanwa, I am Princess Fumiko, chief priestess of Ise Jingū."

I expected the chief priestess to be older, like the empress, timeless and elegant. Instead, she's around my mother's age, with a head of dark shiny hair that is modestly cut and creamy ivory skin. There is a strand of pearls around her dainty neck. Well, okay then.

While our luggage is unloaded, we deliver the correct pleasantries and bows.

"Hajimemashite." The Shining Twins bend at the waist, sweeping into perfect bows.

I rush to follow. "Yoroshiku onegaishimasu."

"Welcome to Ise," she says after, her gaze lingering on my pink nose, my red-ringed eyes. "Now, if you'll follow me." She starts off, and we trot after her. Reina and the imperial guards take up points surrounding us—two up front, a couple at our sides, the rest behind, keeping pace with the luggage cart and porter. Outside, dark cars with imperial license plates idle at the curb. The luggage is loaded into a separate vehicle. I climb in and sit next to Fumiko and across from the Shining Twins.

It is a short drive, around fifteen minutes. Ise Jingū is actually a complex of 125 Shinto shrines divided into two main areas—Naikū, the inner shrine, and Gekū, the outer shrine. All in all, it is roughly as big as central Paris.

"You may settle in this evening and begin your duties tomorrow," Princess Fumiko announces.

The hour is getting late. Darkness descends and we curve around the little town of Ujitachi-chō. I can just make out the simple architecture—buildings with roof tiles and wraparound verandas. It is easy to feel as if we've been swept back in time. Here is the spiritual home of the nation. Here Amaterasu is enshrined. And this is where the sacred mirror of the emperor is kept—a piece of imperial regalia and one of the Three Sacred Treasures. According to legend, Amaterasu hid in a cave after her brother, Susanoo, threw a flayed horse on her weaving loom. Without the sun goddess, the world plunged into darkness and hunger set in—crops withered and died. The mirror was used to lure Amaterasu out. Life was restored. The people rejoiced.

I'm jerked from my thoughts as the smooth road turns to gravel. We've arrived. The guesthouse is topped with a hipped and gabled roof. The windows are lit with warm yellow light. The dark forest winds around the property, like a piece of unfurled green velvet ribbon. Outside the vehicle, I inhale. The air is cool and lush and clean. And it's quiet. There isn't the usual cloud of imperial staff waiting to greet us outside the door. Strange.

Princess Fumiko opens the front door, and we step through, pausing in the genkan to exchange our shoes for slippers. Again, it is uncharacteristically silent. Missing is the hum of the staff as they rush around. Absent is the clatter of pots and pans in the kitchen as the evening meal is prepped. Stranger still. A little ominous now, too.

Reina and the imperial guards disperse about the property. Fumiko addresses us with a congenial smile. "It is an incredible honor the empress has taken such a special interest in your stay. She chose your accommodations herself. Please, follow me."

Her slipper-clad feet pad along the hardwood floors as she guides us down a hall. She slides open a single door. "Your quarters," she says.

I peek in and my eyes widen at the sparseness. It's a tatami room, and bare save for a single light fixture hanging from the ceiling with a pull thread. Fumiko removes her feet from the slippers and walks across the room. She slides open a closet door. "Bedding," she says, gesturing to three folded futons, comforters, and pillows. "Clothing has also been provided." Simple white pants and tops hang on hooks. "Please be ready at five thirty a.m.," she says.

She exits the bedroom. Her tone and pace are brisk as she shows us through the rest of the house—another tatami room with low table and chairs, a communal bathroom, and, finally, the kitchen, where she picks up a basket from the counter and says, "Your phones, please." At this, Akiko, Noriko, and I all curl our hands to our chests, clutching our devices. "Please," she says again, shaking the basket at us. "The empress wishes you to focus on your duties and family relationships. And she believes this will best be accomplished without distractions." With the reluctance of Tamagotchi taking a bath, I drop my phone into the basket. Akiko and Noriko keep theirs a moment longer before relinquishing them, too. Then the three of us stand there, still a little shell-shocked. I'm not sure what I was expecting, but this wasn't it.

"Thank you," Fumiko says with a focused smile. She opens a cabinet in the kitchen and places the basket in it. With a twist of her hand, she clicks the lock and slips the key into her pocket. I watch as it sinks down. "Well, I'll say goodnight, then. Remember, five thirty tomorrow morning." She pivots to go.

"Chotto matte, kudasai," Noriko calls out, a desperate tilt to her voice.

Fumiko stops, turns back to fully face us. "Yes?"

"Sumimasen. What about . . . What about dinner? I'm hungry," she says with a wobble.

"Sō desu ne. Onaka suita no!" *I agree. I am hungry,* Akiko whines.

"Of course, of course. Sumimasen." Fumiko returns. She opens a cabinet door and removes a pot. Then she goes to the fridge and fetches vegetables, laying them on the counter. "My suggestion is to start with something simple. Perhaps vegetables steamed in dashi. But feel free to be as inventive as you like."

Akiko's jaw drops. "You want us to cook?"

"For ourselves?" Noriko clarifies with a note of nervousness.

"You are smart, capable young women. I am sure you will figure something out. Now, if you will please excuse me. I must be up early for my duties as well."

We watch as she goes, as the door closes. Oppressive silence descends. Akiko and Noriko slump down into a pair of chairs.

"Don't worry," Akiko whispers to her sister, a catch of vulnerability in her tone. She pats Noriko's hand in an alarmingly human way. "We'll figure something out." She then stands and ventures to the cupboards, rifling through them. Moments later, she emerges with a package of noodles. "I will make us soup," she proudly announces.

I cross my arms and lean against the wall, finding it all kind of fascinating, like the time I saw a bear at the zoo trying to figure out how to lie in a hammock. I watch as Akiko places the pot on the stove and turns a red knob all the way over, passing the ignition. The room immediately fills with the smell of gas. Akiko frowns, clearly wondering what she's done wrong. She places a hand over the burner. "It's supposed to be hot."

Noriko smiles encouragingly. "Ganbatte."

"Oh my God." I flick the burner off and rush around the kitchen, springing the windows open wide. "Are you trying to kill us all?" I stay by the window, breathing in the fresh air. Akiko stares at me. She has no idea. "Just sit down. I'll make us something."

Akiko slinks off back to her chair. They are mute as I do my own inventory of the kitchen. I fetch a loaf of bread, butter, some cheese, and a frying pan. I fire up the stove, and while the frying pan heats on it, I butter the bread and place cheese on it. The frying pan sizzles with butter . . . and I am struck by a memory. Mom and me in our kitchen in Mount Shasta. *Can I help?* I asked, age five, dragging a stool from the bathroom to the Formica counter. *Of course,* Mom said, smiling then showing me how to butter bread. Ten minutes later, I slide plates in front of Noriko and Akiko.

"What is it?" Akiko picks up the sandwich and sniffs, bewildered.

"Grilled cheese," I say, mouth already full.

Akiko nibbles. "It's okay."

Noriko dives in. "It's good."

Right. I pretend not to hear her or notice the way they

both devour their sandwiches. The twins speak to each other as if I am not present. They bemoan missing their favorite shows this evening. Wish they could go to a local onsen. And the clothes we will have to wear—so bad.

After I'm done, I brace my palms on the table and stand. "I'll make you a deal," I say, wondering why I'm doing this. What I did in a past life to deserve the Shining Twins as relatives. What kind of karmic retribution this might be.

Akiko bristles. "What kind of deal?" There is a suspicious glint in her eyes.

I clear my plate, dumping it into the sink. Eriku said it's hard for them to trust. I am intrigued. I lean on the counter. "I'll cook for us if you do the dishes."

Akiko and Noriko intake sharp breaths and turn to each other. Unspoken words pass between them. I am just about to throw my hands up in the air and say forget it when they come to a decision.

"Deal," Akiko says. "Only . . ." She pauses. Her brow furrows as if she hates admitting the next part. I frown at her, waiting. "You're going to have to show us how to do dishes."

19

Our luggage is still in the car and we drag it out and inside. Akiko complains she broke a nail. We bathe and get ready for bed. The Shining Twins make their beds as far away as possible from me in the room. And without asking if I'm ready, they turn off the light. I find my way in the darkness to my futon. I reach for my phone to set my alarm. Too late, I realize I don't have it. How are we supposed to wake up? I open my mouth to ask the twins but they're already asleep, breaths deep and even.

I turn on my side and curl up. My thoughts are over-crowded and my heart achy. Seeing the photo of Akio, with another woman, ripped open a wound I thought was heal-ing. I had tried to bury myself in studying, in my parents' engagement, even in Eriku. But it's all resurfaced now. The hurt. The pain. And more. It's hard to admit, but I wonder if Akio really *was* right. Was our relationship just too diffi-cult? Is it true what Akio said? Have I been naive thinking we could make it work? Was our relationship constructed with rickety sticks? Were we simply not built to last? Has Akio found someone better suited for him, someone who shares his day-to-day life? I bet she's a pilot, too. Is Akio happier now? Am *I* happier now?

With Eriku, it kind of feels that way sometimes. I have more in common with him. It's easy and fun. I feel a total tug-of-war between the two, Akio and Eriku. What side am I on? Neither—I am in the center. Stuck in a pit of emotional mud. In my last seconds before sleep, I think about getting up and checking the kitchen for a clock to set, but then I drift off.

I wake to Akiko by the closet, slipping on her top. Noriko's futon is already rolled up and stowed away. "What time is it?" I ask.

"Near five o'clock," she says. "Your snoring kept me up all night. It's really bad. You make this wet, gasping sound, like you're drowning. I finally gave up around four and stayed awake." That said, she floats from the room.

I dress in the plain clothes from Fumiko and do my business in the bathroom, then make my way down the hall. Noriko is sitting at the table in the kitchen while Akiko braids her hair, tying it with a red ribbon. They don't notice my approach, and I pause, my hand on the doorframe.

"We need our phones back," Noriko says quietly, gaze downcast. She twiddles her thumbs. "Do you think she's been eating? Getting dressed in the morning?"

Akiko squeezes her sister's shoulder, then returns to braiding with nimble fingers. "Mama will be fine."

Noriko bites her lip. "I don't know, Aki-chan. She's used to us calling every day. Who will check on her?"

My heart cracks open for the two. Their worry clings to me and sticks, filling me with sympathy. Now, it feels wrong to eavesdrop. I enter the kitchen and throw my hands out wide. "Ohayo! What sounds good for breakfast?"

Akiko frowns at me. I paste on a smile before rattling around the cupboards, prepping for the morning meal. I set the rice cooker. Retrieve the frying pan from the drying rack. Fetch some eggs from the fridge.

"Can I help?" Noriko asks, her braid finished.

"Um, sure," I say, keeping my voice casual. I hand her a knife and cutting board with some veggies, setting her up near the fish griller. "I'm going to make omelets. Can you chop the peppers and onions?" The way she grips the knife, it's clear she's never held one. Very gently, I pry it from her fingers. Maybe something without a pointy end. "Cancel that. Why don't you whip the eggs?" I crack one into a cup and hand it off to her after demonstrating with a whisk.

By the time I am done cooking, the sun is rising. Akiko and Noriko are curled up in their chairs, a pair of kittens basking in the warmth. Unlike the grilled cheese last night, they dig right into the omelets and scoops of rice. We eat in silence except for the clink of ohashi against our bowls.

The ride to the temple is smooth and quick. Noriko picks at her nails, worried. At one point, Akiko murmurs to her sister, "Stop. Yamete. It will be fine." I stare out the window and pretend I don't hear.

Fumiko greets us at the shrine and I find her easy smile deceptive. White gravel crunches under our feet as we walk together in silence to an imposing brown torii gate, the boundary between the human and spiritual world. We stop and bow, then enter through the left side (the center is reserved for spirits; it is where they pass through). Then we pause again at the temizuya to cleanse our hands and mouths. And finally, we are at the actual shrine. Stone steps lead to a simple wooden building. At the altar we bow two times, clap twice, pray, and bow once more—giving thanks to the gods.

It's hard not to be overwhelmed. Overcome. The steps we've just taken are the same that every imperial family member has taken for over a thousand years. It is somber and peaceful and my throat thickens at being a part of this ritual. I glance at the twins. There is a sheen to their eyes. Do they feel it too? How we are tied to the land and to each other?

"This way," Fumiko says after another moment. She leads us farther onto the grounds where public access is limited.

Our duties will be behind the tall wooden fences where no one can see us, Fumiko explains. Each gust of wind brings the sound of tinkling bells. A Shinto priest waits for us. Dressed all in white, he holds three straw brooms. He bows and hands one to each of us.

"Now you sweep," Fumiko announces.

I look out, assessing the area. The landscape is vast. White gravel pathways stretch into the forest like an infinite labyrinth. "For how long?" I venture to ask.

Fumiko tilts her head at me. "Until it is done."

Noriko peers at the gray sky and shivers—it's cold where the sun goddess dwells. "What if it rains?"

"You get wet," says Fumiko.

We set to work, and for a while, Fumiko watches us, heels crunching fallen leaves, then gesturing for us to sweep them away. When she is gone, the Shining Twins and I mostly ignore each other. There aren't any snide comments or looks. An hour into sweeping, Akiko and Noriko stop and duck under a rope to lean against a cypress tree. I stop, too. You can't see the river from here, but you can feel it, the water in the air. I turn my face up, letting the coolness coat my cheeks.

The priest comes out of nowhere, the clap of his hands like a whip cracking. With a generous smile, he motions for us to continue sweeping.

Lunch is brought to us, simple bento boxes, and then the priest escorts us to the other side of the property. The day passes in one long, agonizing silence. When Fumiko returns to release us from our duties, she inspects every inch of the area, ensuring all the pathways are clear.

Back at the house, Akiko examines Noriko's hands. On the palms, the skin is red and puckered. In the bathroom, I find some ointment and bandages. "Here," I say, handing them off to Akiko.

Akiko tends to Noriko while I start on dinner, using the pan to make a quick stir-fry. "You need this?" Akiko asks before putting away the bandages and ointment.

"No, my hands are fine." I address Noriko over the vegetables I'm slicing. "You held the broom too hard."

"We should listen to her," Akiko says sagely. "She's used to more hard labor than we are."

For some reason, her comment doesn't elicit the same anger it usually does. "Sō desu," I say drily. I dump the vegetables into the pan and they sizzle, the air filling with the smell of fried onion. "Totally have peasant's hands."

"Is that how you were raised?" Noriko inquires, and oh my God, she is asking an honest question.

"No." I stir the veggies. "I wasn't raised doing hard labor.

But my mom did teach me to use a broom and make food."
I scoop rice into bowls and set the stir-fry next to it.

I'm halfway into my dinner when Noriko asks, "What did you mean when you said we couldn't help the way we are, because it's what we were raised with? That we're products of our environment?"

Stunned, I chew thoughtfully and swallow. I vaguely remember what I said. All of it is kind of blurred in an angry, regrettable haze. But I know enough that I wasn't my best self. "Oh, um. I shouldn't have said that. I'm . . . Gomen nasai." I just apologized to the Shining Twins. I wait for a beat for the sudden chill of hell freezing over.

"You're right. You shouldn't have said that," Akiko snipes. There is a deep, unhappy pause. "But you meant it, didn't you?"

I exhale tightly, pinned to the spot by Akiko's and Noriko's ferocious gazes. "I did. . . . I do mean it. I can't imagine what it was like to grow up in the spotlight like you two have. But it wasn't fair for me to toss something like that in your face. I don't think you can help it, actually." They are victims of circumstance, I realize. It still doesn't forgive what they've done. Sometimes you can't change things, but you can understand them.

"That's fair," Noriko states matter-of-factly.

The dust of the conversation settles around us. I can't hear anything outside except for the occasional night insect. The twins go back to eating and cut me out again, talking only to each other.

·   ·   ·

That night, I creep from our room and into the kitchen. The wood is cool beneath my bare feet as I approach the cabinet with our phones in it. In my hand is a bobby pin. I bend down and peer through the crack.

"What are you doing?"

I jump. Pressing a hand to my chest, I swivel. Akiko stands near the sink.

"You scared me." I give her my best what-the-hell stare. "I thought you were Fumiko."

I turn back around and fit the bobby pin into the lock, jiggling it. The pins give way, and there is a decisive click. *Ha.* Nailed it. If Mariko could see me now, picking locks. She'd die. Very un-princess-like.

I dig out our phones, finding Akiko's with the sparkling case and Noriko's with a leather-embossed cover. I walk to her, hand outstretched. "Here." I offer her both phones.

She assesses me for a beat. "Why are you doing this?"

I shrug, try to play it off. *Because you're sad and concerned about your mom, and I'd want someone to do this for me if the situation were reversed.* "I'm sorry for the shitty things I said to you outside the empress's office."

Akiko blinks. She takes the phones from me, nails scraping against my palm.

"Oyasumi." *Goodnight*, I say, turning.

I'm halfway down the hall when Akiko's voice stops me. "You were wrong about the dress for the sultan's welcome banquet. It wasn't a trick. Noriko was excited for you to wear it. She was so proud of her choice. Then when you didn't wear it and made up that excuse about threads . . ." She pauses. "I purposely showed you photos of Akio." She sticks her nose up in the air. "I . . . I don't like it when people hurt Noriko."

"I see." I inhale at the shifting reality. Suddenly all my interactions with the twins are reframed. Have I been the villain, too? Have I misjudged them? Yes, at times, I have. "Well then, I'm sorry for that, too. I didn't mean to hurt Noriko's feelings. I'll apologize to her in the morning."

She stares at me. "Okay."

I stare at her. "Okay then." We're both waving white flags now. It's a little much. More than I can handle. "Well . . . um, good talk. Night." I slip away, escaping to the main room with my phone. Once alone, I stay still, allowing the moment to sink in. We didn't say as much, but I do believe a truce was just declared in the hallway. Wonders never cease. Blowing out a breath, I sit at the low table and fire up my phone. I've got to tell somebody this news.

But . . . my thoughts are derailed by the *Tattler* article. By Akio. As if possessed, I open it up. The photos are, of course, the same. I close out of the web browser and delete my search history. Then I scroll through my contacts, landing on Akio's name. My thumb hovers over the call button. *What am I doing?*

On an inhale, I press it. A pit forms in my stomach as I listen to the line ring. I count the number. One. Two. Three. It cuts off to voicemail. The pit rises to my throat as I hear Akio's deep and melodic voice asking the person calling to leave a message. I swallow. A few tears squeeze out. I hang up right before the beep. For a while I just sit there, my body feeling heavy.

Why did I think he was waiting for me? Pining away in

Nara? Stupid, stupid girl. No more waiting for him. *Yes, my heart agrees.* No more dwelling on Akio, on what might have been. *Yes, yes,* my heart agrees even more. No more hope of a reconciliation. Maybe it all is for the best. Akio is where and with someone he should be. I deserve the same.

I open up my texts and tap one out.

Me
Hi.

He answers almost immediately. I use my sleeve to wipe under my nose.

Eriku
She lives.

Me
Sorry I've been MIA.

Eriku
Do I need to inform the authorities?

Me
No. I'm exactly where I'm supposed to be . . . I think.

Eriku
And where's that?

I slump back and sit crisscross applesauce in the low chair.

> Me
>
> Sweeping temples with my archnemeses. Scratch that . . . frenemies now maybe, I'm not actually sure.

> Eriku
>
> Is that supposed to be a metaphor or something?

> Eriku
>
> Can I call you?

> Me
>
> Okay.

> Eriku
>
> Calling.

The phone rings, and I answer it with a soft, "Moshi moshi." My voice sounds a little thick; if Eriku notices I'll tell him I'm tired. It's been a long day.

"So," Eriku says, sleepy and smiley. "Temples, archnemeses, I feel like there is a story."

I yawn. "It's a long story. How much time do you have?"

"For you?" he asks, then drops to a low rumble. "All night."

It takes a while for me to fill him in on everything that's happened since we saw each other at the garden party. When I am finished, I say, "So that's it. Here I am."

"There you are," he says back warmly.

"How about you?" I ask softly. "How has everything been?"

"Good. So good. My father hasn't mentioned me taking over the family business in days. All he wants me to do is to keep doing what I am doing. He even said I might continue at university after all, since you'll be going there in the spring. Which wouldn't be so bad, you know. I could see us around campus," he says, low and husky, and it wraps around me like a hug. "The cafeteria food is severely underrated."

I smile huge. I could see us there, too. But . . . "I haven't gotten in."

"*Yet*," Eriku says with emphasis. "Anyway, the weight of my father's thumb has firmly been lifted."

"That's amazing," I say, my heart elated for him.

"I know," he says, then sighs deeply. "Everything is so good, it makes me apprehensive."

We chat a little more, and when I go to bed, I fall asleep easily.

The days and nights blend together in a tangle of sweeping, planting trees, and painting fences. I make sure to apologize to Noriko about the dress. We're civil. Cordial. And we even cooperate. Akiko chops vegetables. Noriko sets the table. I cook. We work as a well-oiled if silent machine.

On our last day, Fumiko bids us farewell at the shrine.

"I will report back to the empress that you have done well," she declares. A priest steps forward, our uniforms folded neatly in his hands. "A souvenir," Fumiko says as the priest distributes them. "To remind you of your stay."

At the train station, Akiko dumps the white clothes in the trash. Noriko gives a small smile and, with a shrug, dumps hers, too. They wait for me to do the same. I hug the uniform to my chest. I probably won't ever wear the clothes again. At least, I don't think I will. But I feel kind of sentimental about it. It's a souvenir of this strange, transformative time. Where I let Akio go. Where I found . . . something.

"Everything go okay?" Reina asks as we load up. I'd seen her during the week but hadn't spoken to her.

"I think so," I say, stepping inside the coach. Akiko shifts and moves a bag from the bench across from her and Noriko. She raises her brows at me in silent question. *You coming?* I duck my head and take the open seat near them.

20

Mr. Fuchigami and Mariko welcome me back to the palace. "I trust your stay was productive," Mr. Fuchigami says as he greets me in the genkan. I toe off my shoes and shove my feet into a pair of slippers.

"It was," I say. For the first time in half a year, I am not even a little bit pissed at the twins. Witness my miracle. "Is my dad around?"

Mariko shakes her head. "The Crown Prince had a commitment with the Grand Duke of Luxembourg."

My mother is out of town with the empress. We've exchanged texts. *I am home,* I wrote in the car. *Glad to hear it, on my way to a bird photo exhibition. Call me later?* she'd replied. I promised I would.

We round the corner into the family room. "Your Highness," Mr. Fuchigami says. "Your mail." There is a glint in his eye as he bows and presents a handful of letters on a silver tray along with a platinum letter opener.

I drift over to him. On the top is a letter. The return address reads *The Examination for Japanese University Admission.* My EJU scores.

The letter is slim and light in my hands, but it might as well weigh a thousand pounds. I swallow and stare wide-eyed at Mariko, whose expression teeters between excitement and nervousness. "Open it," she encourages.

I draw in a long breath and swivel, walking a few feet from Mr. Fuchigami and Mariko. I position myself by the window. A gardener in a khaki safari hat is on his hands and knees, checking a sprinkler.

With a twist of my lips, I slice open the letter and pull out two sheets of paper. I bypass the introduction and go to the second page to the actual scores. They are broken down by subject. Japanese as a Foreign Language—three hundred sixty out of four hundred fifty. Japan and the World—one hundred sixty out of two hundred. Biology—eighty-five out of one hundred. Chemistry—eighty-one out of one hundred. It takes me a moment to calculate it all.

"Gōkaku shita." *I passed*, I say quietly, then whirl around to face Mr. Fuchigami and Mariko. "I passed," I say more loudly, jumping up and down. "I passed. I passed. I passed." I pull Mariko in for a tight hug. She goes stiff in my arms at first, then awkwardly embraces me back.

"Omedetō gozaimasu." *Congratulations*, she whispers as I let her go.

Mr. Fuchigami sweeps into a bow, a rare smile gracing his face. "Yes, congratulations."

I beam at them, clutching the letter to my chest, letting the moment linger.

"Let me see," Mariko says, taking the scores from me to read through them.

Mr. Fuchigami clears his throat. "Izumi-sama," he says quietly. Mariko is a few feet away and doesn't seem to hear us. "I wish to apologize for not knowing of the discord between you and your cousins. Had I known . . . I would never have suggested spending additional time with them. I don't wish to cause you strife."

I tilt my head at him, and the warmth inside of me expands. First passing the EJU and now Mr. Fuchigami admitting he cares about me. "You know, it's actually okay. I mean, it wasn't before, but now that I've had the chance to get to know Akiko and Noriko better, they're not so bad." I grin. "We're not best friends or anything, but it's all good. No more breaking vases."

Mr. Fuchigami rocks back on his heels. "Excellent."

"We almost forgot." Mariko steps forward. "There is a second piece of mail I believe you may be interested in."

My brows dart in. "Oh?"

Mariko presents the silver tray again with a letter postmarked from University of Tokyo. I flip it over in my hands. It's slim, like the EJU scores. I know from watching Noora, Glory, and Hansani opening their college acceptance letters that they usually arrive in thick manila envelopes. Dread unfurls in my stomach. I stick my thumb in the corner and tear into the letter, plopping down on the sofa as I do.

To: Her Imperial Highness Princess Izumi

University of Tokyo requests your presence for an interview . . .

It goes on with scheduling options, in person or by phone, and dates. My heart pounds so loudly I can barely hear my voice when I say, "I've been invited for an interview." I twist around. Mariko and Mr. Fuchigami are grinning at me. This is something I've never experienced before. It's how I imagine climbers feel when they reach the peak. Staring down at the land, remembering each tiny footstep. I made this happen. This moment is mine.

The first person I call is Eriku. He agrees to meet me at the Imperial Library. It's raining, but I don't care. I rush from the car and up the steps, waving the letters at Eriku and sliding on the red marble floor. He's there waiting for me on the other side of the brass turnstile. I pass through, and at the same time, I am shouting, "Eriku! I passed, and I've been invited to an interview at University of Tokyo!" I say it all in one breathless breath, smiling so hard my face hurts.

He grins, opens his arms, and I fall into them naturally. He holds me close. I feel the press of his cheek in my hair, his breath against my ear as he says, "Congratulations."

I look up, step away, surprised by the display of affection. Our eyes meet, and warmth spreads slowly through my veins like honeyed molasses. "Um, th-thank you," I stutter out.

Eriku smiles softly. "You worked hard for this. Yoku ganbarimashita." *You did it*, he says.

I blink, too frozen, too many sensations zipping through my body, to respond. Eriku's eyes are crystal clear, sepia-toned and sincere, and somehow, vulnerable. The letters crinkle in my hand and the moment is broken.

Eriku clears his throat and plucks the letters from me.

There is a slight blush to his cheeks as his gaze slides over the scores and University of Tokyo letter. "The interview dates are only a few weeks away." He levels me with his eyes. "We'd better get started if you want to be ready."

"We?" I ask on a hopeful note.

"Of course," he says simply, a side of his mouth hitching high. "I know exactly what they'll ask you. I've been interviewed by universities six times."

"You sure? You were only supposed to tutor me for the EJU," I say.

"I'm sure," he says with a decisive nod. "I want to help you. It's what you do for someone you . . . I mean, it's what you do for friends, right?"

I study him up close. Blood rushes into my cheeks. "Yes . . . yes, that's exactly what you do for friends."

"Okay, let's hear your best jikoshōkai!" Eriku says a little too enthusiastically. He sits straight in his chair. Upbeat and ready. We've switched it up a bit recently, opting to study at home, in the palace, rather than in the library. Tamagotchi chews on a slipper under the table. It's day three of practice for my interview. I'll be expected to answer personal and academic questions. But before all that, I will be asked to deliver a jikoshōkai, a self-introduction.

I rise from my seat as slowly as possible. I'm having sudden flashbacks of when I first came to Tokyo and gave a jikoshōkai. I rambled on about myself, my stinky dog, and then it's all one terrible, humiliating blank. Now, I swallow and clear my throat. "Watashi wa Izumi Tanaka desu. Amerika kara kimashita. Ringo ga suki desu." I say something about Tamagotchi and Mount Shasta, how much I love Japan and apples. Finished, I press my lips together and stare helplessly at Eriku. For once, he's not smiling. That bad?

"Okay," he offers, nodding and thinking. "Time for an upgrade. First, remember to read the air—kūki wo yomu. A university interviewer is probably not interested in your love of apples." Eriku talks me through the more nuanced and polite way of introducing myself with "to mōshimasu" instead of the more common "desu." And how I should always say my family name first, then my given name.

"Got it," I say, although I'm wondering if I'll ever get this language right.

"Let's move on to questions." Eriku picks up a note card from the table. "What's your biggest weakness?"

I nibble my lip and roll the question around in my head. "I guess . . . I guess I am a perfectionist?" Not true. My biggest weaknesses are academics, Tamagotchi, and my mother. But I don't think I am supposed to answer that way. At Eriku's grimace, I say, "Wrong answer?"

Eriku withdraws a pack of M&M's from his bag, rips it open, and lets the candy spill onto the lacquered, shining table. He puts his finger on a green piece and slides it to me. I pick it up and place it on my tongue, letting the shell and chocolate melt in the heat of my mouth. Eriku reclines, watching me for a few seconds. I dart my tongue, lick my lips.

He coughs, shakes his head, and looks away. "The correct answer is something like, 'I focus too much on details,' or 'I have trouble asking for help.'" Behind Eriku, the clock with zodiac animals strikes noon. He slides another M&M to me. "If you say 'I'm a perfectionist,' it doesn't answer the real underlying question being asked. The interviewer is searching for insight on how you work with others and how you'll overcome your faults."

"Got it." I scribble out a note on the card. Then write in capital letters: *I AM A PERFECTIONIST* and cross it out.

Woof.

I perk up, hearing a new dog. Tamagotchi scrambles from under the table and darts around frantically.

"Sorry," Eriku says. "I brought Momo-chan with me today. I promised her I'd take her to the dog park after. I thought she'd be fine in the car for an hour or two since the weather is so cool. But apparently, she needs me." Momo-chan barks again, the sound deep-throated. "And she is also hungry."

"All that from a couple of barks?" I stack my note cards in a tidy pile.

"I'm fluent in Momo-go," he says. *Go* means language.

At the front door, Tamagotchi is going wild—pawing and yipping.

I stand and walk with Eriku to the genkan. He has on a pair of track pants with a sweatshirt today. He slips on his shoes and looks up, smiling at me, big and bright, set at ten thousand watts. I clench and unclench my hands at my sides. He approaches me, Tamagotchi whipping around us in a tiny tornado.

"Izumi," he says gravely once we're only a few inches apart. He casts me a smoldering look. "I'd like to suggest something"—he licks his lips—"but please tell me if it's too early for this."

I swallow. "Okay."

He hesitates, runs a hand through his hair, and it sticks up everywhere. "I think it's time we took our relationship to the next level. . . ."

I glance around. The entryway is empty.

"You do?" My eyes settle on his tentatively.

He nods, serious, and stoops to grasp my hands, holding them fervently. It's such a simple thing. Us touching. No big deal. Just my heart rolling around like a chinchilla in new wood chips.

"I do," he says on an inhale. "I think it's time . . . well, I think it's time our dogs met."

Eriku lets his smile loose. And it's so free, so contagious, I have to look away.

That is how I wind up outside of the imperial palace, holding Tamagotchi's leash tightly as Eriku fetches Momo-chan from his car. The back window is rolled down, and an enormous Saint Bernard hangs out. Drool cascades from her jowls, puddling onto the gravel. Tamagotchi growls, pulling at the leash. Psycho dog. Come to think of it, this probably isn't the best idea.

Reina saunters up next to me. "He should be punished for letting that dog drool all over the car."

"Reina!" I say, kind of shocked.

Eriku opens the door. Momo-chan drops from the car and lumbers forward. And oh my God, she is so cute I could die. Tamagotchi breaks from the leash and rushes toward her. I close my eyes. I should have put the imperial vet on standby. But then . . . it's quiet. I pop open an eye, then the other, ready to see carnage. Tamagotchi has rolled onto his back, and Momo-chan is sniffing his belly. Her thick tongue darts out, and she licks him. *Licks him.* Tamagotchi shudders, his body convulsing in what I can only describe as pure ecstasy.

"Well, now I've seen it all," Reina says, then wanders off.

Eriku smiles. "I think they like each other."

What an understatement. Momo-chan collapses onto the ground, and Tamagotchi curls up next to her.

"I have mentally and emotionally subscribed to Momo-chan's fan club," I say, walking toward the dogs.

Momo-chan rolls to her side. Tamagotchi adjusts too, lying in between her legs, his back curved against her belly. Just so many wishes fulfilled in one magical moment. I always thought I was a one dog kind of woman, but Tamagotchi *and* Momo-chan—sign me the eff up.

"I thought you said your dog was mostly wild." Eriku leans against his car, swinging the keys around his finger.

"He is. This morning he ate an entire plate of dorayaki. I don't even know how he got it since the plate was way up on the kitchen counter." Tamagotchi defies gravity. It makes him even more special in my mind. Superdog.

Eriku laughs. He kneels and rubs Tamagotchi's belly. I wince, waiting for my stinky dog to try to chomp his fingers off. But Tamagotchi stretches, and all I can see are the whites of his eyes. From the car, Eriku produces a blanket. He spreads it out. And I sit down to stroke one of Momo-chan's buttery-soft ears. "Momo-chan is Tamagotchi's love language," I murmur.

"Love language?" He sits down beside me. Our knees touch; I don't scoot away.

"It's how people like to give and receive love—gifts, cuddling, labor, positive affirmations, that sort of thing."

"I see. So what's yours?" He raises a brow at me.

"What's my what?" Momo-chan's giant head is in my lap now. And it's kind of all my dreams come true, lying in a puppy pile. I could die here.

"Your love language?" he prompts.

"Oh, I don't know." I pucker my forehead. "All of them, I suppose." I give him an embarrassed grin.

He lets it sink in for a moment, scratching Tamagotchi's nose. "Me too."

21

That night I stare out my window, watching the winter sun slowly sink beneath the tree line. I'm cozy in a pair of leggings and a sweatshirt with my interview note cards fanned around me on the bed.

A knock sounds on my window; I startle seeing the twins peering through the glass. "Jesus," I say, holding my chest. I rise and unlatch the door to open it.

They wear little dresses, heart-shaped necklines with flouncy skirts. "We're going out," Akiko announces, floating into my room. She sticks her nose in my closet, then flicks on the light. "It's worse than I thought," she calls out, disappearing around the corner. I hear the sound of hangers clinking together. Clothes fly as they're tossed on the marble island. "You don't have anywhere close to enough cashmere!"

"We want you to come with us," Noriko declares. She's staring at the picture of the AGG and me. The one where we're dressed all in denim. Her nose twitches like she smells something offensive.

Akiko returns with a silver number I borrowed from Noora on New Year's two years ago and kept. She tosses it at me, and I catch it. "It's going to be fun. Let's go out, turn it up," she says.

"Uh, it's Wednesday?" I say, mouth agape.

A tiny smile kicks up the corner of Akiko's mouth. I

admit, she can be kind of charming and persuasive when she wants to be. "Say yes," she says.

"I'm pretty sure that's not how consent works." I pause, feel the slinky fabric, feel myself melt again for the twins. It's official. I've started to fall under their spell. Plus, I need a break. "But okay."

Before we leave, I tap out a quick text to Eriku.

> Me
>
> **Heading out with my twin cousins. I may need a rescue.**

He answers right away.

> Eriku
>
> **Walking Momo-chan. Text me the address. Will meet u there.**

The three of us climb a set of stairs suspended from the ceiling, surrounded by dark space. Below us, bodies writhe on a dance floor. Above us is a balcony cordoned off with a velvet rope. A burly bouncer unclips it and allows us to pass.

Akiko trails her hand over a glass wall. "The glass is special," Akiko shouts over a dance remix by The Weeknd.

"We can see out, but they can't see in," Noriko says.

"There aren't any cell phones or cameras allowed in here. It's members only, owned by the Ohnos." She glances back at me, and at my blank expression she says, "Descendants of the Fujiwara clan. A Kuge family, former nobility."

At that, I nod. After World War II, the class system in Japan was abolished. Aside from the inner imperial court, the peerage was disbanded. While families don't hold titles, they maintain their social statuses and influences—they're considered the outer court.

We sit at a table with candelabra centerpieces. Heavy red velvet curtains drape the coffin-like wooden walls, sconces blazing in between them. So, all in all, a vampire bar. A waiter brings us menus embossed with holly leaves.

"We *have* to get the lobster. They're from the Michelin restaurant next door. They have them overnighted from Nova Scotia," Akiko says, then she frowns. "Come to think of it, let's get two."

"They're small," Noriko chimes in.

I place the menu down. There aren't any prices. Which doesn't mean everything is free. It means that everything is so outlandishly expensive that the only people who would order anything from it are the kind who don't need to worry about money. "I'm not sure if I'm hungry."

Noriko orders a bottle of Boërl & Kroff to start and the waiter leaves. I sit kind of awkwardly. My dress is a little short, and I am unsure if crossing my legs will make it better or worse.

Within moments, the waiter returns with the bottle of champagne in a silver tub. He uncorks it with a flourish and pours it into frosted glasses, handing one to each of us. I sip, and oh my God, it's good. Sweet and tangy and bubbly. I ask for a glass of water. Last time I was out on the town was with my cousin, and I drank too much and landed in a garbage cage—long story. But it was one of those moments when you believe, yes, it *is* possible to puke up your own organs. Since then, I've dedicated my life to never reliving the experience again. For each drink of alcohol, I will take one drink of water.

"Idea!" Akiko says. "Let's play a game. A shot for every lie the tabloids say about us."

She doesn't wait for any of us to agree. She flags down the waiter to order a bottle of vodka along with caviar and also requests the most recent edition of the *Tokyo Tattler*. Shots are poured. The food arrives. Noriko uses a tiny spoon to paint a toast point with caviar and crème fraîche.

Akiko opens the *Tattler* and reads the first headline she sees aloud. "'Ms. Tanaka's Affair with Skirt-Wearing Neighbor . . .'"

I spew my water. "What?" I snatch the paper from Akiko. There is my mom's staff picture from College of the Siskiyous, then a grainy photograph of Jones on his property. "It's a sarong!" I say. "And it's a total lie." Mom and Jones have *never* been romantic. I drink a shot and chase it with water.

I pass the paper to Noriko, and she reads aloud. "'Princess Midori will not be at any public events for the next week while she attends a seminar with the Ladies' Red Cross in Hokkaido.'" Akiko and Noriko both down the shots.

At my questioning gaze, Noriko explains. "The Imperial Household Agency comes up with these 'seminars' or 'retreats,'" she says. "Really, she refuses to leave the palace."

"Is your mother all right?" I ask. The dim lighting, how close we're sitting. Makes me feel bolder. Riskier. I'm asking questions I'd probably never ask.

Akiko shrugs. "Depends on who you ask. The Imperial Household Agency says she is fine."

"But she isn't," I press.

In my mind, there is a snapshot of the kitchen in Ise. Of Akiko gently braiding Noriko's hair. Of Noriko wringing her hands with worry. *Do you think she's been eating? Getting dressed in the morning?*

"When we were little, we used to stand in her doorway." Noriko turns to her sister. "Remember that? She used to let us come in, and we'd cuddle in her bed all day, watching old movies. She likes Audrey Hepburn," Noriko says to me.

"She says she could have been the Japanese Audrey Hepburn, had she continued acting," Akiko agrees, nibbling more caviar. "That's why I bought these earrings." She points to her lobes, where two very heavy three-carat vintage diamonds hang. "They once belonged to her."

The vodka turns in my stomach. I am suddenly aggressively sad for the twins.

"Are you *crying?*" Akiko shrieks.

I swipe at my nose. "No. Of course not."

Noriko rolls her eyes in a what-are-we-going-to-do-with-you sort of way.

The night goes on—the happy vibe returns. We shoot vodka and drink to all the lies the tabloids have written about us—there's a tattoo on my butt cheek, Noriko had a secret nose job, Akiko still sucks her thumb.

I lean over the table and grin lazily at Akiko and Noriko. My stomach is full. I am caviar-drunk. "I used to call you the Shining Twins," I admit with relish. "Like from the

Stephen King movies. You know, the creepy twins in the hallways. 'Come play with us,'" I intone in a chilling voice.

Akiko and Noriko smile at each other, doing that weird thing where they speak without using words, just their eyes. "We like that," Akiko declares.

"You do?"

There is the tiniest amount of caviar left. I scrape it out and butter a toast point. Better not let it go to waste. See how I conserve things? My mother would be so proud of me.

"Oh yeah," Noriko agrees.

"It's kind of like, 'Is that the wind or are we breathing down your neck?'" Akiko giggles.

Noriko leans over, our noses nearly touching. Her breath smells of vodka. "It means we're powerful."

All of a sudden, Akiko brightens at something over my shoulder. "Well, well, well, look who just arrived."

I turn and Eriku stands behind the red rope. I wave enthusiastically and pop up to greet him. As soon as he's past the guard, I go to hug him and stop short. I let my arms fall and nod instead. "Hi," I say awkwardly.

He touches my wrist, and it's so quick I almost believe I imagined it. "Hi back. Nice dress." His eyes roam down, stopping at the mid-thigh hemline.

"My cousins picked it out," I say, then blurt, "I feel very naked right now."

Eriku smiles at me lazily, gaze darkening . . . or it could be the dim lighting.

"Konbanwa," Akiko says behind me.

"Konbanwa," Eriku says, bowing low. "Nakamura Eriku to mōshimasu."

"Oh, we know who you are," Noriko says. "You're the Nakamura scion."

At his sides, Eriku's hands curl into fists.

Akiko's eyes sharpen. "Are you dating our cousin?" she asks him.

"Um, no. I mean, yes," Eriku says.

The twins appraise him for two very uncomfortable moments.

"Do you want something to drink?" I catch his wrist and drag him to the table. We settle into our seats. Akiko and Noriko on one side, Eriku and me on the other.

While Akiko and Noriko adjust their dresses, Eriku leans over and whispers in my ear. "You and the twins, huh?"

His warm breath skates down my neck, and gooseflesh raises on my arms. "Yeah." I roll my empty champagne glass between my hands. "I think this is one of those situations where now that I've fed them, I have to keep them."

"They do kind of look like they want to eat me. And not in a good way."

They *are* watching Eriku like a pair of sociopathic kittens, weird smiles on their faces.

"Yeah, I'm not sure what their deal is. But maybe it's better if you don't make any sudden movements." I grin.

A waiter drops off an Aooni IPA beer for Eriku, and he pulls a long swallow. I wonder if he's remembering the death and dismemberment clause in the NDA he signed.

Akiko picks up the *Tattler* again and flips it open to the society page, explaining the drinking game. She trails a long blush-painted nail down the column. "Oh, here's something about Eriku," she says. "Or about your family.

It says that your father is considering a merger with Sasaki Transportation."

Eriku glances away and rubs the back of his neck. "Expansion is my father's middle name."

"'That would make the Nakamuras' reported revenue increase from an estimated ten billion yen per year to fifty billion,'" Akiko reads. She peers at him over the page.

Eriku's knee bounces. I lay a hand over it and say, "Eriku is a brilliant musician. He's studying for his doctorate in music composition right now." He stills and places his own hand on top of mine, fingers curling around to cup my palm. I inhale a shaky breath. Oh, wow. Okay.

"Are you really?" Noriko asks, curious.

Eriku nods, clearly relieved to be off the topic of his father. "I wouldn't say brilliant."

"We're going to need to hear you play something," Akiko announces.

Eriku pulls away from me and tugs his ear. "I'm not sure."

Akiko flags down a waiter. "We need the stage and a piano!"

It's all happening before I know it. The music dies down and Eriku is ushered (i.e., forced) down the stairs and onto the stage.

Sorry, I mouth as he glances back up at me helplessly.

I return to the balcony and stand with my nose to the glass. The music has stopped, the dance floor is still. A single light illuminates the piano on the stage. Eriku sits at the bench.

I feel Noriko and Akiko behind me.

"What do you think? He's kind of strange," Noriko re-marks.

"But he could be perfect for Izumi," Akiko replies. "It's good he's not from one of those new tech billionaire families or a hedge-fund guy."

"Oh, they're the worst," Noriko adds with a shudder. "Much too flashy."

Akiko makes a mew of agreement. "Exactly. The Nakamuras have ties to the old shogunates and political power. Plus, they have a former *prime minister* in the family. Not close enough to be a problem for you, Izumi, but close enough to be useful."

"Shush," I say, reprimand in my voice.

"I can't help it," Akiko says. "Judging people comes very naturally to me."

"Konbanwa," Eriku says softly into the microphone. "I'm Eriku."

Someone screams, and Eriku chuckles, low and kind of sexy. Then he starts to play. The beat is repetitive at first, then changes. "*You don't own me,*" he sings. "*I'm not just one of your many toys. You don't own me . . .*" His voice is hypnotic— striking, full of heart, and brimming with emotion. "*And don't tell me what to do. Don't tell me what to say. . . .*" I step forward and press my hand against the glass, struck by his song choice. It's as if he's speaking to his father. Singing the words he can't say, offering all of it to the crowd, to the night, to be taken and carried away. He hits a high note and all my senses come alive. *Life is a song,* he'd said to me.

Silence reigns when he finishes. But then the crowd goes

wild, and he slinks off the stage, jogging up the stairs to me. We meet at the top. He ducks under the velvet rope.

"That was amazing," I say, and I am sure there are stars in my eyes.

He keeps walking toward me, and I take backward steps until we're in an alcove, a crimson curtain hiding us.

"Izumi." Eriku says my name like a prayer. His grin is lazy and sensual. "Are you drunk?" he asks.

"No," I whisper, then I amend. "Maybe a little, but I've been drinking water all night. I still have my wits about me. How about you?"

He shifts closer. "Tipsy enough to feel brave, but not enough to forget."

"Hmm?" I ask, peering up at him, my mind spinning. It's hard to focus when he's this close.

He gazes down at me. "Izumi. I like you."

"You do?" I ask.

"I didn't take my own advice," he quietly admits.

"Your advice?" All I can do is parrot his words back to him.

The tendons in his neck tighten. "I told you not to fall for me, remember?" Vaguely I remember how he'd joked about it. I nod. "But I fell for you." He pauses. "I don't want to fake-date anymore."

The buzzing feeling in me intensifies. I steady myself against the wall.

"Izumi," he says. "What are you thinking?" His eyes land on me, a tortured glint to them. When I don't answer right away, he pushes back his hair and shakes his head. "I'm making an ass of myself."

He pivots to go, and I catch his wrist, ensnaring him. He slowly turns back around, gaze on my hand, then traveling slowly to my face. Heat flows between us. Tension radiates like a force field. The music lowers.

"Don't go," I crack out. "I like you, too."

He grins, and his dimples pop. "Brace yourself," he murmurs, as if he's speaking to himself. "You're going to kiss her now."

His eyes flash in the dim light. He pulls me to him, humming a tune under his breath. It's the Beatles. *Here comes the sun, do, do, do, do.* Is this a sign? A coded message from Amaterasu? That this, Eriku, and University of Tokyo are the right path for me? *Here comes the sun. And I say it's all right. . . .*

Our lips come together and there's no more time to think. His nose nudges mine, and I press up, our mouths falling into a rhythm of a kiss. It is soft and sweet, explorative. Mapping each other, this new, uncharted terrain, and at the same time burying old pathways, old loves. I grab on to his shirt, no choice but to hold on. In between mind-numbing, chemical, blisslike kisses, he hums low in his throat, and I feel the vibrations all the way to my toes. *Little darling, it's been a long, cold lonely winter. . . .*

22

"Do you think she's alive?" someone says.

A palm cups my cheek. "She's warm," a second voice whispers.

"She could be recently dead. Dead bodies stay warm for up to three hours after."

I swat away whoever is touching me. My head pounds, and I groan. I blink my eyes open and hiss at the light. Noriko and Akiko are in my direct line of vision. I clutch the covers and don't recognize the feel of them. I am not in my own bed. "Where am I?" I say groggily.

The night comes back to me in flashes. Shots with the Shining Twins. Eriku singing. Kissing Eriku. *I fell for you.* I let my fingers ghost my lips.

Wow. Okay. Eriku and I are no longer fake-dating. We are for-real dating. I smile at the memory, at how everything felt fine and dandy. After that, there was more champagne, my vow to drink water forgotten, and then . . . oof.

They sit back on their haunches. They wear coordinated pajamas—Noriko in pink silk with white piping and Akiko in white with pink piping. I gaze down and find that my pajamas match theirs, light pink stripes. "You are at our condo in the city. If we're out late, we stay here, but we usually reserve it for our mother." Behind them on the wall is a giant photograph of Audrey Hepburn. It's one I've seen before. Her hair is swept back in a high bun, a tiara circling it.

I haul my body up to lean against the tufted headboard, then palm my head as my vision swims.

Akiko holds a glass of water out to me, and I grab it, drinking thirstily. "You were drunk last night."

Champagne is not my best friend. Champagne is no one's best friend. New life lesson.

"Eriku made us promise to take you home, but we were worried you might not be okay alone. We slept here with you to make sure," Noriko adds.

"Oh. Thanks," I say.

"It's no big deal. We still sleep in the same bed together sometimes. We let you sleep between us." Noriko pauses, touches her throat. "You still snore. I think it's gotten worse since Ise Jingū. It's bad."

"Really bad," Akiko says.

"Awful," Noriko says. "You should have it checked. If they have to do surgery, you could have the bump on your nose fixed."

"Okay then." I peel back the covers and place the glass of water on the nightstand. "I should probably get going. Is Reina around?"

"She's in the apartment below us," Akiko says. "In the guard's quarters. Our parents own the top five floors of this building. The floor above us is empty. Our mother used to let us roller-skate up there."

We're in a high-rise. I see the telltale rooftops of Azabu; the districts here are home to artists and celebrities. I could probably buy the actual Mount Shasta for the price of this apartment.

I stand, toes digging into the cream carpet that feels very much like cashmere. The whole room is off-white, the only burst of color from an arrangement of green hydrangeas on the dresser. "Where are my clothes?"

"We threw them away," Noriko says. "We did you a favor."

Akiko hands me a silk satin robe embellished with chrysanthemum flowers. "You can borrow this." I slip it on, the ivory velvet cuffs heavy against my wrists. "It's Olivia von Halle from London. The Duchess of Cambridge had them specially made for us."

They don similar robes, Akiko's teal with swooping cranes and Noriko's almond with writhing snakes. Noriko claps her hands. "Let's have breakfast!"

In some sort of fugue state, I am ushered through their ten-thousand-square-foot apartment. I spy two whole rooms of rolling racks and clothes through partially open doors, most with the tags still on. I catch the name *Prada* as we continue.

In the dining room, they sit me in a Windsor chair. Akiko plucks a bell from a credenza trimmed in gold and rings it. A door swings open, and women in black uniforms with white aprons stride in, laying silver-domed dishes on the white-clothed table. There is fresh fruit, eggs Benedict in a creamy hollandaise sauce, scrambled eggs with goat cheese, truffle onsen eggs, brioche French toast, steamed rice, miso soup, grilled salted mackerel, rice with a salty pink pickled plum on top—enough to feed an army.

"Do you want some fresh-squeezed juice—orange, mango, pineapple?" Akiko asks as a slim glass with a golden straw is placed in front of her, a split strawberry straddling the edge. I say nothing. "She'll have a mango juice," she instructs one of the maids. The maid bows and scurries off.

Another maid offers me the tray of eggs Benedict. "Oh, um, sumimasen," I say. Using a heavy fork stamped with the imperial chrysanthemum, I spear a bite of egg. It's the best thing I've ever tasted. My hangover is soon forgotten, absorbed by the sauce. "So good."

Noriko smiles. "This is the menu from the Four Seasons in Kyoto. We have it replicated and served here whenever we want."

Akiko sips her juice. "Topic change," she says. "We like Eriku."

My eggs Benedict are gone, so I scoop a spoonful of fruit onto my plate. "I do too."

"We weren't sure at first," Noriko continues. She's eating French toast and wipes a dollop of chocolate cream from the corner of her mouth with a crisp napkin. Behind her, there is a credenza with framed photos. I focus on the Shining Twins as children, literally being fed from silver spoons. "We thought he might be using you . . . for obvious reasons." She makes a face like it all should make perfect sense. "But you two kind of work, like when the Olsen twin dated that overgrown Greek billionaire."

I swallow a piece of pineapple before responding. "We actually were kind of using each other. He's been helping me—"

Akiko waves a hand. "Oh, we know all about that. You

are very chatty when you're drunk. Too chatty. Good thing imperial family members aren't entrusted with state secrets. Anyway, on the car ride here, you waxed on and on about how much you liked Eriku and how you were worried he didn't like you back, but then you kissed. That the whole reason you're doing all this, trying to improve your public image, going to school, is for your mother. Blah, blah, blah." Akiko levels me with a gaze. A maid places a juice near my plate. "We're going to help you."

I choke on my first sip. "You are?" My eyes bulge. "Why?"

Akiko blinks, turning her upper lip on the drop of juice that has fallen onto the Olivia von Halle robe. "Other than it is abundantly clear you need us? We have decided we like you. There's just something about you." She gestures at me. "A softness. Like if I touched you, my hand might sink . . . as if I were squeezing a marshmallow."

"That's unnecessarily descriptive," I say.

"Also, we feel bad about how we treated you when you first arrived," Noriko says. "We know we bullied you."

"Although, you did make it easy," says Akiko.

"Very, very easy," Noriko deadpans.

"We've created a list of everything we'll need to work on. Well, at least we started one. Didn't have time to finish last night." Akiko picks up her phone and scrolls through it. "You are on track academically, thanks to Eriku, but your public image needs an overhaul. We'll start with clothes. Mr. Fuchigami was correct to ask for our help with a dress for the sultan's banquet. But you need far more assistance beyond one event." She pauses. "Obviously."

I curl my fingers around my napkin. If my goal is to win over the press and the public, what she says is true.

"Your current wardrobe is fine for a younger girl, but you're going to university now," Noriko says softly. "You need to appear more sophisticated. We've scheduled private shopping appointments in Ginza today." Ginza is New York's Fifth Avenue or London's Oxford Street.

"I've added you to our group text," Akiko says, and my phone lights up with an incoming message and a new number.

Noriko's lips turn up in a smile I find in no way comforting. "You're one of us now."

I check and there is a message from Eriku, too.

Eriku

Did I really say brace yourself
before I kissed you last night?

I grin and respond.

Me

You did. It was quite the pep talk.

Eriku

Plans today? I'm thinking of taking
Momo for some vegan ice cream.

Me

Vegan?

She's lactose intolerant. Want to
come? I'll buy you a double scoop.

Already Akiko and Noriko are standing, waiting for me, promising to let me borrow something of theirs to wear to shop. And also having a side conversation about how difficult it is to respect me now that they've seen my underwear.

I ask for a rain check and Eriku texts back with an *All good*. I promise to see him later and maybe add some kisses and hearts to my response.

"You ready?" Akiko asks from the doorway.

I nod slowly, head swimming, trying to process it all. "Coming."

23

Hours later, I have crossed some Rubicon where Akiko and Noriko are acting like my new best friends, and, accordingly, they are all up in my business. We spend the morning shopping in Ginza. The twins whisk me away to stores without names that cater to a clientele who depend on discretion. Akiko thrusts options at me but I stick up my hands, too intimidated by the labels and price tags. Finally, she stops. She and Noriko choose items on my behalf, clothing, they promise, that will complement my skin tone, body shape, and even the way I walk. Garment bags are zipped, and shoes are boxed and sent to the palace.

Then we have lunch. The manager greets us as we enter the upscale restaurant. He bows low and escorts us to a back table. "Your guest has already arrived."

"Guest?" I murmur.

"Ichika," Noriko says. "No last name. No kanji."

"She's a"—Akiko puts a finger to her lips, searching for an answer—"supervisor, of sorts."

"She'll be making all the creative decisions regarding you," Noriko adds.

Akiko and Noriko break into smiles seeing a woman with bangs straight across her forehead sitting in a red velvet booth. They scurry across the marble floor to greet her. She stands. Bows are exchanged.

"Hi. So nice to meet you. Hajimemashite," I say to Ichika, sliding into the booth across from her. The twins follow. We're all sitting now. "This restaurant is beautiful." A zelkova beam spans the ceiling and a wall features a giant mosaic of a seascape.

Ichika curls a hand around a frosty glass of water. "Every US president has sat in this booth when visiting Japan since nineteen seventy-seven," she says. Her long-fingered hands flutter to the ceiling, to the art nouveau light fixtures. "The lighting was done by Akari and can be adjusted depending on the patron. It made Reagan appear twenty years younger."

A waiter distributes menus. When he leaves, Akiko says, "It's all about positioning yourself in the right light."

"Exactly," Ichika says in a voice like a slap.

I focus on the menu and consider whether to have the yakiniku-teishoku or shrimp tempura udon. If Eriku were here, he'd order both. "I can see why you brought her to me," Ichika says to Akiko and Noriko. "She's a diamond in the rough, is she not? There is something about her . . ."

"A provincialism," Akiko fills in.

It is almost better than what she said earlier, about me being soft, like a marshmallow. *Almost.* Still, I am not super thrilled with the description. But I don't say anything. Because now I know, behind their criticism is fondness, a protectiveness. Also, the menu mentions the restaurant has a dedicated dessert room—where you can browse and select your own sweet treat. Chocolate always puts me in a benevolent mood.

"Exactly," Ichika says. "Very workable. I haven't felt this inspired in years."

"Yokatta!" Akiko claps her hands.

We order. Our plates arrive. Eating commences, and Ichika takes the lead, starting with my wardrobe. The twins explain what they chose this morning and Ichika murmurs her agreement but has ideas of her own. She forks a bite of salad with choregi dressing into her mouth, chews, and swallows. "You can wear a variety of clothing. But you should have one designer you favor. I suggest Amano."

"Ooh," Noriko hums. "I *love* him."

Ichiko taps out something on her tablet and hands me photographs of his latest runway show. "I see it now. You are a small-town girl who supports the local artist. An up-and-comer like you. That's your brand." She winks at me. "Amano's pieces are flattering with a nod to classical elements, but with a certain modern flair."

Women strut down a white runway. One wears a black silk furisode with flowing kimono sleeves and a lotus flower motif. Another sports a red evening gown with a matching capelet. Another, a turquoise fitted dress with a square neckline and beaded belt. All so pretty. I like.

"In addition to looking the part," Ichika says, placing her napkin next to her plate, "you need a cause to champion. Something charitable but not too controversial."

"Like friendship bracelets for orphaned puppies," I say.

Ichika cocks her head at me. "You're funny."

"Arigatō gozaimasu." I preen a little and sip my water.

"I didn't mean it as a compliment," she says.

"A hobby is noticeably missing from your profile,"

Noriko interjects, using her fork to push a piece of beef through the sauce on her plate.

"What about blood donations with the Red Cross?" Akiko says. "Imperial women have patronized the organization for nearly two hundred years."

"Perfect," Ichika declares. "Upholding such a tradition will contrast well with your more modern clothing decisions." Should I mention that the mere thought of blood makes me squeamish? Too late, Ichika has moved on. "We'll discuss specifics tomorrow."

Tomorrow? "Ashita?" I ask.

"Darling," Ichika says. "We're not done. Not even close. This is just the beginning."

Ichika becomes a regular fixture in my life. She meets me at a spa with the twins. We bathe in iodine-rich amber-colored water, sip diluted apple cider vinegar, and discuss possible publicity opportunities.

There is shopping and more shopping, and the twins help me nail my eyebrow shape. One morning, Ichika shows up at my doorstep with a van of clothing sent by Amano. Ichika palms her forehead at my undergarments. She commands Mariko to run to the lingerie department at Mitsukoshi and find me every bra and panty set that speaks: *woman on the verge of a sexual awakening*. Whatever that means.

"You don't have to," I whisper to Mariko.

But she shrugs it off, kind of amused by it all. Mariko gone, Ichika continues cleaning out my closet.

"This has to go," she announces, holding up a sweatshirt of Akio's. Suddenly, my mood derails.

"Not that," I blurt. I snatch it from her and bury the sweatshirt in a drawer. I actively don't analyze why. And I definitely don't think about how my mother kept a book about orchids with a handwritten poem from my father for eighteen years. There is no parallel. She carried a torch for Dad. My fire has been doused. I'm sentimental, that's all.

The rest of my time is filled by Eriku. When we're not together, we text. *What are you doing? What is Tamagotchi doing? Momo-chan misses him. She* pines *for him.* We study at the palace, perfecting my jikoshōkai, practicing for my interview, which usually ends with Eriku throwing the note cards in the air and tackling me with kisses.

Eriku is continually fascinated by Mount Shasta. He likes to talk about my small town. How it's so different from New Haven, where he lived while going to Yale. I tell him stories about the Asian Girl Gang and feel a pang of longing. I haven't spoken to them, especially Noora, nearly as much as I intended to. No matter—I'll catch up with Noora when she visits in a few weeks—we'll make up for lost time. And Eriku is excited to meet her. We spend an entire afternoon on the Rainbow Gatherers, and against my better judgment, I introduce Eriku to the Grateful Dead. The very next day, he shows up in a shirt with dancing bears. I lament I have lost him forever when he starts spouting Jerry Garcia facts. *Did you know Jerry's* (because they are on a first-name basis now) *first love was country music? He lost the middle finger on his right hand when his brother accidentally chopped it off in a wood-chopping accident.*

I cut him off with my lips. It is very effective.

It's been a whirlwind, and now, this afternoon, I am in a domed arena for the youth equestrian championships. The place smells of horses and hay.

"Thanks for coming with me today." I lean into Eriku. Akiko and Noriko are around somewhere as well. It's a family affair.

"Are you kidding?" Eriku says with a charming smile. He's wearing some sort of divine wool and silk two-piece suit, with a neat little purple pocket square that matches my A-line lavender dress by Amano. A subtle way of signifying our coupledom. "Dressage is one of my favorite things."

"I thought your favorite things were pocket candy and Saint Bernards."

He clucks his tongue. "There is so much you don't know. I also like girls with flowers in their hair."

I grin up at him. My hair is swept back with a headband featuring appliqué flowers—another design by Amano. Eriku smiles, too, but only for a moment. His gaze drifts up to the glass skybox suites, where his father is. And mine. They've met before, I believe, running in the same circles and all that. But this is more. Mr. Nakamura is having a private audience with the Crown Prince. My father is as self-possessed as always, and Mr. Nakamura wears the mantle of a man who has snared a golden goose. When we left them, Mr. Nakamura was regaling my father with tales of the yacht he recently purchased from a dealer on the Mediterranean. All is well.

"Sumimasen, Your Highness." A man with a press

badge steps toward us and bows low. Eriku and I face him. "Do you have time for a few questions?"

I smile. "Of course."

"Sumimasen." Akiko is next to me all of a sudden, Noriko not far behind her. "We need to steal our cousin away for a moment. But we would be happy to pose for a photograph."

"I would appreciate that greatly," the reporter says, waving his photographer forward. Eriku wanders toward the ring. We pose, and he thanks us for our time.

"Never talk to the press without a fully vetted statement," Akiko advises me as the reporter departs. Of course, I remember the sultan's welcome banquet and what I had said to the reporter. *My only hope is that my parents will be allowed to follow their hearts.* How my words were twisted the next day in the papers.

"You're so lucky to have us," Noriko says.

"What would you have done if we hadn't intervened?" Akiko asks. "With the press, you must project an openness all while keeping your mouth shut."

"Yes," Noriko agrees. "Think pleasant and uninformative."

Across the way, Eriku chats up one of the riders, hips loose as he leans against the rail. She stands on the other side, horse leads in her hand.

"Who's that?" Akiko asks.

There is a Gakushūin crest on the rider's blazer.

"I don't know." My forehead scrunches. "Should I know?"

"She doesn't look familiar. Probably nobody, but let's find out her name anyway," Noriko says.

"We wouldn't want her coming in between you and Eriku. We'll start a rumor she shoplifts," Akiko declares.

"What?" I laugh big with disbelief, then sober as I realize they're serious. Really serious. "No," I sputter. "No rumors she shoplifts."

Noriko pouts. "Spoilsport."

TOKYO TATTLER

Imperial princesses wear bold new headbands

November 24, 2022

HIH Princess Izumi made a splash yesterday at the fifty-seventh youth equestrian championships. She wore a lavender dress with an asymmetrical neckline and a flower bandeau in her hair that coordinated with her cousins, HIH Princesses Akiko and Noriko.

At her side was Eriku Nakamura, sporting a Kiton suit with a matching lavender pocket square. While Nakamura has been seen with Princess Izumi, this marks the first time the two have worn anything similar, and we wonder if this means they are more serious than previously thought. Japan definitely approves of the match. "He is her equal," imperial blogger Junko Inogashira says. "I hope I never hear the name Akio Kobayashi again."

Inogashira isn't the only one pleased by the match. It's said that the Imperial Household Council also likes Eriku Nakamura for Princess Izumi. So much, in fact, this may have been a part of what turned the tides in favor of Crown Prince Toshihito's engagement to Hanako Tanaka. "It is a gigantic step in the right direction," our palace insider states. "It might have pushed them past the finish line."

24

Noon the next day, I stand on the concrete steps of the faculty office at University of Tokyo. My interview starts in fifteen minutes.

"You ready? Want to go over anything last minute?" Eriku asks.

Click. The sound of a camera shutter. Ichika gained permission from the Imperial Household Agency to hire a personal photographer. She's contacted *Vogue* Japan to do a profile on my university entrance journey. *It will be like Legally* Blonde *meets* The Princess Diaries, she said. I'm not sure exactly what that means, but I said okay. I am wearing a chic navy suit by Amano. According to this morning's *Tokyo Tattler*, I am now his patron.

"No. I'm okay. Nervous, though," I admit quietly to Eriku.

"You're going to do great," he says. And I kind of believe him. I feel good, and I've memorized all the answers we've studied. "Just be the best version of yourself."

"Your Highness," the cameraman calls out to me. "If you please, go ahead and look up at Mr. Nakamura." I tip up my chin. "Smile." I do, and he snaps a photo. "Thank you." He bows and swipes through the photographs.

Inside, the building is near empty, having been cleared by imperial guards beforehand. Mr. Ueno, a science department faculty member and my interviewer, is waiting for me on the third floor.

When I arrive at his office, Mr. Ueno executes a formal bow. A large mahogany desk stretches between us. I reciprocate and launch into my jikoshōkai. Once finished, I fold my hands in front of myself and smile nervously. Mr. Ueno nods, no smile, and invites me to sit. While I arrange myself in the chair, I go over my self-introduction, my mind spinning. Did I miss something? Last time I practiced with Eriku, I nailed it. What did I do wrong?

Before I can entirely process it all, Mr. Ueno speaks. "Let me start by saying that University of Tokyo is honored you are considering our institution. As you know, the university is ranked number one in Japan. Our alumni include several members of the imperial house, the emperor, and the Crown Prince among them. In addition, we have turned out several Nobel Prize laureates, prime ministers, and innumerable captains of industry. We have a reputation as not only a prestigious but a highly selective school. It is my job as an interviewer to ensure that reputation is upheld. Therefore, I will treat you as any other candidate." A single sheet of paper is on the desk, the questions spaced evenly apart so he might take notes on my answers.

"Please." I invite him to proceed with an open hand, my palm sweaty. My pulse thunders in my ears. "I planned to express a similar sentiment. I wish to be treated fairly and based on my accomplishments, not my birth."

I search his face for any nonverbal cue that he is pleased by my answer. The man could give lessons in poker face. He taps his pen against the desk. "Excellent. Let's begin. . . .

Describe an Asia-related issue that has recently interested you in media. Why did this issue particularly interest you?"

I count to five before answering. *Don't launch right into the question*, Eriku advised. *Wait a few seconds, gather yourself and your thoughts.* "Most recently, I have been interested in Japan's shrinking population . . ." I go on explaining the economic influences, the danger of losing cultural traditions. He scribbles my answers, writing furiously.

The next hour is much of the same, focusing on academics. He doesn't pull any punches. *Some people argue history repeats itself. Do you agree or disagree? Pick an example. A typical conclusion of standard microeconomic theory is that the economy is led by an "invisible hand," and, thus, the role of government should be minimized. Do you think this also applies to environmental policy issues? Why or why not? From a chemical point of view, tell me as much as you can about water.*

My bladder is full and near to bursting sixty minutes later as we approach round two, personal questions. But I don't budge an inch.

"What is your biggest weakness?" he asks.

I draw a deep breath and answer. "I am too detail-oriented. . . ."

And the last ten minutes are idle conversation. "Why did you choose botany to study?" he asks, cocking his head.

"My mother is a professor of botany. I'd like to follow in her footsteps," I say warmly, feeling affection for my mother, not the subject.

Mr. Ueno nods along with my statement, then pushes away from the desk. He stands and bows. "Thank you so much for your time, Your Highness. We will be in touch with an official notification." He pauses, and there is the faintest hint of a glimmer in his eyes. "But if I may, I'd like to personally welcome you to University of Tokyo."

The first place I visit is the bathroom. Then I fly through the double doors of the faculty office and announce my victory with a wide smile. Eriku offers to take me out, but I ask for a rain check. The people I most want to celebrate with are my parents. Eriku and I head in opposite directions, and I call my mother as soon as I am back in the car. A chauffer with white gloves is at the wheel, and Reina beside him.

I'm bursting with the news. As soon as the screen flicks on and I see Mom's face, I cry, "I got in. I got in!" Reina grins in the rearview mirror.

Mom smiles and puts a hand over her mouth. Her nails are manicured, the nail polish a blush color. "That's wonderful, honey." She is also in a car. I recognize the buttery yellow seats of one of the imperial Rolls-Royces.

"We should celebrate." I bounce in my seat. "There is this spa Akiko and Noriko took me to. We could go as soon as you get back next week."

"Oh, I'd love to. That sounds so nice. I could use some R and R," she says softly. "I'm back tomorrow."

"You have all-day tutoring with the empress, then will be attending a private cello concert with His Imperial Highness the Crown Prince," a disembodied voice says to her left. I recognize it as Ms. Komura, her lady-in-waiting, on loan from the empress. She rattles off more of Mom's commitments. "Next free date is five days from now," she finishes.

Mom looks as if she's going to argue, but I stop her. "It's okay," I hurry to say—and it is, it really is. Marrying my father is important to my mom. Therefore the tutoring, the social engagements, are important, too. Mom needs me to be supportive right now. "Five days from now, we have a date."

Mom's mouth is a thin line, but she says, "All right, then. Spa day, here we come." Her focus shifts to someone off camera. Low murmurs. "Honey, I'm sorry, but we've arrived. I'll call you tonight, okay?"

"Of course!" I say brightly.

"Oh," she says. "Happy Thanksgiving!"

I'm taken aback. It is Thanksgiving in the States today. I hadn't even thought of it. We've never spent the holiday apart.

"Happy Thanksgiving," I say, watching her tenderly. "When you get back, we should celebrate that, too. Maybe we can make a pie or something?"

"I'd like that," she says. "Better yet, why don't we make the whole meal, maybe for Christmas, as a do-over?"

"Yes," I say. "A mega Thanksgiving-Christmas feast."

Her car door opens. Light floods the vehicle. "Love you, honey."

"Love you too." We hang up, making kissy faces at each other.

While I was on the phone with Mom, Noora texted her flight itinerary.

Noora

So excited to see you. I wanna
talk details. But I'm home for
Thanksgiving and my parents have

invited every family member over
who lives within a five-hundred-
mile radius. Talk next week?

> **Me**
>
> Of course! BTW I'm pretty sure
> I got into University of Tokyo
> today—no big deal.

Noora

WHAT? Big deal. Major deal. This
calls for a pun . . . whale done!

> **Me**
>
> I totally snailed it.

Noora

☺

Back home, I wander through the palace to the kitchen and find my father eating ichigo daifuku, mochi filled with a juicy strawberry and sweet red bean paste. "I'm spoiling my dinner," he says with a final bite.

"Konnichiwa," I say.

He nods, rinses his hands in the sink, uses a towel, and neatly folds it. I think of the crumpled shirts in my closet. We're quite different, my father and I.

"How was the interview?" he asks, leaning a hip against the counter, fixing me with a serious look. He's wearing a navy sweater over a collared shirt. Thanks to Akiko and

Noriko, I now know what kind—cashmere woven from vicuña fleece.

I step more into the kitchen. "Good," I say, playing it cool. But then I feel that burst of joy again, and it's difficult keeping my expression neutral. "Dekimashita. Mr. Ueno, the interviewer, gave me an unofficial welcome."

His eyes crinkle. "Well," he says with a warmth he reserves mostly for my mom and me. "That's as good as in."

I beam at him.

After a pause, he shakes his head as if in wonder. "You did it."

I inhale, chest puffing. I did it.

I. Did. It.

"Mom and I are going to celebrate five days from now," I say. "Scheduling conflicts."

He nods and peers at his feet. "I am familiar. As a boy, I had to make appointments to see my parents."

I think about Akiko and Noriko. Their parents. My parents. It used to be just Mom and me, but now it's Dad and chamberlains and ladies-in-waiting, too—all pulling for our attention. Is it bad? Or just different?

"Was that difficult for you?"

"It is what I was raised with. But I cannot say I am unhappy you were raised differently." He stands and strolls to me, so we're toe-to-toe. Then he places two hands on my shoulders and squeezes, admiration in his foxlike gaze. "You settled close by at University of Tokyo and your mother by my side, it's a dream come true. We'll celebrate with your mom when she returns, but how about I take you out tonight? Just us. I am so . . ." It's the first time I've seen him at a loss for words. "I am so proud of you." He folds me into a hug.

Dad is proud of me. With Mom, it's pretty much a given. She thinks most things I do are great. When I was four and picked my nose, she'd open her hands, face lighting up, and say: *Look at you, doing something all by yourself, you're so independent.* It's harder won with my father and somehow a little sweeter, a little more meaningful. My eyes well up. I nestle into him, into the feeling.

25

Mid-December, a cold snap sweeps through Tokyo. Overnight, intricate light displays pop up all over the city. My favorite is the Shibuya Ao no Dokutsu, the Blue Cave illumination where the zelkova trees outside of NHK quarters are wrapped in royal blue LED lights and a reflective sheet is laid out on the center of the street. The effect is stunning, as if you've been bathed in ethereal blue light. It's incredibly peaceful and on brand for the actual holiday of Christmas in Japan, which is all about happiness and serenity.

Shoring up the season's greetings is an official acceptance letter from University of Tokyo. Now all that is up for debate is whether I will live at home or in one of the dorms.

Everyone has an opinion. My father bought a new desk and requested one of the rooms in the palace be cleared as a study for me. *It would be nice to have you home,* my mother agreed with a blush. Reina concurs—security-wise, it is easier. On the other side are Akiko, Noriko, and Mr. Fuchigami. As far as public perception, it would be well received if I were making an effort to be an average university student. *The press adores these kinds of stories,* Ichika had said. *We could do a whole profile on your dorm room.* Eriku isn't much help. He's completely neutral. Although he helps me make a pros-and-cons list. Which ends up in a tie. I can't decide. Thinking about it makes my throat dry. Things are getting real.

There is a hint of snow in the air when Noora arrives. Despite our best efforts to talk on the phone more, we didn't have much of a chance to. She was busy with finals. I've been busy with imperial events, Eriku, and the twins. So now, I am hopping from foot to foot and watching by the door for the car to pull up. Where is she? I check the time. Her flight landed a couple of hours ago. The front gate rang and said they'd let the car through. I am ready for my Noora fix.

When I see the black car, I rush out, adrenaline pumping through me and a bunch of balloons in my hand. Tamagotchi is at my heels. As soon as she is out of the car, I catapult into her arms. She's wearing leggings and the Columbia sweatshirt she's sported before. She looks the same . . . but different. There is a new aura about her. A confidence. A maturity.

"You're here," I say, squeezing her. Tears form and my insides are a mess—puddles of gooey love.

"Are you smelling me?" she asks as we disengage. Tamagotchi barks and circles us.

"No. Yes," I say on an inhale.

When we were thirteen, she determined that we should all have a signature scent. Mine is vanilla . . . well, because cake. Hers is gardenia, sultry and intoxicating. She's been wearing the same oil from the Berryvale market since. It's nice to see some things will never change. Only . . . "Your hair!" I exclaim. Subtle auburn streaks catch in the winter morning light.

"I know. What do you think?" She half turns, showing

off the glossy strands that touch her shoulders. "I'm more me than I have ever been."

"I couldn't agree more," I say with a sage nod.

She picks up a lock of my hair. "You should do the same to yours. It would look good on you. Oh! Maybe blond instead?"

I smooth a hand over my hair. "I'd have to check. I'm not sure I'm allowed to dye my hair."

Noora pauses. "Come again?"

I wave a hand like it's not a big deal. "Imperial rules." And actually, general Japan rules. Many schools here don't allow hair coloring. "Come in. Come in." I pull her by the hand to the genkan. I toe off my shoes, exchange them for a pair of maple cashmere slippers, and set down a matching pair for Noora. "Like when we were little." We had this whole thing when we were younger. We pretended to be twins—dressing alike, eating the same foods. We thought no one would notice I'm Japanese and Noora is Persian.

Noora stares in slack-jawed wonder at the opulence as we tour the palace on the way to Noora's guest room. Mariko is already unpacking Noora's suitcase when we arrive. "Hello," Mariko says with a bow. "It's so nice to meet you. I am Mariko, Her Highness's lady-in-waiting."

"Nice to meet you, too. Izumi's best friend since two thousand nine." She pauses and mumbles, "Um, you don't have to do that. I can unpack on my own."

"Are you sure?" Mariko has folded Noora's underwear into neat little two-inch squares. "I don't mind."

"No, thank you very much. I'd prefer to handle it on my own," Noora says, a little bemused and embarrassed.

"All right, then." Mariko turns to me. "Do you require anything else?"

I shake my head. "No. Thank you."

As soon as Mariko slides the door closed, Noora says, "Oh my God, this is intense. I need to catch my breath. You have servants. *Servants.* Is it always like that?"

I hip-check her. "No, of course not. Mariko is less formal when there aren't others present, but she goes into default lady-in-waiting mode anytime we have company."

She sighs big. "I'm definitely not leaving my underwear sunny-side up here." She falls onto the heirloom four-poster cane bed like it's all too much. She can't even stay upright. She moans a little and rolls around on top of the crisp white duvet. "What thread count is this? It feels like butter."

I fall in beside her. "They are high-quality merino wool fabric woven with small amounts of gold carat and silk jacquard, specially made for the imperial family."

"I'm calling my mother and asking her why she never bought me gold sheets." She flips around, and we're almost nose to nose. "Who knew I have been so deprived?"

I touch her hair, pull at the red strands, and smile. "I'm so glad you came."

Noora is here for seven days. She struggles to stay awake the first seventy-two hours but manages to rally with a combination of caffeine and sugar. We don't intend to waste a single moment. First thing, I give her a tour of Akasaka Palace. We have a formal sit-down tea service in the Asahi no Ma room. It's very eighteenth-century France with a Japanese twist.

I unfold my napkin and place it on my lap. "Tell me everything. How is New York? Classes? What is going on with you? I feel like we haven't spoken in forever." We've texted a lot, but it isn't the same.

Noora tracks my movements and does the same thing with her napkin. She sits uncomfortably straight. A butler steps forward and pours us both our tea. She waits until he's done. "Classes are good. I'm taking this one all about Disney films and feminism. It's really fascinating. Duke says . . ."

"Duke?" I quirk an eyebrow.

"This guy." She looks down, blushes, then settles her gaze back on me. "He's in the class. And well . . . um, I'm kind of dating him," she whispers into the cavernous room. Above us is a portrait of a nude Roman goddess cradled in cherry blossom branches, just hanging around, watching us.

I slam my fist down on the table. "Get out. How did I not know this? Why didn't you tell me?"

Noora smiles and relaxes a bit. She tentatively picks up her teacup and sips, "Well, it's kind of new. He's royalty as well."

I stare at her. "Seriously?"

The butler steps forward and offers us mini ham sandwiches. Noora waits until he's gone to speak again. "Sort of. His family owns a large cattle ranch in the Midwest. His father is the beef king of Kansas."

"Mrs. Beef King," I say low. "Maybe you should show him you're really committed and have his name tattooed on your lower lip."

"We're at that point."

The butler comes forward, and Noora goes mute again. I give him a bright smile and say we're okay. Outside the windows, the sky is purple. It's cold and quiet and still.

Alone again, I ask, "It's that serious?"

Noora nods. "That serious. He asked me to come home with him for his spring break. I'm pretty sure he's going to try to get me to milk a cow, which I'm weirdly excited about. And you know me, I am strictly an indoor person." One year for Christmas, I gave Noora a sweatshirt that said Indoorsy. So yeah, I know.

Noora hasn't touched her food. I lean in. "Are you okay? Do you not like it? Want me to order you something else?" It's unlike her to be so passive. So hesitant.

I look to the butler, but Noora says quickly, "No, it's fine. I'm just afraid of spilling something." She glances meaningfully down at the plush purple carpet. Then she very carefully, very deliberately, takes a bite of the sandwich, holding it over her plate to make sure every crumb is caught. "What about you? How are you holding up post-Akio?" she asks after swallowing.

Wow. I haven't heard his name in a while. "I'm okay. Things with Eriku . . ." She knows a bit about him but not everything. I fill her in on what's been happening, how quickly our fake-dating scheme became real.

"You really like him?"

I think of Eriku's lopsided smile, his earnestness. "I do."

"Better than Akio?"

Like Eriku, Akio gives more than he takes. But the similarities end there. Akio is stoic, loyal, an old soul. He is a master of self-restraint and Eriku is exploding colors. I shake my head. "I don't think there is a comparison. They are too different."

That night we spend time in my closet, and Noora is more relaxed without the staff around. "This is gorgeous," Noora says, pulling the black-and-gold-stitched dress my cousins chose for me. Noora holds it against her in front of a mirror. "Did you wear this somewhere?"

I shake my head. "No" is all I say. But I long to. The dress still calls to me.

"I'm trying it on." She throws it on the marble island and strips down. I zip her up and admire it. Our body shapes are similar: flared hips, bigger-than-average boobs. The skirt swishes, floating around her ankles. The V-neck is deep and a little daring. I kind of love it. Could see me in it. It's one of those dresses you feel powerful in. I totally get why Akiko and Noriko had me choose it. But where would I wear it now?

Noora's like a magpie, and a new item of clothing has caught her attention. She wiggles out of the dress and I hang it up, stroking it once and letting it go.

The next afternoon, I introduce her to Akiko and Noriko. I spend an hour prepping her for the meeting—no sudden movements. Maintain eye contact. Make yourself look bigger. Kind of like if you encounter a mountain lion in the wild. "They're not so bad," I say as they approach us. Akiko is wearing a rainbow intarsia knit sweater by Stella McCartney and white leggings.

"You're Izumi's best friend from the States," Akiko says as she slides in across from us. "Hajimemashite."

We're at the members-only club where Eriku sang "You Don't Own Me." But it's daytime and open for lunch. Tables draped in black linen cloths are set up on the dance floor. Servers mill about with white gloves.

"We're her best friends here," Noriko says, snapping out a napkin and laying it on her lap. She is also wearing Stella McCartney, an amora silk fruit print dress, and a chain mail bag that could definitely be weaponized.

"New friends are always appreciated," Noora volleys back. "But they can't replace *years* spent together. Remind me when we met?" She turns to me.

"Second grade," I murmur, unsure of what is happening.

Akiko smiles and it's cold, confrontational. "Isn't there an American saying along the lines of 'Out with the old, in with the new'?" she asks.

Noora stares at them. Akiko and Noriko stare back. A standoff. This is going super well.

"Some things can't be replaced," Noora grits out. "Izumi will always need me for emotional support."

Noriko speaks up. "Well, she needs us, too. We've spent oodles of time together. I mean, look at her." She gestures at me from head to toe. "This is all us. We're the best things to ever happen to her."

"Exactly." Akiko bobs her head. She pauses. "Can you believe Izumi didn't know the different grades of cashmere?"

"Travesty. I convinced her in the seventh grade not to get a perm," Noora says in a clear bid to one-up them.

Noriko shudders. "Thank goodness you talked her out of that. The other day she nearly wore a cardigan twinset," she says.

"It's worse," Noora says, her expression changing from aggrieved to amused. "She was just going to do her bangs, then keep the rest straight."

"Hey," I interject.

Akiko grins and says, "I mean, what would she do without us?"

Noora smiles. The twins smile. They are sharing a joke . . . at my expense. Is it wrong to be kind of touched by this moment? Now, I'm grinning. Akiko gives me a WTF look.

Noora sits back in her chair and crosses her arms. "You two are very . . ." She actively searches for the right word. "Confident. Maybe you're good for Izumi."

"Of course we are," Akiko says.

Noriko sips her water and says, "Izumi mentioned you're going to school in New York."

Akiko leans in. "We've always wanted to go to New York. Get one of those cute old-world apartments that overlook Central Park. Does your place have a view?"

"No, it doesn't. But my dorm room does overlook the HVAC system of the building next door," Noora says matter-of-factly.

Akiko and Noriko find this fascinating, and the rest of the meal is spent discussing how Noora lives in one hundred and fifty square feet of space and shares a bathroom with twenty other girls.

It's on from there. The twins invite us shopping. Noora says she's game . . . although her eyes bug out when she sees the stores and then the price tags. We top the night off at a private karaoke bar. Noora and I perform "Bohemian

Rhapsody," a throwback to our middle-school talent-show days. Somehow, I even convince Akiko and Noriko to wear synthetic feather boas. It is a lot of sake and too many bad dance moves. Really something else.

A few days before Christmas, Noora is still here and it snows. A foot of powder blankets Tokyo, and it reminds me of Mount Shasta. Mom would shove me in a snowsuit and out the door, shovel in hand to clear the driveway. When done, Noora and the girls and I would pillage neighbors' recycling bins for large cardboard boxes to sled on.

Which sounds like an excellent idea.

The butlers refuse to source cardboard for us, but they do produce three premium wooden sleds. Eriku joins us. He brings Momo-chan, who is in heaven, digging up the snow and then rolling around in it, Tamagotchi following her like . . . well, like a lovesick puppy. Noora screams as she shoots down a hill on a sled. I wipe out toward the bottom and roll to a stop, giggling, my life flashing before my eyes. We're half drunk on snow and joy. Eriku is in my line of sight, offering me a hand up. I gaze into his sparkling eyes.

"You have freckles on your nose," he says dreamily.

I touch the bridge of my nose with a gloved hand. "It's, uh, I think it's sun damage," I say dumbly.

He tucks a stray lock of hair gently back into my cap. We're interrupted by the imperial guards, who insist on making sure I am not injured. While they discuss calling the royal physician, we wrap ourselves in plaid blankets and drink hot chocolate with peppermint sticks from silver cups. Eriku is making a snow angel, and Noora nudges me. "He's fun," she says. "You two are a lot alike. He's like the male version of you."

I scrunch my nose. Mom said something similar. "I guess he kind of is."

Eriku lies in the snow now, Momo-chan on top of him and Tamagotchi pawing his other side. He's totally the guy who says: *I support you, you're doing great, should we get another dog?* Akio encouraged me in a different way. I remember night after night playing Go. The way he'd stare at me across the board, challenging me. *Do better. You can beat me. C'mon.*

That night we have dinner with my parents, just the four of us. Hungry from playing in the snow, Noora and I inhale our udon topped with inari age, seasoned fried tofu.

"You okay, Ms. T?" Noora asks.

Mom hasn't eaten much, and there are dark smudges under her eyes. I remember I looked similar the first weeks I was in Japan. When everything was so new and I was trying to learn it all at once. Like me, Mom had been thrown in headfirst. The imperial pace can be grueling. "Fine. Tired," she says, smiling sleepily. "Too tired to eat."

Dad's mouth dips in concern. He touches her forehead. "Do you feel sick?"

"No," she says, dodging away. "I think I need a break, though. I'm looking forward to the next few days with my family." The three of us have managed to block off our schedules for three whole days. Mom and I are taking over the kitchen and cooking our Christmas-Thanksgiving mega-feast. "But I think I'll turn in early." She stands. Dad walks her to her room, and I tug her unfinished noodles to me.

At Noora, I say, "What? It will go to waste if someone doesn't finish it."

She rolls her eyes. "Well, at least share." She scoots closer to me and we polish off Mom's bowl together. Noora makes my world complete.

26

The day before Noora goes home, we head to a holiday market, a replica of the one in Stuttgart, Germany, in Roppongi Hills. We wander the stalls while Beethoven's ninth, "Ode to Joy," plays on overhead speakers.

"So we're down to the last twenty-four hours. Anything else you want to squeeze in?"

Noora's face brightens. "Yes," she says, then stops short.

We've started to draw a crowd. Not just one camera but several have suddenly popped up. Imperial guards swoop in, holding back the tide as they press against their outstretched arms.

"Shoot," I say. "I'm such a dummy. I should have warned you about this." Every place we've visited so far has been private or cleared beforehand. This is our first time in public. "Is it bothering you? We can go. I guess I've just gotten used to it." Noora is frozen. "Hey." I adjust so I am in her direct line of vision. "Want to go?"

She shakes it off. "No, that's okay. I want to see the market."

We carry on, but the casual, laid-back vibe is gone. Noora grows more and more tense as the crowd doubles, then triples. There is an empty stall selling hot cider, and I duck inside. The imperial guards post themselves outside. The owner emerges from the back room. He is gracious and bows deeply, offering us steaming cups smelling of sweet apples.

"Should I give him some money?" Noora asks as we sit in the back.

But Reina has already stepped forward and is paying the vendor. "No. It's on me. Well, the imperial family. I don't carry money," I say. At her expression, I explain. "Royals don't carry cash. It's a whole thing," I say, rotating the cup in my hands, letting the heat seep through and warm them. "So, ideas? Last twenty-four hours?" Her flight departs tomorrow evening.

She shifts back and forth. "What about riding the subway? I've read so much about the Tokyo transportation system. I'm dying to see if I can figure it out like I did New York's."

Noora has always loved a challenge. I imagine she thinks of it a bit like a dissection, following the lines like arteries, seeing what organ they lead to.

A choir starts to sing Christmas carols. I stare into my cup. "I don't know. I'll have to ask. I mean, if you want me to go with you. . . . My father and grandfather ride the subway sometimes, but it involves a ton of extra security and delaying subway schedules."

"Princess Izumi!" someone shouts.

On autopilot, I perk up and swivel toward the voice, switching on a stage smile. A picture is snapped, and the cameraman bows in appreciation.

Noora pushes away her cup and makes a little sound.

"What?" I ask.

"Nothing," she says.

Passive, meet aggressive. "What?" I insist.

She gestures at me. "It's just been weird seeing you like this. Turning it on and off."

I sit back as if struck. "What on and off?"

"The whole princess mode. It's unsettling." She finds a spot on the wall and steadfastly stares at it. "Never mind. Forget I said anything."

"'Princess mode'?" I blurt, then rein it in a bit. "Can we not do this here? People are watching." Harmony is a big thing in Japan.

Noora sighs. "Of course."

As we leave the café, I smile tightly at the owner and bow to the owner. "Gochisōsama deshita," I say, thanking him for the cider. He bows back. The ride in the car is dark and silent. Noora crosses her arms, her jaw firm and unforgiving. She won't look at me.

"I don't understand," I say. "What happened? We've been having such a good time. . . ."

Noora rubs her eyes with the heels of her hands. "We have . . . and we haven't. . . . It's not what happened just now. It's been seeing everyone bow down to you. Elaborate tea parties in palaces. The price of the clothes you buy. Butlers setting up winter picnics while we sled . . ."

"You liked the sledding," I defend.

"I did . . . or I thought I did, but doesn't it make you uncomfortable? Or maybe it doesn't, and that's why I'm so upset. You've changed so much."

My chest gums up with emotions. "It may seem like I'm different, but I'm still the same Izumi inside. You know why I'm doing all this. For my mom," I say into the dense silence.

Noora rubs her eyes with the heels of her hands. "I know, but at what cost? Losing yourself?"

"You don't understand. Japan is a collectivist culture. I'm adapting."

"So conform or die?"

"It's not like that." I squint my eyes and breathe in through my nose. "I don't even know where all this is coming from. Maybe we should just take a moment to ourselves."

"Sounds good to me," Noora says.

We don't talk for the rest of the ride.

It's rounding midnight, and I can't sleep. I am restless. With Noora fuming at me, my life is out of balance, a tilted painting. I slip on my robe, the one Akiko and Noriko gave me, and pad down the hall. I knock on Noora's door before sliding it open.

"Noora?" I whisper into the darkness.

A few seconds pass, and I am about to leave when she answers. "Yeah?"

"You awake?"

"Obviously. I can't sleep."

"Worried about your flight tomorrow?"

"No, dummy. Because we're fighting. We never fight."

I creep closer and sit on the edge of her bed. "Except that one time on your twelfth birthday. Do you remember?"

"I remember."

Her mom had decided to scare the AGG on a sleepover, putting a sheet over a broomstick and waving it in front of the window. The ghost effect was super terrifying. I pushed Noora out of the way to save myself. It's not one of my proudest moments.

"You didn't talk to me for three days," I say. I had to solemnly swear on Tamagotchi that should a real ghost ever appear, I would throw myself in front of her.

"I still feel totally justified." She tilts her chin up.

"Not arguing." I fall quiet for a moment. "What's happening to us?" I ask, twiddling my thumbs.

Noora scoots up and clicks on the light. "I don't know." She releases a long-suffering sigh. "I guess I expected this visit to be more like how we used to be—palling around just the two of us. The entourage and photographers are a lot, honestly. I'm mad at you for having this whole life without me, and I feel abandoned, even though I know I shouldn't. I just don't feel like I'm your number one anymore." She sighs.

I nod along with her words. "I can see that. But . . . I don't think I'm your number one anymore, either. We keep missing each other. We make plans to call but then one of us cancels . . . which is fine," I qualify. "You're busy. I'm busy. There's so much going on. New, exciting classes, friends, boyfriends." We're leading two different lives now. When did we stop sharing with each other? "Can't we just be happy for each other?"

She softens. "Of course we can." She peels back the covers, and I slide in next to her. We sit against the headboard. She fiddles with the sheet. "I'm always happy for you. But everything feels like it's changing. I don't want us to lose sight of each other."

"Me either," I say, and mean it.

"Truce hug?" Noora asks.

I open my arms, and we squeeze each other. We chat for an hour about everything and nothing, and I am feeling as close to her as I have ever been. We're starting to doze off when fat white pieces begin to drift from the sky. "It's snowing again."

I rise and go to the window. There is no question about it—this night is magical. I think that's what best friends do, sprinkle fairy dust on your life. Noora is behind me. We watch for a while as it piles up. The tree branches hang with ice that glitters in the moonlight like spun sugar.

"Hey, Izumi," Noora says. "Just remember when you're asking what Japan wants from you, make sure you ask what you want from yourself, too. Don't bury who you are to become who others think you should be."

My hands ball into fists. It's not that I'm angry. I'm resolute. "I think they're one and the same."

"Okay," she says firmly. She pinches the fabric of my robe. "This is nice."

"The Duchess of Cambridge gave it to my cousins. They let me have it since it's from two seasons ago."

"The Duchess of Cambridge, as in Kate Middleton?"

"The very one," I say.

She clucks her tongue. "To think I felt so fancy when I bought my prom dress from Macy's."

I snake an arm around her, and we lean against each other. I always loved that our hair was the same color. Inky. Black as night. And when we put our heads close together, you couldn't see where I began, and she ended. The colors are different now, but it doesn't matter. Noora and I are evergreen, a single note that will always resolve itself.

The next morning, we ride the subway. I don a hat to go incognito and make Reina dress in plain clothes. Reina is shocked when we don't get off anywhere. Noora is content to ride the rails along with the sleepy, quiet passengers. The thrill is in the discovery, not the destination, she says.

Time flies, and a few hours later, I am hugging Noora outside the palace and saying goodbye. "I'll die if you leave," I declare.

"Dramatic," Noora says back, but she holds on to me for a minute longer than necessary. Her luggage is loaded. The trunk is slammed shut, and a butler holds open the car door—a shiny black SUV on loan from my father. We linger.

"Let me know how everything goes, okay?" she says, worry in her tone.

The Imperial Household Council will be voting any day now on my parents' marriage. I think of Akiko and Noriko. Of Eriku. Of Mom and Dad. Of the acceptance letter to University of Tokyo tucked away in my nightstand drawer. I've done all I can.

"I will." We hug one more time. "I want the family, Noora," I say into her shoulder. I want my parents married. I want to be a unit. Undivided.

"Family is what you make it," she says, releasing me.

I sigh instead of disagreeing. As she climbs into the vehicle, I press a note in her palm. A waka poem I penned for her.

You and me, we are
hair and gum, peanut butter
and jelly, Post-it
notes and paper, tires against
a road, we stick together.

Christmas Day, Mom and I blast carols through the palace. We make a mess in the kitchen, making a turkey and stuffing, whipped mashed potatoes, and a green bean casserole. Last, we roll out dough and bake fresh apple pies. Mom's cheeks are dusted with flour, and her eyes are bright and shiny.

A few hours later, the table is a wreck, plates scraped clean of food, half-empty glasses, silverware glinting in the firelight. But we wait to clear it. Instead, we move to the fire, our bellies near bursting.

Dad hands Mom an envelope, and she tears into it with a quizzical smile. "What on earth?" she asks, staring at the folded piece of paper. "Architectural designs?"

He nods. "I'm renovating the garden and palace to include a state-of-the-art composting system and rainwater-collecting stations."

"Mak," she says. Then she leaps across crushed wrapping paper to hug him, and peppers kisses on his face.

He chuckles, smoothing her hair. "You like it?"

"Love it," she says. Then he whispers something in her ear that makes her blush hard and giggle furiously.

I'm next. Mom and Dad give me a University of Tokyo

sweatshirt. I peer down at my Mount Shasta High School T-shirt and say, "Is this your not-so-subtle hint that it's time to retire this?" The hem is fraying, and there is a small hole in the armpit.

"You're on to bigger and better things now," Mom says.

"Open the next one," Dad encourages.

It is large and wrapped to perfection in furoshiki tied in a gorgeous knot on top. I shed the cloth. The box says *Louis Vuitton*, and inside is a backpack with their famous checkerboard pattern.

"For school," Dad says. "Your cousins helped pick it out. Apparently, it's a must-have on campus."

"This is way too nice," I say.

They have a few more gifts for me. It's a university theme: pencils, notebooks, a brand-new laptop. On the outside, at least, I'm totally prepared for university.

The best gift of all comes from the grand chamberlain. He knocks and enters, snow melting on his jacket. "Extreme pardon, Your Highnesses, Ms. Tanaka. We have received a message from the Imperial Household Council."

We freeze in our spots.

"They were set to meet tomorrow," Dad says.

"They had planned to, but the prime minister had a last-minute scheduling conflict. They moved the meeting to this afternoon. It was unanimous. All ten agreed to the marriage. Congratulations." He bows.

We sit for a moment in pure disbelief. Happy tears track down my cheeks, and Mom's, too. Dad grabs a bottle of champagne and pops the cork. Toasts and lots of hugs go around. Later that night, we watch *Miracle on 34th Street.* A hazy glow of happiness surrounds us.

I text Eriku from my corner of the couch.

Me

Engagement approved.

I follow with a string of party hats, champagne, and streamer emojis. Eriku answers right away with a picture of two dogs hugging.

Eriku

I knew it would go your way. Do
you want to know what Jerry
Garcia said about love?

I text him a thumbs-down.

Near the end of the movie, Mom falls asleep. She snores. Dad watches her instead of the television. I go back to the movie. It's all been worth it.

TOKYO TATTLER

Crown Prince officially engaged

December 26, 2022

While most of Tokyo is eating KFC and quiet this time of year, the Imperial Household Council held a secret meeting Christmas Day. Their topic: a second vote on the marriage between Hanako Tanaka and Crown Prince Toshihito. We'll be hearing wedding bells soon. The council voted unanimously in favor of the engagement.

"While certain members wish the Crown Prince had chosen someone younger and from a similar background, The Crown Prince has made his choice clear," a palace insider says.

Earlier this year, the couple was under much scrutiny. Critics worried about Ms. Tanaka's pedigree or lack thereof. They were fearful of her environmental positions, political leanings, and commitment to her own career. Growing up in the United States, she had no knowledge of the imperial family's internal workings. The Imperial Household Council used her daughter as a template for how Ms. Tanaka might adjust to royal life. It is well known that HIH Princess Izumi's entrance into high society was rocky, from her sensational affair with her imperial guard to her delay in choosing a university or course of study, with a million missteps in between.

But since, the mother-daughter duo has turned things around.

HIH Princess Izumi has forged a serious relationship with Eriku Nakamura, heir to the Nakamura shipping dynasty. "The Imperial Household Agency is very pleased by their connection," our palace insider states. "They would love to see a union between the two but understand that may be premature." In addition, the princess has recently announced her acceptance to University of Tokyo with coursework planned in botany. In a public statement she made to *Vogue* Japan, she said, "I am honored to be following in my father's footsteps and attending the same university he did. I am also honored to be following in my mother's footsteps with my major." The princess also has a new hobby, volunteering with the Red Cross.

Ms. Tanaka has undergone a makeover of sorts as well. "Ms. Tanaka has been very committed to her studies with the empress," the Imperial Household Agency said when asked about Ms. Tanaka's recent activities. We managed to catch Ms. Tanaka waiting for the Crown Prince outside the imperial palace after he finished a jog in the nearby Chiyoda Ward (see picture). Ms. Tanaka was patient and elegant in a winter white pantsuit. Perhaps she knew what we didn't, that a wedding would be in her future sooner than later.

27

The Christmas tree is gone; the pine needles are swept up and deposited into trash cans. The happy glow fades, and schedules resume. A barrage of wedding gifts is delivered to the palace, and it's a practice in maze navigation getting out the door. There is a paulownia wood bedding chest, paintings, and silk tapestries featuring storks to represent fertility, then an actual fertility deity statue. And thousands of cards, congratulating my mother.

Ms. Komura, Mom's demure lady-in-waiting, is now permanently on loan from the empress. Mom can't turn a corner without being peppered by questions. "What kind of flowers are you thinking?" Ms. Komura asks early one morning. We sit in the living room. Catalogs of the imperial jewels are open on a tufted ottoman. Mom must decide what tiara she will wear on her wedding day. Will it be a diamond floral tiara featuring chrysanthemums or a tiara with diamond scrolls and a matching necklace?

Mom lights up. "Orchids. I love orchids."

I nod eagerly in agreement.

Ms. Komura's tiny bow-shaped mouth dips into a frown. "Orchids aren't in season. We'd have to have them flown in or specially grown. The public may frown upon such an expense."

Mom's brow crinkles. "I can't have orchids?"

Ms. Komura shakes her head. "I don't think so." She jots a note down on her phone. I've never seen someone's thumbs move as fast as Ms. Komura's. Her phone rings. "Sumimasen. I have to take this. When I return, we'll schedule your fitting for the jūnihitoe."

"Jūnihitoe?"

Ms. Komura smiles. "Hai. Your dress for the ceremony. You'll have two. The traditional twelve-layered garment, then a white gown." Her phone rings again. "I really must take this." She scurries off.

Moms sits for a moment, a little stunned in the wake of the tornado known as Ms. Komura.

I scoot closer to her. "You okay with all that?"

Her brow puckers. "I suppose so. I mean flowers, the dress, those are small things," she says. "I guess if I had my way, it would be a touch simpler. But all this is a means to end, right?"

"Right," I affirm, rubbing her back and giving her my best supportive smile.

Eriku accompanies me to the emperor's year-end luncheon the next day.

"You might be sitting in the same seat where George H. W. Bush vomited in the lap of the prime minister just as wagyu beef was being served," I tell Eriku. He's my date, all turned out in a custom suit.

Eriku touches his chest. "And all my life I thought learning and music were my passions . . . but this is truly life goals. It's an honor."

I grin. There's always something about the end of the year. Though New Year's Eve here isn't the same as in the States. In Japan, families quietly gather to clean and make preparations for New Year's Day. There is noise around midnight but not fireworks or lips smacking. Rather, it's the sound of bells rung 108 times, a Buddhist tradition to rid humans of earthly desires. I like that. The promise of starting fresh. A slate wiped clean. A heart more open.

Dessert—chocolate chiffon cake dusted with powdered sugar—is placed in front of us. While we eat, a world-renowned violinist plays. Soon enough, tables are cleared and mingling commences. I catch Eriku in conversation with the prime minister. He bows low to me. "Congratulations, Princess," he says. "On both your parents' upcoming marriage and your admission to University of Tokyo." I thank him, and he turns to Eriku. "Please thank your uncle for his phone call the other day. I enjoyed catching up with him. It is always nice to talk with someone who has been in the trenches, so to speak." Eriku promises to do so, and the prime minister bids us farewell.

"Your cheeks are pink," Eriku says, loud enough to be heard over the crowd. We're near a set of doors and he leads me through them to go outside.

"What was that all about? I didn't know you and the prime minister were such good friends," I say with a mystified smile as we slip farther away from the building.

We stop in a section of grass, near a heater where the snow has melted away. Trees block us from the rest of the party. "Oh, that," Eriku says. "Remember I said I had a former prime minister in my family?"

Warmth from the heater radiates and seeps through my dress—light blue velvet with a square neckline. I even have a little matching clutch. "Vaguely."

He steps forward, leans down so we're almost nose to nose. "Well, I may have called him and asked him to put in a good word about you and your mom with the current PM."

"What?" I stare up at him, my eyes saucer-wide. "You did that? Why?"

He straightens but stays close. "For you, of course," he says, then shrugs. "It's not that big of a deal."

It is a big deal. At least to me. But not to Eriku. He was born into this world. A favor is his to ask, a privilege. I don't begrudge him for it. But I see. I see how fortunate I am. How lucky. "Eriku." My voice is thick, my chest cluttered with emotions—sincerity, gratitude, and affection. I bow my head. "Arigatō."

"Like I said, it's nothing." He places a single peck, soft and sweet, on the cheek. "Akemashite omedetō gozaimasu." *Happy New Year*, he says, voice raspy and lush. Eyes locked on me.

"Happy New Year," I say quietly, gravel in my throat.

I consider the lines of his face, the way his mouth has a perpetual upward curve, how his lower lip is slightly larger than the top.

"Izumi," he says, loosening his hold. "You know . . . You know you've changed my life." He shakes his head as if in a daze. He takes my hand, places it on his chest, right over his beating heart. "Because of you . . . I feel so different now. My father hasn't changed, but I feel like *I'm* changing. I've thought about what you said. It's okay to want his approval as long as it doesn't mean sacrificing my happiness, and I'm thinking about making some changes. Maybe moving out, or . . . I don't know. I just know I want something else. And that's not all. . . . I mean, you've introduced me to the Grateful Dead. . . ."

I stifle a laugh and curl my fingers into his shirt, thinking I might hold on to him forever. "I can't tell you how much that means. It's the same for me, too. You've changed me."

It's true. I am different now. Months ago, I wasn't sure what I wanted. School or gap year. But now . . . now, I've traveled so far down the princess path. Accomplished and seen so much. When I look back, I was afraid, I think. Afraid of failing, of not living up to all the expectations. And Eriku helped me accomplish all of what I set out to do. I can't thank him enough.

Eriku bites his lip and lowers his head. His approach closer is slow and lazy. He rests his forehead against mine. There isn't any music, but we sway. Although it's probably what Eriku's soul is made of . . . inky blue notes. "Izumi, Izumi, Izumi," he says again and again and again, my name a song in his mouth. Our lips touch. I press into him, and the world fades away.

"Izumi?"

A voice slices through the white noise. Recognizing it, I break away from Eriku. Slowly, I turn my head. . . . "Akio?" I ask hazily. Is this a dream? He's wearing a plain black suit. I know the feel of it under my palms, had kissed him in it when he was my guard. I step toward Akio, my hands open, reality sharpening. "What are you doing? How did you get here?" I stumble over my words, reeling with shock. Still, I draw closer to him. It's weird seeing him right now. In the stark light of day. In front of me.

I know Eriku is behind me, but I can't turn; I am falling too deep into Akio's eyes. How they glitter with misery and darkness.

Hurt is etched all over Akio's face. So much pain it will give me nightmares. He opens and closes his hands in a helpless gesture. "I'm sorry to barge in like this. I saw the papers, your parents' engagement," he says in a fragmented burst. His brows draw in. "I'm doing this wrong. Look . . . may we speak?" His eyes narrow on Eriku, and his voice becomes hard. "Alone?"

I look back at Eriku, unsure. Questions nag at me. What is Akio doing here? Why do I care? And what are all these emotions bubbling up all of a sudden? I shake my head. "I don't know—"

"Five minutes. That's all I ask," Akio says flatly. "I know you don't owe me anything, but . . . hear me out? Please." The way he phrases that last word. *Please.* So wild and with such quiet desperation, it yanks at me.

Eriku clears his throat. "The man has something on his mind." He steps forward, takes my hands, and kisses me on the cheek. "I'll be right inside." He wanders off, snow crunching beneath his heels as he disappears.

I shiver, and Akio says, "You're cold."

He starts to strip off his jacket, but I put out a hand. "No," I say, anger curled around the one syllable.

He flinches and shrugs the jacket back on. Then he lets out a long breath. "I'm making a mess of this."

"What *is* this?" I scowl.

He hangs his head and says, "Machigaeta." Then his eyes rise to mine. "I made a mistake," he says louder.

I clutch my chest and stagger back. Months ago, I remember holding my phone, wishing he'd text or call. Trying to manifest those four little words into reality. *I made a mistake.*

"I never stopped thinking about you. I can't stop thinking about you. About us. I know you've moved on, but—"

I snort. "You've moved on, too."

He looks at me with unflinching eyes. "I did not."

"I saw you in the papers with a female cadet, holding hands." Tears rise. "I tried to call you after, but you didn't answer."

He huffs out a foggy breath; his muscles tense under his jacket. "A car was coming. The tabloids very cleverly cropped out that part of the picture. I was pulling her out of the way. As for your phone call," he says, "I'm sorry I didn't answer. It's my biggest regret. I sat there watching your name flash against the screen. I didn't know you had seen the papers. Your parents weren't engaged yet. I thought I was doing what was best. . . ."

Anger replaces sadness. *He White-Fanged you.* "Very noble of you."

He stares up at the gray sky. "It's not noble. I've been a coward."

I have the distinct sense of whiplash. My heart sinks to my stomach. "What?" I ask, my voice a reedy whisper.

His expression morphs with anger. "What I said about leaving you . . . doing what was best . . . it was true, but I was also afraid. Of not being good enough, of never being good enough. Can't you see? You are a princess. I'm just a civil servant. I was trying to save you a lifetime of that, but myself too," he spits out.

I cringe. "I made you feel that way?"

"No," he answers, low and scratchy. "Never. But others did."

I nod slowly, knowing this to be true and having witnessed it firsthand. The papers. The guide on my tour of University of Tokyo. *How could I have expected to stay in your golden orbit forever?*

"I've been running scared." My chest squeezes at his words. "But I don't want to be afraid anymore. I don't want to let others' opinions keep us apart. That's why I'm here now. I should have come sooner. Seeing your parents' engagement gave me the courage, that's all. But I've come back."

The dam on my tears bursts. I swallow rapidly to keep from crying out. Akio is in front of me, taking my elbows, touching my cheek, holding me gently. "Radish, I still care about you. I still want to be with you. Is there still a place in your heart for me?"

Blood rushes in my ears, the sound of a wave toppling me over. "Eriku" is all I say. But in my mind's eye, I see him. The laughing boy who has made me insanely happy.

Akio shifts and glares for a moment, then his scowl lifts. "I know you're with him. I didn't think this would be easy." He steps back and thinks. Restrategizes. "You need time. I've surprised you. I understand. I'll leave you for now . . .

but Izumi, I'm not going *anywhere*. I'm willing to fight for you." He kisses my cheek. The opposite one Eriku just grazed. "I'll call you."

I blink, and Akio is gone. The warmth of his touch bleeds away. Minutes tick by. But I can't move. Hot tears streak down my cheeks. *Akio came back.* He was right here in the garden with me. And now he wants a second chance. A ragged breath shudders through me. I've moved on. Haven't I? Guilt stabs at me. Is it possible to care equally for two people? My insides cave in. The space around me seems to shrink smaller and smaller.

My back turned to the palace, I don't sense his approach.

"Didn't think I'd find you crying," Eriku says quietly, circling until he's in front of me.

"It's not . . . I'm not . . . I-I'm . . ." I stutter, not sure what I'm trying to say. Why I'm bothering to deny it. I'm a mess. I thought I might never see Akio again. Thought I'd locked him away in a chest, let him sink to the bottom of my heart.

Eriku searches my face, frowning deeply at what he sees. "What did he say to you? Did he hurt you? Should I notify my second to prepare for pistols at dawn?" he jokes with a ghost of a smile.

I swipe at my nose. "He wants me back. He's asked for another chance. Says he's going to fight for me."

His Adam's apple bounces. "And what do you want?"

"I don't know." I shake my head. "I'm confused," I whisper.

"I see," he says.

Dread builds in the back of my throat. I'm on the precipice of losing Eriku. "No, you don't." I stare up at him wide-eyed. "I thought my feelings for Akio had faded. They haven't. But it's equal to what I feel for you. You've made me so happy. You've made me feel so alive. I cannot imagine my life without you . . . or without Akio," I finish. An ache forms in my temples.

"Okay," he says calmly. I shift my focus to him, and his eyes are squeezed shut. His hands balled into fists. "I am not confused. I do know what I want. And I won't settle for less. I've done that with my father. I won't with you. I deserve to be first in someone's heart." He pauses, opens his eyes.

"I understand," I say. Eriku is making the decision for me. It's kind of a relief.

"I don't think you do." His eyes are strong and steady—a fortress. "I deserve to be first in someone's heart. I'm going to show you *I am* first in yours. Akio wants to fight for you. I will too. I'll be in touch soon," he promises. My chest constricts.

And Eriku walks away, in the opposite direction of Akio. Leaving me stuck in the middle.

I cry myself to sleep. Many tears soak the pillow. Every time I close my eyes, I see Akio and Eriku. Memories swirl. Akio thumbing my cheeks while I sat on his lap. *I like it better when you win.* Eriku pushing a piece of candy across the table to me. *Scents and flavors create specialized neurological pathways.* Akio dancing with me in the living room. Eriku lying next to me in the planetarium . . . I am in turmoil. Eriku or Akio? I know one thing for sure. A heart divided cannot stand.

28

I don't tell Mom about what's happening with Eriku and Akio. She doesn't need that weighing her down. She doesn't need to worry about me. Instead, I paste on my happiest facade even as Akio texts me waka poems:

Akio

I am headed back to Nara.

Akio

I'm sorry I left
you. Two times I've made you cry.
What happened to my
promise to take your sorrows,
my vow to bury them deep?

Akio

In Nara now.

Akio

Ten p.m., I saw
you cal. I didn't answer.
Foolish me. I thought
it better to be lonely,
than be loved and insecure.

Even as Eriku sends gifts. Flowers. Candy. Grateful Dead dancing bears. A hand-painted portrait of Momo-chan and Tamagotchi lying in front of a blazing fireplace on a fur rug.

The palace becomes even busier. The traditional engagement ceremony, the Nōsai-no-Gi, is held. Because my mother has no close living relatives, the Imperial Household Agency finds distant cousins in Japan who are presented with gifts—two large fish, six bottles of sake, and five bolts of silk. Then my father issued his formal request for marriage, which my mother humbly accepted. It hallmarks the official engagement of my parents.

There is an engagement banquet where we stuff ourselves on smoked salmon, sea scallops, and strawberry bavarois. I miss Eriku's presence, him laughing at my elbow and cracking jokes. But if I'm honest with myself, I miss Akio, too. His dry humor, his steady warmth. I am a mess. A heart-wrenching, brain-confused mess.

Crates of 1982 Chateau Mouton Rothschild wine arrive for the wedding. The empress declared my parents should be married as soon as possible in the spring—no reason to let the Imperial Household Council delay things any longer. The papers publish stories about my parents. *The two are so in love, they can't wait for their happily ever after to begin.*

The wedding is two months away when Mom is fitted for the sumptuous twelve-layer gown she'll be married in: the jūnihitoe. The same pair of seamstresses who fitted us for the garden party return. The first seamstress distributes the twelve layers throughout the room, each one a different color and textile. "Weighs twenty kilograms," she explains.

"Forty-four pounds," Mom says, twisting the ring on her left hand. The Japanese don't do engagement rings, but the empress gifted my mother an emerald the size of a cherry tomato.

I toss her an encouraging smile. "Might need to start lifting weights."

"First layer," the seamstress says. "Please remove your robe."

The seamstresses work in tandem. Noora texts me, and I answer her. When I look back up, they are three layers in, and Mom is sweating. "You okay?" I whisper. "Want me to get you some water?"

"Dame. No drinking in the dress," the seamstress interjects. The whole getup costs more than three hundred thousand dollars.

"I'm okay, honey," she promises with a thin smile.

I move so I'm in front of her. "Want to go over my course schedule with me?" I ask, bringing it up on my phone. "I'm trying to decide what classes to take."

"Sure," she says, heavy-lidded eyes focusing on me.

"Obviously, I am going to start with some biology coursework," I say to make her happy. Even reading the description makes me sleepy.

She regards me, her expression wary. "Do they have a course on native plants? I enjoyed that as a freshman. Lots of fieldwork, if I remember correctly." Her voice is a little less shaky now.

"Let me look." I make a big deal of scrolling through the catalog.

The fourth and fifth layers go on. Mom stands still, and

her chest rises and falls rapidly. "How much longer?" she asks.

"Almost done," the seamstress reassures her. "Next layers are quicker."

"It's really heavy," Mom says.

Ms. Komura buzzes in. She bows, quick and efficient. "Sumimasen, Hanako-san. A few items while you're still." She smiles. "I've emailed you the wedding week schedule. You will see a press conference on the itinerary. I've included another attachment with speaking points. You will most likely be asked about your position in America."

"My position?" Mom parrots. "I've taken a leave of absence."

Ms. Komura bobs her head. "I am aware, but of course, now that you are marrying the Crown Prince, you will need to resign."

Mom seems taken aback. "Oh, I hadn't considered that. . . ."

"Hold still," one of the seamstresses says, fiddling with her collar, making sure the outer layer is flat. Mom goes quiet while they finish up and step back, bodies parting like curtains so Mom can view herself in the mirror. The whole look, alternating shrouds of reds, purples, and yellows, is opulent and excessive. It is topped off with a green brocade coat. The garment hasn't changed in one thousand years.

"Oh," Mom says, trying to place an arm to her chest, but the sleeves weigh her down.

"Don't touch," a seamstress chides. "Sawaranaide kudasai. Oils from your fingers will ruin the dress."

Mom's hands flutter uselessly to her sides.

"What do you think?" the same seamstress asks.

"Kirei," the other seamstress says.

"Very beautiful," Ms. Komura says. "Now, about your job. I realize you've taken a leave of absence. But you'll have to pen your letter of resignation soon."

Mom sways. "I'm sorry. . . . I'm . . . I'm so warm." Her eyes flick to me. They are feverish, bright, and remind me of a rabbit I once saw in the woods behind our house, its leg caught in a trap. I ran all the way home. Jones helped me free it, but it stuck around, and we fed it field grass and named it Sugar Magnolia.

"Are you okay?" I don't recall moving, but suddenly I am in front of Mom, holding her clammy cheeks.

"Yes, no." Her voice is paper-thin. "I'm having trouble catching my breath. I think I'm having a panic attack." Her chest hitches and she curls her shoulders, hunching over. My hands fall away. "I need this off."

I glance around. The seamstresses are frozen, twin confused smiles on their faces. Mom's movements are shaky as she strips off the green outer layer, letting it pool at her feet. She's draws in a breath, each inhale and exhale more frantic than the last. She starts working at the belt.

One of the seamstresses says, "Stop. You'll ruin it."

I jump into action. Batting Mom's hands away, I undo the obi belt. Together we strip the layers from her shoulders until we come to the hakama ties. But they're too tight. "Help me," I beg. Ms. Komura is useless, stock-still with her phone in hand. One of the seamstresses brushes me aside and deftly undoes the knots. While she works, I reassure Mom, murmuring things like *You're okay, just breathe, I am here.* Somewhere I hear the echo of my own childhood. Of my mother's voice when I skinned my knees or fell from the monkey bars, knocking the wind out of me.

Mom is in her underwear now. She's still shaking. There are indents on her belly from where the hakama was tied too tightly and cut into her skin. The jūnihitoe crumples at her feet like shattered jewels.

"Mom." I catch her eyes, and they are wild and frightened.

"Zoom Zoom," she whispers, body sagging. "I can't stay here."

"Okay, okay," I soothe—hot tears streaking down my face. I swipe them furiously away.

"Please," she says. "Get me out of here." Every line in her face is etched in what I can only describe as anguish.

"You can't leave," Ms. Komura says, reanimating, but I ignore her.

My chest aches. When the rabbit felt better, it dashed off into the woods, taking refuge in a hollowed log. "Okay," I say again. "Okay." I can't stop repeating it. I'm not sure if the word is more for her or for me.

I help her into her own clothes. Pushing her limbs through a T-shirt and sweatpants, it's like dressing a doll. She is shaking so hard.

"Mariko!" I yell as I snake an arm around Mom and frantically charge with her down the hall.

"I am calling the grand chamberlain," Ms. Komura says behind me.

Mariko appears, eyes widening when she sees Mom. "What happened? Ms. Tanaka, are you all right?"

Mom hides her face in her hands. "I don't want anyone to see me."

"It's just Mariko," I say calmly. "She's going to stay with you while I get a car for us."

Mariko opens her hands. "You stay with your mother. I'll find a car." She dashes off. In no time, an imperial vehicle idles at the curb. A guard steps forward to open the door, and I help Mom into the car. She curls onto the seat, a crumpled piece of paper. Another guard advances to the driver's seat, but I stop him. "No," I say firmly. "Just Reina."

The guard looks to Reina for permission. She nods, and he backs away. I climb in after Mom and promise to call Mariko soon. Then we're gone, Reina in the driver's seat.

"It's going to be fine," I say to Mom as we whip through the streets, destination unknown. It's close to Valentine's Day, and stores feature chocolates and hearts.

I can't take her back to the palace. She won't want to face anyone right now. And I can't take her anywhere public; no hotels, either. I need somewhere quiet, private, where she will have space, calm, peace. My mind races, turning over the impossibilities before finally, I have an idea. I tell Reina where to go, then relax back into the seat.

"Don't worry." I hold her close. "I'm going to take care of you."

29

"Here you go." Akiko sets down a silver tray laden with a teapot and cups on the glass-and-gold coffee table. Mom is on the cream couch, legs curled underneath her, cheek turned away. She hasn't spoken since we arrived. There are no more tears, but there is a blankness to her that's even more concerning—she is detached, hollow, removed. Noriko hovers nearby. Their apartment was the only safe place I could think of to bring Mom.

"Thanks," I say.

"We sent most of the staff away," Akiko says. "They have all signed NDAs and can be trusted, but our mom never likes having too many people around when she isn't feeling well."

There is some symmetry between the twins' mother and mine. Princess Midori was hounded by the press; she buckled under the weight of all the imperial expectations. What other choice did she have but to withdraw?

Noriko steps forward and speaks very, very quietly. "We also have a physician on call, just in case."

At this, Mom starts. "No doctors."

"We'll be okay," I tell Akiko and Noriko and swallow against a lump in my throat. I kind of love them—a lot. Mom trembles, but I think it's all that adrenaline still coursing through her body. "Would you mind giving us a moment?"

"Of course not," Akiko says. "Let us know if you need anything."

As soon as we're alone, I busy myself pulling a blush-pink cashmere throw from the end of the couch and draping it around Mom's shoulders. Then I pour her a cup of tea.

Her hands tremble as she accepts the cup and saucer from me, but she doesn't drink. Instead, she places it on the end table. Her color still hasn't returned. Her complexion is waxy.

She rubs her eyes.

"Mom," I venture. "Maybe we should call a doctor."

"Honey, it's fine," she says. "It's just . . . it's been a rough couple of months. And Ms. Komura mentioning resigning from my job was a tipping point for me. Subconsciously I knew I might not be able to keep it but . . . I love my job. It was too much, all at once."

Months? I watch her and wonder why I didn't see this sooner. How tired she is. How she's been withdrawing, letting Ms. Komura make decisions for her.

The answer is easy. I was too busy looking at her through a kaleidoscope of hearts and weddings and second chances. Too caught up in my determination to succeed at my goal of getting her engaged, of obtaining the family I always wanted. I didn't stop to think about what *she* wanted. I thought I knew. But we haven't been talking as much recently—*really* talking.

She inhales and rests her head back on the couch. "I'm not sure I can live this way."

"How?" I ask dumbly, still trying to catch up with the situation.

She levels me with a steady gaze and purses her lips. "Zoom Zoom," she says. "I'm miserable, and I've been keeping it from you because I was trying to protect you."

"What? Why?"

Mom smiles gently, her brow heavy with sadness. "Honey, I know you want your father and me to get married. It's what you've always wanted, even before you knew who your father was. This is your dream."

"It's not your dream?"

She sighs. "Your father is my dream. Not the princess part."

She fixes me with a look, forehead creasing. "I don't know who I am anymore. That's the problem. I've lost myself."

"I've been keeping things from you, too," I say before I can stop myself. "So much has happened. I don't know why I didn't come to you." I swallow against a flurry of conflicting emotions. Could Mom and I be in similar positions? Doing things to make other people happy? "Akio and I overheard a conversation between the chamberlains and steward—"

"Wait. What?" Mom lasers in on me.

"Back when you and Dad were first engaged. Remember that day in the office, when you learned the Imperial House Council conducted a pre-vote?" I wait for her to nod before going on. "When the chamberlains and steward left, Akio and I listened to their conversation in the driveway. They talked about how my relationship and my indecision on whether to go to college or not were affecting the council's poor opinion of you." Her brow furrows. I can't stop. The floodgates have been opened. I get it all out. How Akio broke up with me. How I started fake-dating Eriku. "All of it. Applying for university. Majoring in botany . . . I thought—I thought that's what I had to do so you and Dad could get married," I stammer on the verge of tears. I finish with the end-of-year luncheon, and Eriku and Akio asking me to love only one of them. "I've made a mess of things," I finish, feeling better having gotten it all off my chest.

"Oh, honey," she says with a somber frown. "You did all that for me? For us?"

I nod, perching on my knees. "Of course I did. I love you," I say. "I want you to be happy."

Mom gives a derisive snort. "Look at us." She leans her head against the couch. Her eyes are filled with liquid, too. But it's not from panic. Now she's just sad. "How did we get here?" I recognize the question as rhetorical and don't answer. "I don't think I am meant to be a princess. How am I going to spend the rest of my life doing what others tell me to?" Her hands clench into feeble fists. "It's like I am participating in my own dissolution. Seeing my life played out in the tabloids." All too well, I remember my stance on the press. *Did I die? Did someone I love die?* Not exactly. But the room is filled with heaviness of grief—the weight of a spirit succumbing.

"So you don't want to marry Dad?" I ask, my voice small. You never think of your parent as a real person. At least, I haven't that much. I always believed my mom was impenetrable. Forget superheroes. She is the one made of steel. But now I see. She is a woman first, susceptible to pain like everyone else.

She shakes her head. "I want to marry him. I love your father, I always will, but I don't know if it's enough. How do

I explain?" She pauses. "When I found out I was pregnant with you, I was so afraid. Afraid of what the imperial family might do to you, worried a life in the clouds would mean you'd never touch the ground. Does that make sense?"

I nod gravely. "It does."

"But I realize now that I was afraid for myself, too. I always thought I was so strong, but I'm not. . . . . It's too much pressure. And I have given all I have to give right now." Her chin trembles, and twin tears track down her cheeks.

I understand. The press and the Imperial Household Council made her feel like she was worth a little less because of her age, because of her job, because of the way she grew up. When someone tells you over and over again there is something wrong with you, pretty soon you start to believe it, and then you'll do anything to fix it.

Automatically, I think of Akio. *I've been a coward.* But that's not true. It's not cowardly to be vulnerable. It's actually the bravest thing you can do. There are too many rules. Who made them up? Why should we follow them?

My phone rings, the word *Dad* flashing on the screen. "It's Dad."

"I'm not ready to talk to him," she says with a sniffle.

My lips twitch, and I click off my phone. There is a large television on the wall. "Do you want to watch a movie or something? Forget about it all for a while?"

Mom says sure, and she opens the wrap, inviting me in. I go to her, and she hugs me with one arm. "I don't want you to worry," she says.

"Kind of impossible not to," I say back. I twiddle my thumbs. She really scared me.

"I'm sorry," she says. "I don't want you to sacrifice anything else for me anymore. You got it? That's my job."

"Got it," I say, laying my head on her chest. Her breaths are steady and slow. "But you shouldn't have to sacrifice yourself, either."

"Thank you, honey," she says into my hair.

Akiko and Noriko have all of Audrey Hepburn's movies. With the press of a controller, I dial down the lights and switch on *Roman Holiday*. It's at the top of their watch list under "Favorites." During the film, I wonder about Akiko and Noriko's mom. How many times has she lost herself in a movie about a princess who escapes her rigidly controlled life for the day? My bet is a lot.

Forty-eight hours pass. Akiko and Noriko stay with us, for the most part. We spend our time watching their entire Audrey Hepburn catalog. We cook together. Play cards. Mom wanted to disappear. And I admit, I was on board. She's not the only one who is hiding. Up here, in this tower, reality is on pause. I try not to think about Eriku. *I deserve to be first in someone's heart.* Or of Akio. *I still care about you. . . . Is there still a place in your heart for me?*

In the late afternoon, my phone rings. Dad again. He's been calling nonstop. We're in the kitchen. Mom has a rolling pin and is showing the twins how to make pie. I don't have to say who it is.

I hold the phone, letting it ring and ring. "I'm not ready," she says into the pie crust. Akiko lays her hand over Mom's. The two have struck a bond. It's not as evident with Akiko, but she and Mom are both natural caretakers. I see the way Akiko hovers over Noriko, their mother. The way Mom hovers over me. Yeah, they get each other.

"I'm going to talk to him," I say.

Mom ducks her head—silent permission.

I slip away into the hall. "Hi," I answer.

"Izumi," he wrenches out. "Finally." I'm quiet for a moment. "Izumi," he says, insistent. Louder. "Where are you? Are you with your mother? Are you okay? Is Hanako okay?" He sighs with frustration. "I don't understand. I'm going out of my mind with worry."

I lean against the wall, letting my toes curl into the plush carpet. "I'm with Mom. And she's okay. Physically, at least. I mean, I think." She's eating and smiling. But wears her sadness like a shroud. She's like spun glass—still, beautiful, and so incredibly fragile.

"I don't understand," he says again, voice tight.

Did you know most students buy their own textbooks? My chamberlains had the authors annotate and personally deliver them to me, my father said in the garden before proposing to Mom. I tilt my head, fold my hair behind my ear. "Dad," I say carefully. "This has all been a lot for her."

"I know it is. But once the wedding is over—"

"I don't think it's just the wedding," I interject. "It's the whole life. Not being able to make your own choices. You grew up in this world. You know what to do. How to navigate the narrow passageways of culture and etiquette, and expectations. But Mom doesn't . . . and I'm not even sure she wants to. The gowns, the social engagements, they aren't her."

"Are you saying she doesn't want to marry me?" His voice is lower now. Bewildered. Sad.

"She loves you," is all I say.

He inhales. "But not the institution."

I frown. "I'm sorry."

After a while, he speaks again. "Izumi," he says, even and smooth. "Tell me where you are."

I shake my head. "I can't. I promised."

"I can probably find out," he throws down, frustrated, then softens to a more persuasive tone. "But I'd rather you tell me. Let me come speak with your mother. Let me make this right."

I sigh and rest my cheek against the wall. "We're with Akiko and Noriko. . . ." I tell him where because we're family and we belong together. He promises to be here soon. We hang up, and I hope I did the right thing.

The whole apartment smells like apple pie. We pile onto the couch with blankets and pillows, plates in hand, to watch *Roman Holiday* again. The twins know the dialogue by heart and mouth the words, even copying some of Audrey's mannerisms, touching their hair when she does, smiling when she laughs.

Near the end, when Princess Ann is greeting the press, gazing up at Gregory Peck and saying she is so happy, a shadow darkens the doorway.

"Hanako," Dad says. We whip around and stare at him. He inclines his head. "May I come in?"

"How did you find me?" Mom asks. So much lies

between them, so many unspoken things—it stretches the air taut.

The credits roll, and Akiko flicks on the lights.

"I told him," I say. I blink at Mom. "Sorry." Her mouth thins, but I can see in her eyes, she's not angry. "He's worried," I quietly say to Mom. "But we don't have to leave."

"You can stay here for as long as you want," Akiko says. "She can stay here," Akiko tells my father.

"Of course." His voice comes out thick. "I'd never make Hanako do anything she didn't want to." He may be speaking to Akiko, but he only has eyes for my mother. "Can we talk?"

Mom shifts. "Okay. Okay, sure."

"We'll give you guys a moment," I say, shuffling out with Akiko and Noriko. I pause in the hallway. I press a finger to my lips, telling Akiko and Noriko to stay quiet. We crowd around each other and listen. There is the sound of swift footsteps, and I peek around the corner. Dad is at Mom's side, kneeling at her feet—bowing to her.

"Hanako," he murmurs, smoothing down her hair. "My dearest Hanako." It reminds me of the poem he'd written to her in a book she always kept on her nightstand. It's the one I found last spring, what started my journey to Dad, to Japan.

My dearest Hanako,

Please let these words say what I cannot speak:

I wish I were as close
To you as the wet skirt of
A salt girl to her body.

I think of you always.
—Yamabe no Akahito

Yours,
Makoto "Mak",
2003

"What has happened?" he implores. "Talk to me."

"I'm not sure I can do this," she says, and she sounds like a little girl. Like me when I had tried to ride my bike without training wheels. *I can't do it.*

But this isn't like that. It's not something you persevere through to come out the other side, wind in your hair as you ride into the sunset. I keep thinking about the way Mom looked in that wedding dress. Her face pale. Body about to collapse. *Did I die? Did someone I love die?*

"What part? The wedding? Being with me?"

She waves a hand, encompassing the room, the whole imperial institution. "All of it," she says. "I love you. I have always loved you, but this is too much. I'm losing myself."

His nostrils flare and his lips thin, then he softens. "Sweetheart." He kisses her hands and stands upright. He paces for a moment, lost in tormented thought. Then he stops suddenly, a light dawning. "I'll abdicate, then." The words are like a knife thrown across the room. I still. So do the twins. Our mouths part.

Mom gives a strangled laugh. "Of course you won't."

"I am serious," he insists, gaze locked meaningfully on Mom.

"You can't abdicate," Mom says. "I'd never ask that of you. You would be so unhappy. I just wish we could go back to the summer. When we were first engaged. That was such a wonderful time. When nobody knew." Mom's voice is full of longing.

Dad adjusts so he's closer to her. Their shadows merge on the carpet, two figures hunched against the wind. "I promise you, we'll figure something out," Dad says earnestly. "But please . . . please, stay with me. Don't run."

My heart beats a static rhythm in my chest, waiting for Mom to answer. She takes her time mulling it over. Maybe she's thinking about eighteen years ago. When she'd learned she was pregnant with me. She had run then. How does she think things turned out since? Would she do it again? Does she regret it? Or was it the right solution, and would it be now? We've talked about it, but we haven't put our place in Mount Shasta up for sale yet. Mom still has a safety net. A place to fall.

Finally, she answers. "Okay," she says. "We can try to work it out." She doesn't promise to stay, though, or not to run. I suppose it's the best she can do.

We stay the night at Akiko and Noriko's apartment, Mom and Dad in one room and me across from them in another. We all feel the need to be close right now.

It's late, and my phone is in hand, note page open. I blink and see my father kneeling before my mother. *People bowed to him, but he never asked me to.*

I chew my lip and tap out a poem. For her. For him. For me.

I will keep you safe
gather around you like a
shield, like a barn in
a storm, like the fire around
the sun, let me shelter you.

30

With a heavy sigh, I pick at a piece of dorayaki in the kitchen. I can't find comfort in food right now.

"Hey." Dad walks in. "Can't sleep either?"

Outside, the garden is dark, wind whips through the trees, and ice shards have formed against the windows. We have been back at the palace a mere twenty-four hours. Not much has changed. Dad dismissed the staff. Mom sticks to her room. Sometimes change is hard and slower won.

"Yeah" is all I say, my chest filled with sand. I can't help feeling as if something is slipping away.

"You hungry? I could make you something." He opens the fridge door and sticks his nose in.

I remember Mom telling me more about his college days. *He didn't know how to make a cup of soup.* "I'm okay," I say, and pick up the dorayaki and bite into it. Ugh, it tastes like chalk.

"Izumi," he says, expression dark. "Do you *want* to go to University of Tokyo?"

The question catches me so off guard I choke on the dorayaki. "What?" I swipe at the corner of my mouth.

He spreads his hands on the gleaming countertop and levels me with a gaze. "I spoke to your mother just now, and she told me you enrolled in university and started dating Mr. Nakamura in some misguided attempt to help us."

Dad can be very direct. I totally feel the full weight of the Crown Prince right now. I get why the chamberlains sometimes tremble in his presence. When he wants to be, he is a force.

I wait a moment, carefully chewing and sorting out my answer. Wondering if I should come clean or say Mom was mistaken. I decide to be honest. The truth will set you free and all that. "I was trying to help," I squeak.

He inhales and nods, staying silent.

A gentle hum emanates from the refrigerator and lights, filling the room. Dad waits. That's how he's different from Mom. She leans in, peppering me with questions, cajoling me with my nickname—*Zoom Zoom*. Dad leans out. Neither is necessarily wrong. Maybe it's strategic, though. Because I can't stand the lull and naturally seek to fill it with word vomit. Distantly, I remember reading somewhere that silence is a common interrogation tactic.

"As for wanting to go to University of Tokyo, I'm not sure." I trace the edge of my plate with a finger. It feels good to say it. As if I have finally set down a hundred-pound weight I've been carrying uphill. I glance up at him. His face is tight and drawn. "It's just that I'm not really academically inclined. I know I scored all right on the EJU, but I had to work my ass . . . sorry, my tail off."

I leave out Eriku and Akio. How deeply I feel for them both. I met Akio first. Something inside me is naturally wired for him. Akio is a push. I am the pull. We're opposites, and it works. But then there is Eriku. We're twin souls. He and I are the same.

One isn't the loneliest number. Three is.

"I see," he murmurs.

"I'm sorry," I rush out. "I don't even know if I should go to college. You and Mom have accomplished so much." And what have I ever achieved? How will I ever compare? I tuck in my chin. "But then again, I suppose it's my duty to study something benign and uncontroversial like mollusks."

"Mollusks?" I glance up, and his eyebrows have hitchhiked to his forehead. His expression changes and he regards me tenderly, then circles the counter until we're closer. "Izumi, the last thing I want for you is to follow someone else's path. I grew up with everything predetermined. What I ate, where I went to school, who I fraternized with." He told me once his friends were hand-selected by the empress. "Chamberlains controlled my life, and I have been letting them up until now. It is what I have been trained to do, to look outside myself and please others. I didn't see that I have been conditioned to want certain things. For the public to love me. To be a humble servant. To choose the crown first and always. But I am changing that as of today. I'm sorry it's taken me so long to figure it all out. I'm also sorry you've been under the assumption you needed to do or be someone else for that to happen."

"I want you to be proud of me." I blink. Right here in this kitchen, I remember him hugging me the day I received my unofficial welcome to University of Tokyo. There is a thickness in my throat, and I struggle to free the words. "I just . . . I just don't want to disappoint you or anyone." I turn away, don't want him to see me cry.

He inhales and slowly exhales. "The only thing you could ever do to disappoint me is denying who you truly are."

I'm still trying to digest what he said. What it means to me, how it applies, so I divert the conversation. "How's Mom?"

If he's surprised, he doesn't show it. "She's better, I believe. The quiet has been good."

"What about the wedding?" I ask. "Has she said anything about it? I mean, I don't think she wants a big imperial wedding."

He shakes his head. "No word on any of that. In the meantime, I don't want you to worry. You do you," he says with a sparkle in his eye. Another euphemism I taught him. He squeezes my shoulder. "I have every confidence you will figure it out. I am going to go check on your mother."

One week passes. Time marches forward. Dad makes a formal announcement he is reducing his duties for the next three weeks. He lets the staff return but at a reduced number—no butlers, a handful of maids and valets. Even the dog walker has been reassigned.

It's the three of us—Dad, Mom, and me. We cook our own food. Play games. Watch movies. Walk in the garden. Pretend the world isn't waiting for us to figure out our next steps. Japan wants us back. Akio texts me late one night and it's the last I hear from him.

Akio

The more I tried to
forget you, the more I remembered your smell, your

smile, the way you made me feel
like the sun grazing my skin.

Eriku keeps sending gifts. I leave them all unopened.

I hate the distance between us. It's not fair to keep them hanging on. But I can't quite let go. It's selfish to want them both. I'll have to make my choice soon. This can't last.

I heard Dad on the phone this morning in his office. Someone inquiring about the wedding. He noticed me and gently closed the door. I didn't hear his answer.

It all comes to a head that day at lunch. "The empress called this morning," my father says, holding my mother's gaze for one breathless moment. "She wants to know about the wedding. I'm afraid I can't put her off much longer."

Tamagotchi sits at my feet, and I pause, feeding him a little scrap. Mom sets her ohashi down and stares at her half-eaten grilled sawara. Dad shifts and places a hand over hers. "Hanako," he says quietly. "I am committed to you. It is still my desire to marry, and my offer to abdicate is still open."

When Mom looks up, her eyes are liquid. "I don't know. But Mak, the thought of a big wedding, a thousand guests, all that pomp and circumstance . . ." She trails off.

"What if . . ." I chime in, an idea forming. "What if you could have the wedding without all of that? Something smaller, with just us?" I remember her saying she wished it was all simpler. Like when their engagement hadn't been approved yet.

"That would be nice," Mom says, but then shakes her head. "The empress would never approve of that."

Dad and I meet each other's eyes, hope glinting off our faces.

"Okay," I say slowly. "Amendment. What if you had a small wedding before the big wedding. Something just for us, then something for the world." Sometimes it doesn't have to be either/or—it can be both.

Mom turns to Dad. "Is that possible?"

"Anything is possible," he answers. "But Hanako, it means you'd be choosing this life. You would be the Crown Princess of Japan, empress someday."

Mom draws in a breath. "It may not seem like I've been doing much these last few days, but I have been giving what I want a lot of thought." Her mouth curls with a soft smile. "I want to marry you, Mak. I want to stay in Japan. And I will take on the duties and customs required of me. But I also want to control my life in ways that are important to me." Another deep breath. "I want to keep working. I don't know if it's possible, but I'd like to email College of the Siskiyous and inquire about teaching some online courses. I understand as a member of the imperial family, I'm not allowed to earn an income, and this would be a big change. Maybe I can donate the money or volunteer, but I need this . . . and if I can't be at the College of the Siskiyous, I'd like to seek a position in Tokyo somewhere." Mom stops suddenly, as if winded.

Dad nods once, spine stiff. "Okay. Done. What else?"

My pulse quickens.

"While I appreciate your mother introducing me to Ms. Komura, I would like to choose my own lady-in-waiting," Mom says with a tilt of her chin.

"Also done. What else?" He's scooted closer to her, on the edge of his seat. I'm pretty sure if she asked for the sun, he'd say yes.

"I'd like time with just you. I'm sorry if it's selfish. The state dinners, events are fine, and I'll attend those, but I want us to have time alone together. I want your undivided attention," Mom says with gusto.

A twitch tugs at Dad's mouth. "Done," he says. Then he draws a little closer to Mom, their knees touching. "But you should know it doesn't matter if there are a thousand people in a room. My mind has always been singularly focused on you." Dad is smooth.

"You make all of it seem so easy," Mom says, watching Dad with suspicion.

Dad settles back in his chair. "It won't be easy. I won't pretend it will. But the best things seldom are. I promise to support you in your choices and dreams. And I promise to never take our time together for granted."

I pitch forward in my seat. It's a re-proposal of sorts. Dad isn't on one knee. The table is a mess. Mom is wearing a T-shirt stained with compost. I'm right here, and Tamagotchi has horrible gas. None of it is right. But somehow, all of it is right.

"Okay, Makotonomiya, Crown Prince of Japan," Mom says with a smile. "Let's get married."

31

A week later, my phone chimes with a text.

Noora

In five words or less, start a fight
without including politics.

Glory and Hansani's responses pop up almost instantaneously.

Glory

Speed walking is a sport.

Hansani

Hot Pockets are overrated.

I giggle.

"What's so funny?" Mom asks, resting her chin on my
shoulder. "'In five words or less, start a fight without including politics.' . . . I don't get it."

I set my phone down and twirl around. Mom fidgets
under my stare. She's wearing a dress—a light blue flowy
crepe gown with a sheer chiffon skirt. Her wedding dress.
Because today, she is getting married. When we shopped
for what to wear, Mom tsked at anything white. *I'm pretty*

sure the jig is up, she said at the virginal color while tapping my nose. To which I covered my ears.

Today her back is straighter. Her smile is brighter. I pluck a bouquet of orchids out of its vase and hand it to Mom. "You ready?"

Her hands tremble as she takes the flowers but not from panic. From joy. Both emotions can make you weak in the knees. "One more moment." She eyes herself in the mirror.

"You look beautiful," I assure her. She's done her own makeup today. A natural look with a little blush and gloss. She didn't need too much. She's glowing with happiness.

"You look beautiful, too," she says.

I peer down at my dress, at the black chiffon with gold stitching. It's the dress Akiko and Noriko picked for the sultan's banquet. It's a little too fancy, but I don't care. I'm wearing it because I like it. Because it makes me feel good. It is such a gift just to be a girl in a pretty dress.

Mom squares her shoulders. "I'm ready," she announces.

We hook arms. I'll be escorting her down the aisle, or rather to and through the greenhouse. We're ending how the proposal began—a woman and a greenhouse and the man she loves.

Outside, a breeze ruffles Mom's hair and brings with it the smell of compost. I scrunch my nose, but Mom just laughs. It's perfect for her. There have been sun-showers on and off today—fox rain. And we get caught in one on our way. Our hair is dry but frizzy by the time we arrive at the greenhouse.

The greenhouse's metal-and-glass door is propped open. Mariko stands next to it, holding Tamagotchi by his leash.

He's wearing a little tux, the bow tie already askew. He curls his lip at me.

We start down a white carpet. Dad is waiting at the top of the aisle along with Akiko and Noriko, who are wearing elaborate Oscar de la Renta confections. They look like beautiful pieces of cake. They are the other two bridesmaids along with me. Next to Dad is his brother, Uncle Nobuhito, the twins' dad. Mom wanted to keep the wedding small, intimate. Mr. Fuchigami rounds out the guests, as he's officiating.

We'd hit a bump in the road planning the impromptu wedding. We needed a palace official to make it legal and binding. I'd tentatively brought it to Mr. Fuchigami, with whom I told my mother I have a very special relationship.

"It's extremely unorthodox," he said, unsure.

"It is," I said.

"It's not how things are usually done," he said.

"You're right," I said.

"I feel that you are being very agreeable so that I will be agreeable," he said.

I grinned at him.

"Your parents plan to then have a larger ceremony according to the Imperial Household Agency's wishes?"

I nodded eagerly. Dad and Mom had a five-hour-long meeting with the emperor and empress where Dad stated his intention to marry Mom in a private ceremony. It turned into a negotiation. The empress demanded a proper wedding at a later date. Dad and Mom were prepared to concede. The empress gave her blessing but wouldn't be present for the vows today. Their Majesties are entertaining the king of Bhutan.

He rubbed his forehead. "It's not traditional. Not right.

But I suppose," he muttered to himself, "I have always danced a little left of center. Jaa. I'll do it."

I beamed and executed a formal bow. "Thank you."

Now, Mom and I reach the end of the aisle. I hug her, and my sinuses burn as I try not to get emotional. Dad takes Mom's hand. They've written their own vows. Dad promises to love, honor, and support Mom. Mom promises along the same lines, but adds not to run when things get hard.

They seal the deal by saying, "Chikaimasu." It's over in a few moments, and Mr. Fuchigami declares the two married.

After, we have cake and hojicha, roasted Japanese brown tea, in the garden. The air is crisp and cool, and I should have worn a jacket, but my chest is fuzzy with warmth and romance.

Still, there is a shadow cast over the day. Eriku and Akio. I miss them both with an ache so acute it steals my breath. It is also disturbing how easily I go back and forth between the two. How do I shut off these feelings? The heartache runs deep—each trench carved by Akio and Eriku.

"It's a shame your mother didn't opt for something more extravagant," Akiko says, examining her nails.

"When you get married, please make sure there are at least some guests to see our dresses. This is a waste of Oscar de la Renta," Noriko adds, glancing down meaningfully.

"Thank you," I say sincerely. "For all you did for us. For my mom. For me." I regard them intently, liquid gathering in my eyes.

"It's not a big deal," Akiko says with a sniff, clearly uncomfortable.

Human emotions. So messy.

"Um," Noriko says to Akiko. "I think she's going to try to hug us."

Before they can object, I wrap them up in my arms, embracing them both. Akiko pats my back awkwardly, and Noriko is stiff. "I love you," I say, releasing them. "And I know you love me, too."

I blow them a kiss and trot off to my mom, swiping a piece of nutty cake off the table as I go by. I shovel a bite into my mouth.

"Still happy?" I ask her. My dad is chatting with his brother.

"The happiest," Mom says with a silly grin.

"Well, I guess my job is done, then," I say wryly.

The truth? I'm not sure what to do with myself now that Mom and Dad are tied up neatly in a bow. I chew my lip, thinking of Akio and Eriku. Who is first in my heart?

"Honey," Mom says. "You have that wrinkle between your brows when you're overthinking something. Is it the school thing? Want to talk about it?"

I shake my head to say no, then launch into it. "How did you know that Dad was the one?"

Mom blows out a breath. "You know, I don't think there was ever a defining moment. I wasn't ready for love or marriage when I had you. I had to grow into myself some more, into my own self-worth. I think that's why your father and I needed time apart. When I was younger, I felt so dull around your father next to his Crown Prince shine. But now that I'm older, I don't have those same insecurities. Seeing him with you has changed my mind. And I am genuinely happy, too. Does that make sense? Or have I made more of a mess of things?"

"It makes sense," I say. "So love is a choice?"

She keeps her tone quiet. "Love is many things, and it manifests at different times in different ways for people. For me, it was kindness, time, growth, encouragement . . . *space*. It's worth it, though. All these years apart from your father, I don't regret them. It's the climb that makes you appreciate the view."

The sound of silverware clinking against glass draws our attention. My uncle makes a toast. While he congratulates the couple, I wonder again how my heart can beat for two people.

But I'm going to make a decision. And one thing is certain. No matter what, I won't have any regrets.

I forcibly blink against an onslaught of emotions as I bid Mom and Dad goodbye that evening. They are leaving for a quiet honeymoon in the Yaeyama archipelago in Okinawa Prefecture.

Mr. Fuchigami stands behind me. "I guess that's it then," I say to him, watching the car disappear down the drive. Mariko has already turned in.

"Is there anything else you will need this evening, Your Highness? Perhaps a second secret wedding?" His mouth is a straight line but his eyes glimmer. Mr. Fuchigami is making a joke.

"Mr. Fuchigami." I inch closer to him. "May I ask you a personal question?"

He opens his hands. "I am at your disposal."

"What is love?"

His brow furrows. He's sorry he stuck around. Should have gone home with the rest of the guests earlier.

"Are you married? I'm assuming not, because you don't wear a ring."

"I am a confirmed bachelor," he states.

"Did you ever want to get married? I mean, have you ever been in love?" I ask, then think better of it. "Sorry, too personal. You don't have to answer that." I start to brush past him, but his voice stalls me.

"I didn't ever consider marriage," he announces. "I began working for the Imperial Household Agency straight out of university. I've dedicated my life to the institution. Does that answer your question?"

"Yes," I say. "Thank you." That's a kind of love, I think. I give him a faint smile. "Have a good night."

He bows low. "Oyasumi nasai."

Alone in the palace, I cross my arms, tapping my feet against the floor. It's dark, and I'm restless. Even though the weather is bitingly cold, I decide to go for a walk in the garden. I bundle up in a long down coat and step outside. Wind whips against my cheeks, but I press on, deeper and deeper into the gardens, passing the greenhouse where my parents were married. The remnants of the ceremony are still present. Ribbons flap in the breeze, branches try to hold on to their leaves.

Soon, I am in the East Garden, which is open to the public but closed now at night. I cross the wide lawn, a dark figure moving steadily through the dark, through the evergreen pines.

Then I am at the former castle tower. The ruins I saw kids climbing when Akio broke up with me. My breaths come out in foggy puffs as I ascend the ramp. The stone foundations are wide and large—ominous and forbidding, meant to keep intruders out. I step on a ledge and heave myself up until I am sitting on the rock wall. Mom says the climb is worth it. She is so right.

The imperial estate stretches before me, backlit with the Tokyo high-rises. Icy patches in the pathways shine in the moonlight and reflect the city—the cold stings my nostrils. But I keep still and close my eyes. Let myself sink, down and down. Past what I have been conditioned to want. Past what others want from me. Past what I am expected to be. Past the push and pull between duty and family and pursuing one's own desires. My blood hums.

There are no distractions now. Mom and Dad are married. Akio and Eriku are miles away. What better place to find yourself than in silence, in the dark? Who am I? What do I want?

My mind settles. I urge Amaterasu, the past, to speak to me, to tell me my future. But it's not ancient voices that rise. It's my mom. *How am I going to spend the rest of my life doing what others tell me to?* My Dad. *The only thing you could ever do to disappoint me is denying who you truly are.* Mom again. *Love is many things . . .* Noora. *Family is what you make it.*

Akio. *You just need to figure out where your proclivities lie.*
Eriku. *Life is a song.*

When I open my eyes, I have the answers I seek. I know what I want. I know who I want. I slip my phone from my pocket and text Noora.

> **Me**
>
> You were right.

She replies instantaneously.

> **Noora**
>
> I usually am. Remind me about what, though?

I climb down from the tower. My fingers are frozen as I text her back.

> **Me**
>
> I've been trying to do the right thing for everyone but myself. But I think I've figured it out now. I'm going to stop trying to please everyone.

> **Noora**
>
> Yesss!

> **Me**
>
> Get ready for Izumi 2.0. I'm totally evolving.

Noora

What do you think your final form
will be?

Me

IDK, probably something
winged and glittery.

Then I add,

Me

I'm going to keep the clothes,
though.

Noora

I feel like that's a given.

I laugh, and it is carried away in the wind. That's fine. Tokyo can have it. I know what to do. It's not what I should do, maybe. But it's what I want. I have the answers now. School. Eriku or Akio.

That night, I sleep soundly but wake before the sunrise. I kneel on my bed and watch the light streaking through the tree line. Dawn is coming. I won't close my eyes.

32

I ring the bell for the third time. Tokyo is nothing but blue sky today, but still bitterly cold. I am wearing a camel wool coat, the lining in pink silk. Wind whips around my ankles, flipping up the edge of the jacket.

"Should have called first," Reina says behind me.

I raise my hands and rattle the gate. "Surprises are the salt of life. They make everything tastier," I answer.

"Salt gives you high blood pressure," Reina mutters.

"If you want to wait in the car, I understand," I say.

"Can't," Reina volleys back. "Have to stay, be prepared to take a bullet for you." She's in a mood. It might have something to do with me dragging her out of bed in the wee hours of the morning.

The intercom buzzes, and a woman answers, "Hai."

"Yes. Hi," I say into the box. "I'm here to see Eriku."

"Dare desu ka?" she asks.

"Oh, um, Izumi—"

Reina bends to the box and speaks. "Her Imperial Highness Princess Izumi is here to see Mr. Eriku Nakamura. Onegaishimasu." Her voice is very "or face the wrath of the crown."

The gate clicks and swings open.

"That was effective," I say to Reina as we walk through a courtyard with manicured trees.

"I'm cold," she says.

We're in the middle of Tokyo, and the sounds of the city bleed through, but not the sights. High brick walls enclose the mansion. An archway frames the front door, which is open. A woman in a maid's uniform swings into a low bow. She mutters honorifics in Japanese. We toe off our shoes and place them on the rack, and she apologizes profusely that the slippers aren't new. Then we're escorted through the house. Gleaming marble floors. Grecian columns. A double spiral staircase and a sleepy Eriku at the top of them.

"Izumi?" He jogs down the stairs, clearly happy to see me. Momo-chan ambles down, too, sniffing my feet.

"Sorry to show up out of the blue," I say. He's wearing sweatpants and a Grateful Dead tee. There is a small gold chain around his neck. His hair is messy, untamed. My veins flood with warmth seeing him.

He shrugs, smiles. "Surprises are the salt of life."

"That's what I just said," I say, heart skipping.

He grins. "So . . ." he trails off.

"Can we talk?" I ask.

His smile inches down. "Sure," he says. He holds out a hand, gesturing to a living room with tufted sofas and floor-to-ceiling doors leading to a stone patio.

Reina turns to the maid. "My security team is going to need access to the house to check the perimeter. In addition, I will need the names and birthdates of everyone present on the grounds." The maid is deferential and scurries off, Reina behind her.

Eriku and I settle in the living room. Me on a silk damask loveseat and Eriku in a chair with gilded arms.

Momo-chan saunters over. She huffs as if the six-foot walk was positively exhausting and lies down at his feet, jowls spreading on the Persian rug.

"This is a nice house." I chew my cheek and focus on the white marble fireplace. "Are your parents home?"

He shakes his head. "They're in Osaka for the weekend." He pauses and peers at me with a hopeful look in his eyes. "I'm happy to see you."

"I'm happy to see you too." I scoot to the edge of my seat. "Listen . . . that night in the garden . . ." I hesitate. "You told me all the ways I changed you, but I didn't get to tell you all the ways you changed me." I stop short.

He leans forward, elbows resting on his knees. He looks tired. I wonder if he's been sleeping. "Go on."

I pick at my thumbs. "When we met, I think we were in similar places in our lives." Both standing at a fork in the road, unsure if we needed to leave the park or forge our own path within it. "Our lives are hyper-controlled, and we, or at least, I, was trying to figure out how to fit into my parents', and the imperial institution's, ideals." I take a breath and let it out. "I thought I had to conform or rebel. That there wasn't any middle ground. But there is. . . . You've taught me it's okay to succeed. You just can't sacrifice your total happiness for it. You have to know what you want, at the end of the day."

"And what is it, exactly, that you want?" His voice comes out as a rasp. He's asking about himself. His place in my life.

"I want to go to school," I say with finality, fists balling in my lap. "I've earned my place at University of Tokyo. But I don't think I'm going to study botany. I think . . . I think I want to study literature. It's another thing you've shown me. We're both artists, you and me." Eriku with his music. *Life is a song.* Me with my poems. "And I want you . . . as my friend." Eriku palms his head, fingers splayed in his hair. "I'm sorry . . ." I squeeze my eyes shut. "You're amazing, and we're so alike, but . . ." Eriku is a free verse. Passion, energy, and rhythm. But Akio . . . Akio *is* waka, carefully composed, controlled, polished, and elegant. There is something timeless about him. Everything would be—and was—so easy with Eriku. But he doesn't challenge me enough. Not like Akio does. Love is so many things. And for me, it's a push and a pull. "I'm sorry," I say again, because what else is there to say? "Are you angry?"

A wave of tension ripples through the room as he regards me, brown eyes deepening to pools I could jump into. "No. I'm sad. I'm disappointed, but I'm not angry."

"I wouldn't be where I am right now without you."

He tries smiling, but it doesn't quite catch. "We're probably going to have to work out some sort of custody agreement for Momo-chan and Tamagotchi to see each other."

"Jones has an ex-partner he shares a dog, guinea pig, and five chickens with," I say. "I'll ask him for some tips."

Eriku slumps back and gazes at the coffered ceiling. "I wish I were Jones sometimes."

My shoulders are tense. That off-the-grid lifestyle is really appealing to Eriku. I think back to the song he sang onstage, at the members-only club—"You Don't Own Me." I remember all the moments Eriku told me he was happiest. Living in the States and going to college. Fake-dating me. Then actually dating me. All because he was out from under his father's thumb.

"Eriku . . ." I start, then cut myself off. The idea is kind of wild. But then again, so is Eriku. Plus, sometimes love is space. Mom needed it from Dad. Eriku might need it from his own father. "Eriku, have you ever thought about living in the States again? Mount Shasta is really lovely in the spring, and you know, the Rainbow Gatherers come for the summer. We still have our house there. Plenty of room for you *and* Momo-chan." Silence then as my words sink in. "Forget it," I say at his bent head. "It's a crazy idea."

"Izumi," Eriku says, raising his gaze to meet my eyes. His expression is lighter, nearly buoyant. "You had me at Rainbow Gatherers."

I grin. He grins back.

"Apologies, Your Highness, you would like to go *where* now?" Reina stands in front of me, blocking the imperial vehicle I am about to board outside of Eriku's house.

I peer at my phone, at the second stop in my make-it-right tour. "Nara Air Base. Here's the address." I flash her the screen.

She purses her lips. "I am familiar with it."

I smile brightly and tuck the phone into my pocket. "Great."

"Is this an official imperial visit?" Reina asks. She produces a phone from her pocket and scrolls through it. All the imperial schedules are sent to the guards.

"Not an official visit. But my day is clear." I skirt around

Reina and open the door. Clutching the edge, I say, "We should get going. It's a long drive."

Reina hesitates a moment before closing my door. She slips into the driver's seat and adjusts the rearview mirror so she can see me. "Mr. Kobayashi, eh?"

I nod. "Yes," is all I say—because I am a boomerang. I will always return to Akio. The question is, am I too late?

33

Predictably we get stuck in traffic, and I bounce my foot as we wait for cars to inch along. Soon enough, we are out of the city and cruising. A snow-capped Mount Fuji looms in the distance.

At the base, we are stopped and held at a guard tower. A man in fatigues with a clipboard pinned under his arm approaches the car. Reina rolls down the tinted window. He recognizes the imperial plates, me in the backseat, and sweeps into a formal bow. Before Reina can stop him, he's radioing someone.

"What's going on?" I fidget in my seat.

"He's calling the base commander." Reina taps her hands on the steering wheel.

"That seems unnecessary. Can't you just tell him I'd like to visit Akio?"

Reina rests her head on the seat back. "Too late." Things are happening. The radio explodes with chatter.

I scowl. Within minutes, vehicles stream toward us, lights blinking. They park in a semicircle, and the giant black gate swings open. Reina and I step from the car. A man in an officer's uniform with flower epaulets bows low to me. Soldiers line up behind him. I am embarrassed from the tips of my toes to the top of my forehead. Luckily, the cold air cools the blush on my face. The air is a bit briny, smells of fish and salt.

"Your Imperial Highness, what an unexpected but welcome surprise. I am Base Commander Hasegawa." He sweeps into another bow, officer's cap under his arm. His jaw is square and mean-looking. I'd definitely avoid this man in a dark alley.

"Please excuse the intrusion." I open my hands. "But I am here to see one of your officer candidates. Akio Kobayashi. If you could just point me in the right direction . . ."

The base commander turns to another officer. He barks something in Japanese that I can't quite catch. There is a flurry of activity. Officers confer with one another and make phone calls. Three whole minutes pass. I actively try not to tap my foot and check my watch.

"We have located Airman Kobayashi," the base commander says. "He is on the flight deck. I will escort you there," he announces with finality.

"Are you sure?" I ask.

"Please, I insist." He signals, and the soldiers slam back into their vehicles. This isn't a man who is argued with often. He might give my father a run for his money. I'd like to see the two of them in a room together.

"All right, I'm sorry to trouble you." I climb into the back of his shiny SUV. Then we're speeding through the base. During the very short drive, the base commander explains all of Nara's local attractions and invites me to dinner at his home this evening, which I politely decline.

The cavalcade slows and stops at an airfield. "Ah, here

we are," the base commander says. "If you wait here, I will make sure you are outfitted with the appropriate safety equipment, then have Mr. Kobayashi brought to you." Soldiers dart around with noise-canceling headphones and orange flags. Pilots in flight suits load into planes. I search the landscape for a familiar set of broody eyes.

I see him. Know him by the way he holds himself. Perfect posture with his hands behind his back, an old habit of the imperial guard he couldn't shake. I am out of the car and running.

"Akio!" I yell, darting across the airfield. The sound of engines rumbles and drowns out my voice. My hair and jacket fly in the wind. I am a streak of camel and pink against the greens and grays and blues. "Akio!" I yell again. He is on a ladder, stepping into a Kawasaki T-4. I am only a few feet away when he finally notices me.

"Izumi?" he booms, astonished and climbing down. He's wearing an olive-green flight suit that brings out the honey color of his eyes. He scowls, his gaze darting to the propellers, to the planes, to the airmen wearing helmets. "What are you doing here? It's not safe."

"I had to see you," I yell over the roar of the engines. The cold whips through my hair and stings my cheeks.

He curses and steps forward, closer to me. A helmet hangs loosely from his hand. "Here, put this on." I take it from him and hold it, playing with the straps. For a moment, I trace the lines of his face with my eyes. Letting my gaze linger on the slices of his cheekbones. He's speaking again. "What are you doing here?" he asks again.

Suddenly, I am at a loss for words under his heated

stare. I miss him so much. It leaves me breathless. It hurts to look at him. It hurts more not to see him. "Why did you stop texting me?"

He lifts his brows. "You drove all the way to Nara to ask why I stopped texting you?" he shouts over the noise.

"No," I shout back. "I have some things I need to say, and I wanted to say them in person." I pause, not sure where to start, then land on what's happened recently. "I went to see Eriku this morning. He's helped me with so many things. Finding myself, helping me discover what I'd like to study. I think I'm going to major in literature. He's helped me understand I don't have to walk the same path as everyone else."

It is so much easier to be led than to blaze your own trail. Actually, "blazing" sounds too easy. It is more rigorous than that. Pulling up weeds. Unearthing trees. Laying down gravel. It's hard work becoming who you are. Is there really a right way to be a princess? A woman?

Akio's face hardens. "I hope you two will be very happy together. Is that all?"

I shake my head. "No, that's not all. I don't want to be with Eriku. I want to be with you." I stomp my foot with desperation. The final engine cuts off just as I wildly holler, "I love you!" The base commander, Reina, and the hundred or so soldiers hear it and can barely contain their smiles. "I love you," I say more quietly.

"Izumi," he says, low and harsh.

I hug the helmet to my chest, emotions running amok. I think about how I haven't heard from him for weeks. "Are you done fighting for me?" Humiliation inches up my spine; it bleeds through me at Akio's silence.

At last, he opens his mouth and speaks. "Never. I'll never be done fighting for you. How can I? I love you, and you fight for the things you love."

"What?" I hold my breath, hoping I haven't misheard. If this is an illusion, I will die. Die.

"I love you, too," he says. "Now, will you put the helmet on?" He takes it out of my hands and places it on my head. It's too big and tilts forward. "I'd kiss you, but we have an audience," he says gruffly.

I shove the helmet up so I can see. Soldiers stand around, legs braced apart, hands behind their backs with smiles as wide as an ocean. I duck my head and careen into him, wrapping my arms around his waist. A hug is okay. His chest rumbles under my cheek. "I was planning on camping outside your bunker if need be," I say, grinning up at him.

"Unnecessary," he says. He squeezes once and releases me. Applause goes around until the base commander barks an order for everyone to mind their business and return to work.

"I should probably go." Akio rubs the back of his neck. The muscles in his face tense. "It's my first time piloting."

"That's amazing!" I say, smoothing out my trousers. "I guess I'll call you later?"

He nods, thinking. "I actually have leave starting this evening. But I understand if you have prior commitments. . . ."

"I don't have anything," I blurt. "I'll wait—that is, if you want me to."

"It's settled, then," he says.

"Go," I usher him away. "Fly your plane. I'll be here when you land."

The base commander lets me stay. We climb the steps to the flight tower. There, I hear him through the radio. See his plane roll down the runway and slice through the air. It's exactly where I should be. Watching Akio take flight.

That night, I'm in the backseat of a taxicab with Akio. The streets of Nara are sleepy. Lights blink out in windows. Storekeepers shutter their shops. I have a hat on my head courtesy of Akio, and I am wearing one of his sweatshirts. We're holding hands, and every so often, Akio squeezes my fingers. There is a giddiness coursing through us—a kind of electricity. Reunited at last.

"Reina is going to kill me." I lean against his shoulder, a sigh rippling from my mouth.

"Blame me," he says. I grin up at him, and he smiles back, white teeth flashing in the dark. His hair is still damp from his shower. We've given Reina the slip, ducked into a cab, and sped away.

"Where do you want to go?" he asks. "Get something to eat?"

"I'm not hungry," I say.

"Walk around a park?" he asks.

"Too tired," I say. "Let's go somewhere private. Maybe a hotel?" Six months without Akio is too long. I want him all to myself. Don't want to wait anymore to feel him, to touch him.

"You sure?" His voice drops, and his eyes flare.

"I'm sure."

He leans forward and gives the driver directions, then

kisses my knuckles. "It's not the best, but it's nearby and private."

The cab stops outside of what looks like a traditional Japanese house. It has wooden engawa verandas and rain gutters to carry rainfall off the eaves and down the decorative kusari-doi rain chains. I wait outside while Akio checks us in, ducking my head when a group of teens passes. He reemerges, key in hand, then leads me up a narrow staircase.

The room matches the exterior. The ceiling is high with exposed wooden beams. A bamboo light fixture resembling an old lantern casts a warm glow, almost like firelight. And a queen-sized bed with a snow-white duvet is right in the middle. He shuts the doors and turns the lock with an audible *click*. It's suits us, both of us.

"Is this okay?" he asks with a swallow.

I walk the room, letting my hand trail over the bed. It's simple. Perfect. He hovers near the door. If he tries to make a run for it, I might tackle him. "It's better than okay." I have a sudden thought. "What you said . . . about not being worthy, not staying in my gilded orbit, you know it's the opposite, right?"

His mouth twists into a frown. I can tell he's going to disagree.

I go to him. "It's me who's not worthy of you."

He shakes his head. "That's not true."

I ball my hands into fists. "It is. Can't you see? I'm a mess. I have no idea what I'm doing. I keep making all these mistakes. I will probably spend my entire life making mistakes. Just . . . just stick with me, okay?"

He grasps my hands and holds them against his chest. "You have me. You have always had me."

"Your heart is beating so fast," I whisper.

"I . . . I didn't think I would ever see you again. Except for in magazines. That I'd be cursed to watch you forever from afar." He touches my face, my lips.

"Will you kiss me now?" I ask. "It's been an awfully long time."

"Too long," he agrees. The deep timbre of his voice reverberates through me—an infinite echo. I feel his hands on my waist, his hands in my hair. It's fine. Everything is fine now.

"I love you," I say.

"Say it again," he says near my ear, and I feel a little kiss there. A nibble.

"I love you."

"I love you, too," he says back. Three very little potent and powerful words.

I go still and pull back. "But why did you stop sending me poems?" I ask, heart in my throat. I've never felt so vulnerable. Fear shoves its way in. Akio hurt me when he left. His reason was altruistic. But who's to say he won't do it again? Maybe I'm stupid for trusting him again. Or brave. Yeah, that.

"You didn't reply," he simply answers. "I was waiting for you. I didn't want to be . . . forceful."

I sigh. "We need to work on our communication."

He chuckles and lifts a hand to my chin, and holds me there. I close my eyes and kiss his cheek, the corner of his mouth, then finally, *finally* his lips. He growls low and opens his mouth, and the kiss turns from gentle to more. It's difficult to decide where to put my hands when I want to put them everywhere all at once. Buttons are undone. Shirts are slipped off.

"Oh God, Akio," I murmur in between mind-numbing kisses.

We stumble back to the bed, and Akio asks me if it's okay, and I say, "Yes, but um, do you have something? You know, for protection?"

He gazes at me, fierce and intent. His voice is thick. "I do."

All that taken care of, the kissing and clothes-shedding resume. Soon we're under the sheets. This is what I want.

I can't sleep. It feels as if I have been plugged into a socket. I am all lit up. Wiry. Akio snoozes next to me, the sheet pulled to his chest. My phone is out, and between tapping out verses, I steal glances at him. He hasn't moved. When we first met, I thought he might be a vampire. Now, I can confirm it. He sleeps like the undead.

"I can feel you watching me," he murmurs, eyes still closed.

I cast my phone aside and prop my chin on his chest. "I'm just taking you all in. Making up for lost time."

His hand cups my head and plays with my hair. He cracks an eye open. "Radish," he says.

"Maybe, later on, you could get your uniform and try it on for me." I shift and try to contain my wince. The truth is, I am a little sore, but in the best way.

His hand trails down and strokes my bare upper arm. "Are you objectifying me?"

"Most definitely." I lean into him, angling my head for a kiss.

"What's that?" he asks, after lifting his lips from mine.

I follow his line of sight to my phone. The screen is still lit up. "Oh, just the poems I've been writing." I reach to shut it off and put it on the nightstand, but he stops me, wrapping his fingers around my wrist.

"Read them to me," he commands.

Uncertainty rises. "They're silly."

He pulls me back down and closes his eyes. "Read. Now."

"I've forgotten how autocratic you can be," I huff out, settling in the crook of his arm.

The corner of his mouth kicks up into a smile. "Waiting," he says.

I scroll to the top and start at the beginning. With the waka poem about Japan's shrinking population and dying arts. *Who will live here now that you are gone?* I finish with my most recent work—the poem about my mother, myself.

I see you shrinking
smaller and smaller. Giving
your time, your smiles, your
energy. Yet, it is not
enough. They'll have your bones, too.

When I am done, Akio is silent.

"Like I said, it's silly. That's why I'm going to take some

classes, to improve. I'm sure I have lots to learn." I fiddle with the sheet.

He opens his eyes, and they are pools of honey. "Those poems are amazing." I blush and hide my face in his chest. He tips my chin up, making me look at him. "Seriously, amazing."

Then he kisses me, and I feel the world sigh.

Less than twenty-four hours later, Reina bangs the door. She's found us. Akio is due back on the base, and I am expected back at the palace. We linger in the hotel's courtyard. Akio's eyes flash to mine. "What happens now?" he asks. The morning air is cool and somber. Our little bubble has burst.

Two cars idle at the curb. Ready to take us in separate directions. "What happens now"—I smooth my hands down his chest—"is you go back to school, and I start school."

It's different from the last time we were reunited. When he'd quit his position as my bodyguard and sent me a rainbow key chain with my name on it (a long story). Back then, I'd run from the palace and straight into his arms, declarations of forever on my tongue. That day Akio said he'd wait for me as long as it took. But now . . . now we aren't waiting for each other. And I think we both know it. We're two trees growing side by side, but distinct. We have our own root systems. Our own pathways to the sun.

He rests his forehead against mine. "I'll call you."

"I expect you to."

We kiss. Once. Twice. Three times. He opens the car door for me, and I blow him a kiss in the rearview window. He waves. I don't know what the future will bring. Right now, we're together. And I hope we stick. So that's how we leave it. With hope.

34

Six Weeks Later

**Don't forget to jiggle the toilet
handle after you flush so it
doesn't run.**

I tuck my phone in my pocket and pull my dorm door closed, locking it with a twist of my keys. The hallway is littered with international students. I wave to my neighbors I met over move-in weekend—an engineering major from Hungary and a global ethics major from Botswana. Mom regaled them with stories about Gary, my imaginary friend when I was eight, who made me eat so much gum I had to go to the doctor. I had to bite my fist from screaming at her to stop.

Reina joins me and taps her watch. *Late,* she mouths. My phone vibrates. I pull it out in the elevator and see Eriku has answered.

**Got it. Do you think your mom
would mind if I took down the**

picture of you naked in the
bathtub? It's really charming,
but . . .

The photograph is an eight by ten and hangs promi-
nently in our bathroom in Mount Shasta. I am four years
old—rear up, cheeks glistening, and bubbles all around. I
tap out a response as I head toward campus.

Me

IDK. It's kind of a classic. But I
guess . . .

Me

Other than that, everything else
okay?

Eriku

More than okay. Jones is teaching
me how to make a bongo drum
this evening. He's adamant we
need to be shirtless and barefoot.
Something about connecting to
the land?

Jones has totally taken Eriku under his wing, and Momo-
chan, too, even though he disagrees with the pure breeding
of dogs for aesthetics or genetic superiority. He also doesn't
believe dogs should be leashed, trained, or collared.

Wind rushes through a row of beech trees, and the clock tower comes into view. Reina is behind me, losing her mind I'm sure. If we're not twenty minutes early for everything, we might as well be late. I text Eriku back and quicken my steps.

Me

Do it. Life is a song, right?

Eriku

One hundred percent. Life is a song.

We sign off. Two more texts come through. Noora sent a gif of a man with a mustache throwing glitter. We both know what it means. She's excited about my first day of classes. She wants to hear all about it. She also has something she needs to tell me. Call her later. Yeah, all that from an animated picture.

And finally, there is a message from Akio.

Akio

Good luck today.

I send him a glittery thank-you. We talk on the phone—a lot. But I've only seen him once since our night in the hotel in Nara. And I can confirm now for everyone that Akio has worn his uniform for me. Expectations exceeded. I can't help but grin.

I am still smiling as I slide into a hardback green chair in a lecture hall. I pop open my notebook. A youngish woman with a heart-shaped face and a navy suit enters and stands at the podium. "Ohayō gozaimasu," she says, smiling gently. "I am Imai-sensei. Welcome to Poetry 1A." An aid distributes the syllabus.

I chased Mr. Ueno, my interviewer, down and blasted him with a whole speech about following my passions—which weren't botany. Bless the man, he listened, then directed me to the registrar to change majors. It was a lot less of a big deal than I thought it would be. Still, filling out the form, crossing out *botany* and writing in *poetry*, felt momentous, like an arrow hitting its mark. I have also reconsidered my hobby. No blood donations or Red Cross for me. I'm thinking something having to do with animal welfare; Mr. Fuchigami is looking into it.

The professor goes on, "To start with, I always ask if anyone would like to read their work." Students shift uncomfortably in their seats and refuse to make eye contact with her, lest she mistake it for volunteering.

I chew my lip and raise my hand.

"Hai, yes, please," she invites. "Dōzo."

I stand next to my seat. My palms are sweaty, and my phone slips in my hand. My grip tightens as I read:

We used to hide in
forests of green ribbons,
waiting to be found, now
we seek open spaces to

fill with our voices. See us.
See me. SEE. ME. Here I am.

I slip back in my seat when done, and another student rises to read his work. I'm sure the poem will leak to the tabloids. They will interpret it however they will. Let them. Life is a poem. I'm going to write it.

ACKNOWLEDGMENTS

Writing a book during a global pandemic is no joke. Luckily, I have some amazing people in my corner. As always, I am ever so grateful to my partner, Craig, and my twins. Yumi and Kenzo, everything I do is for you (and for me, too: I am such a better mom because I get to write). Trust me when I say you three are my real happily ever after. I am grateful to my parents, who instilled a love of reading and writing in me. And to my siblings, all of you, including extended family and friends: thanks for your enthusiasm, love, and overwhelming confidence. Also, thanks to Carrie, whom I call friend now, for being such a fabulous reader and assisting in bringing Japan to life in this book—I could not have done it without you.

To my agent, Erin Harris: I am incredibly grateful for your unwavering support. Thanks for taking my super cry-y phone call while visiting your parents; it was above and beyond. (I'm sorry again, Mr. and Mrs. Harris.) And thanks to Joelle Hobeika, an editor with a sharp mind and a kind hand. Additional gratitude to Josh Bank and Sarah Shandler and the whole Alloy team. I'd also like to acknowledge John Ed de Vera, an amazing artist without whom neither of the beautiful covers for *Tokyo Ever After* or *Tokyo Dreaming* would exist.

A BIG thank-you to my editor, Sarah Barley, at Flatiron

for believing in Izumi enough to let me write a second book. And thanks to the entire Flatiron team: Megan Lynch, Malati Chavali, Bob Miller, Nancy Trypuc, Sydney Jeon, Jordan Forney, Claire McLaughlin, Erin Gordon, Vincent Stanley, Frances Sayers, Keith Hayes, Kelly Gatesman, Emily Walters, Donna Noetzel, Brenna Franzitta, Katy Robitzski, Emily Dyer, and Drew Kilman. Thanks for everything you do in front of and behind the scenes.

And to the book community, thank you! Lastly, some intrepid readers might note these acknowledgments are similar to those in *Tokyo Ever After*. Please know that just means that I am doubly thankful and it's a wonderful place to be—I am happy times two.

ABOUT THE AUTHOR

When Emiko Jean isn't writing, she is reading. Before she became a writer, she was an entomologist, a candlemaker, a florist, and most recently, a teacher. She lives in Washington with her husband and children (unruly twins). She is the *New York Times* bestselling author of *Tokyo Ever After*, *Empress of All Seasons*, and *We'll Never Be Apart*.

emikojean.com
@emikojeanbooks